USA TODAY BESTSELLING AUTHOR
DALE MAYER

Yowls in the Yarrow

Lovely Lethal Gardens 25

YOWLS IN THE YARROW: LOVELY LETHAL GARDENS, BOOK 25
Beverly Dale Mayer
Valley Publishing Ltd.

ISBN-13: 978-1-773369-94-5
Print Edition

Books in This Series:

Arsenic in the Azaleas, Book 1

Bones in the Begonias, Book 2

Corpse in the Carnations, Book 3

Daggers in the Dahlias, Book 4

Evidence in the Echinacea, Book 5

Footprints in the Ferns, Book 6

Gun in the Gardenias, Book 7

Handcuffs in the Heather, Book 8

Ice Pick in the Ivy, Book 9

Jewels in the Juniper, Book 10

Killer in the Kiwis, Book 11

Lifeless in the Lilies, Book 12

Murder in the Marigolds, Book 13

Nabbed in the Nasturtiums, Book 14

Offed in the Orchids, Book 15

Poison in the Pansies, Book 16

Quarry in the Quince, Book 17

Revenge in the Roses, Book 18

Silenced in the Sunflowers, Book 19

Toes up in the Tulips, Book 20

Uzi in the Urn, Book 21

Victim in the Violets, Book 22

Whispers in the Wisteria, Book 23

X'd in the Xeriscape, Book 24
Yowls in the Yarrow, Book 25
Zapped in the Zinnias, Book 26

Boxed Sets and Bundles
https://geni.us/Bundlepage

About This Book

Riches to rags … Marriage is wonderful … Divorce can be ugly … Chaos surrounds both …

Doreen has had enough of her estranged husband's antics, but, when he shows up dead in the garden outside her favorite Chinese food restaurant, she's horrified and anxious. And, of course, in the eyes of the rest of the world, … guilty.

There's no Doreen for her to call to help out this time, … but she knows Mack has her back, although he's being questioned too. The police force rallies around her, as their history rips apart her former life and finds out that all her suspicions about Mathew were correct, and he'd been in deep trouble.

The trick now is to make sure that said trouble died with him and won't carry over to Doreen. Good luck with that. Between her animals, the police, and every other well-meaning resident trying to help, Doreen knows she could be in bigger trouble than ever …

Sign up to be notified of all Dale's releases here!
https://geni.us/DaleNews

Chapter 1

Late October, Friday Morning ...

AFTER A LOVELY night's sleep and a lazy morning inside, Doreen decided to treat herself to Chinese food. Mack was due to come by for lunch, and she thought maybe she could pick up enough for both of them. She had a little bit more money at the moment, and, besides, after the last case closed, she deserved it.

She was pretty sure food therapy wasn't a good thing to get used to, but it was awfully tempting to just keep turning to food every time something good was going on. As she walked down to the Chinese food restaurant that she loved so much, animals in tow, she stepped inside and looked at the menu, just as Mr. Woo came out from the back and asked, "One dish?"

She smiled at him. "Hey, I was hoping to get a couple dishes."

"You always get one dish."

"I'll have company this time," she replied.

"Ah, two dishes."

She winced. "Maybe three."

He looked at her. "Big spender." But his face was splitting into a big smile.

"Not really." Finally settling on three dishes that would hopefully fill her and Mack, she placed her order. With lots of money coming, she wondered if she would ever get used to spending it.

"You wait fifteen minutes." Then he shooed her out the door.

She went outside and sat down on a bench. All kinds of noises came from all around the place. A normal city day. As she sat here, she sniffed the air and smiled.

Mack had plenty of work to do at Meredith's place, but they had unearthed Dennis yesterday, much to everybody's relief. So, of course, Kelowna was just abuzz with all the news. Doreen didn't really want to get caught up in too much of it, but there was only so much she could avoid.

She'd talked for hours with Nan on the phone but had resisted going down to Rosemoor, pleading tiredness. Even now, as she sat here with the animals all around her, she was feeling pretty whomped. But it was a good tiredness.

Goliath wandered over to a shrub and disappeared behind it. She stood up and walked over. "Goliath, come back," she ordered. His head poked through the bush, looked at her, and then he disappeared into a huge cluster of yarrow plants. She smiled at the multicolored flowers.

"Look at the size of those blooms. I've heard you can make tea out of that stuff." She wondered whether that was an old wives' tale or something she could trust. She'd come a long way, but she still had a way to go in terms of knowing what she could do and couldn't do with plants. Google helped, but it also confused her more often than not.

When Goliath started to hiss and snarl, Doreen raced into the shrubbery, looking for him. "Come out of there," she called to him. She found other flowers, dandelions, and one azalea bush, but this cluster of yarrow seemed to go on and on along the back into another corner. She kept following it. "Goliath? Goliath, come here."

Thaddeus poked his head out from behind her curtain of hair. "Goliath," he called out. "Goliath. Goliath, come here."

She glared at him. "You could have told me that you could call him earlier," she muttered.

"*He, he, he, he, he,*" he snickered at her side.

She just sighed. What was she supposed to do when Thaddeus was so completely wise and yet such a little snot sometimes?

"Goliath!" Another howl came, and that was followed by a different animal sound, and all of a sudden the air was filled with cat cries. Doreen raced in that direction, and then out came a spindly-looking cat, who glared at her and sauntered off. Goliath finally came out, strode toward her, his tail up and all puffed out, having had quite a battle. Yet he was strutting, as if he had won the spoils of the war. And something was in his mouth.

Doreen groaned. "What did you find?" she scolded. "Who did you steal it from?"

Of course the other cat was gone, and there was no further sign of him.

Goliath didn't need to steal food from anybody, as he had plenty of food at home. But, as he approached her, he stood up on his back legs and put his front paws on her thighs, and she saw something plastic in his mouth. She snatched it from his mouth. He didn't want to let it go right away, but eventually he released it.

She looked at it and gasped. "Where did you get this?" she cried out in horror. She raced around to the back of the garden and stopped. She pulled out her phone, and her voice was shaking.

"What's the matter, Doreen?" Mack teased. "I told you that I'll be there in a little bit."

"No, no," she cried out. "You need to come now."

"Doreen, what's the matter?" he snapped. "Are you okay?"

She took a deep breath. "I'm okay, at least for the moment, but I'm not going to be okay for long."

"Stop making cryptic comments, and tell me what's going on."

"You need to come to Mr. Woo's Chinese restaurant. I was buying lunch for you and me, and I was waiting for it to walk back home because you were supposed to be there."

"Yes, I'm in the vehicle heading your way. What's the matter?"

"Meet me here now, please." And, with that, she ended the call.

It seemed like an hour, but it was probably not even five minutes before Mack whipped into the parking lot.

He saw her, hopped out, and came running over. "What's the matter?" he cried out.

She stepped back a bit and pointed, and then she held out the plastic item in her hand. "Goliath brought me this, so I went and took a look."

He looked at what was in her hand, frowned, and stepped around the corner. He came back, his face grim. "This is all Goliath brought you?"

She nodded slowly. "Isn't that enough?" she asked. "That's Mathew's driving license," she cried out. "And that's Mathew in that garden bed, isn't it?"

Mack nodded ever-so-slowly, his gaze intense and

searching. "I'm sorry, Doreen."

"Sorry won't quite cut it right now," she declared, staring at him. "Somebody killed Mathew."

"Yes. Do you realize what this means?"

She nodded. "Oh, I know what it means. I'm suspect number one."

Chapter 2

A STILLNESS FILLED the air, almost the quiet before the storm.

For the first time in her life, Doreen knew exactly what that meant. She had a sense of holding on to something so fragile, so breakable, that even the slightest breath would shatter it. Soon the news would get out, and everybody would know, and her phone would ring, and everybody would wonder if she had done this—if she had murdered Mathew.

Doreen sat here at home, staring at her phone for at least the fifteenth time, reassuring herself that she'd turned off the ringer. Mack had sent her home as soon as he could, but she still got sideways looks from all the cops, even though they should have known better. Mack told her to wait, just wait by the phone, and he would call her.

He hadn't called, and she had surely spent hours in the dark abyss of her mind. Yet, no matter how she felt about it, it had only been an hour. An hour in which time stood still. An hour in which her heart didn't know what to do. She had alternately mourned, cried, rejoiced, and then felt horribly guilty, only to have the vicious cycle start all over again.

With her phone's ringer off, she wouldn't hear a call coming through. However, she kept hoping she would see the missed call. Then she would return Mack's call, but she didn't want to deal with the rest of the world. She *couldn't* deal with the rest of the world.

That sense of being breakable, that sense of fragility, that sense of her world coming apart at the seams was so strong and right in her face. She saw no way out of the upcoming blowback, the media frenzy, her phone ringing off the wall, and people knocking on her door. Everything was blowing up, and she had no way to stop it. She didn't even know if she should. Would some people say this was the next step of her life?

It was the next step, just not the step she had expected. Obviously not the step she had wanted.

She had no ill will toward Mathew, but she also knew the world around her wouldn't hear that or believe her. They wouldn't listen to that. They would think what they wanted to think. When she first had been confronted with Mathew's death in the back of Mr. Woo's restaurant, she was certain that no one would believe she could do such a thing.

However, the longer she sat here in the aftermath, the more she wondered if a lot of the world would think the worst and wouldn't bother to get the answers or seek the truth. They would just judge her and laugh because it had nothing to do with them. *That* she could understand—but the rest? Not so much.

Back in the never-ending silence, contemplating her marriage, its breakdown, the pending divorce, Robin, and everything that led up to this day, Doreen wondered if this could have been avoided.

She didn't want anything from Mathew. She didn't want

so much money that it would cause him any hardship. She went over all her conversations with Nick, again and again in her mind, wondering if she had somehow wrongly given him the impression that he should push, when she didn't want that.

As far as she was concerned, that forceful division of the marital assets was not needed at all. Nick would probably say that she was due part of Mathew's money after her fourteen years of marriage, that this was not her fault, and that it had nothing to do with her. However, in her heart of hearts, she knew it had everything to do with her.

"How could it not?" The thought was killing her.

She and Mathew were in the middle of a divorce that the media would say was an ugly one, even though she didn't know what that meant. It's the only divorce she'd ever had. It had been a bad marriage, but there was no reason for anyone to get hurt, or worse, to get killed over it.

"Was there such a thing as a nice divorce?" Doreen asked aloud. "Was there such a thing as an amicable divorce? Truly? … Did people get along and sit down and sign paperwork together, after congenially working out a settlement considered equitable for both parties? Is it possible to go separate ways and still be good to each other? If so, how?"

Her questions were all over the place, and there was no coherency in her thoughts. Mathew had come up to Kelowna—to apparently sign the divorce papers—so she didn't understand what had happened between his arrival here and her finding his body.

Had she been afraid of him?

She wanted to say no, not anymore, but a small part of her had to answer truthfully, and that answer was yes. That part of her was relieved to know any wife-beating scenario would never happen again. She was guilty of feeling relieved about that, yet that wasn't the same thing as actively killing someone or even arranging somebody's death.

She'd heard too many stories, had seen too much, over these last seven months of investigating cold cases to not know how the world would react. When the news finally broke, and the media got a hold of it, she would be crucified. She was the most logical suspect. And the news would harp on this "fact" until proven otherwise. Maybe not even then. People would most likely remember this period of thinking Doreen was capable of murder. They would say that she'd learned so much in solving cold cases that she figured out how to kill her husband and how to get away with it.

She gave a bitter laugh because, if that were the case, she surely wouldn't have put him in a garden beside the Chinese restaurant, only to be the one who found his body. That would have been a little too obvious, even for her.

As the time passed, with still no word from Mack—or anybody else for that matter—Doreen got more and more worried that something else was going on that she didn't know about. She half expected the police to arrive at her front door and arrest her at any moment. She didn't even know how they could possibly come to that conclusion, yet everything in her world was coalescing to that point.

When her phone lit up, she reached for it, then checked who was calling. *Nick.* She sighed but answered it. "Hello," she replied, the single word coming slowly and quietly.

"Doreen," Nick greeted her. Then his tone sharpened. "Are you all right?"

"Am I all right, after finding the body of my soon-to-be ex-husband, where I was picking up Chinese food to provide a meal for your brother?" she asked, her words spoken in almost a monotone. Then came a slightly hysterical laugh, which she couldn't contain. "I'm fine, *just fine.*"

"I want you to buck up now. I'm trying to get up to Kelowna, but I'm at the airport. No matter how hard I try, I'll still be an hour or two."

"It's fine," she muttered. "No rush." Then came an odd silence.

"You don't sound okay."

"No, I'm probably not okay," she admitted in between short hysterical chuckles. "I don't even know what to think anymore. I've been sitting here in the dark, just waiting for time to go by, waiting for Mack to call and let me know what's going on. But, to be honest, I know he won't tell me anything. He can't. It's his case. It's a pending case," she said, her voice almost a whisper.

"No, not in this case especially, he won't talk to you at all."

She nodded, but, of course, Nick couldn't see it.

"Look. Stay where you are, don't go out, don't do anything. You have a habit of answering calls without checking who it is, but now would be the time to listen to me. *Don't* answer the phone unless it's Mack. I'll be there as soon as I can. Got it?"

"Yes," she whispered. Then, with her voice rising hysterically, she continued. "Nick, you're a divorce lawyer. Are you also a criminal lawyer as well?"

"No, I'm not," he stated, then hesitated. "Do you need one?"

She stared at the phone. "Are you asking me if I killed him?" she cried out. "Because that's a whole different story than needing a lawyer."

"You're right," he told her calmly, "and that's why I

didn't ask that because you didn't." His tone was strong with conviction.

She closed her eyes, feeling the hot tears behind them. "No, I didn't kill him. Yet, for a lot of the world, that is a truth nobody will care about." And then she started to cry.

"Hold on, Doreen. Just hold on," he repeated, his tone rising in worry. "What about getting your grandmother to come up? Can she come over and visit you? Can she stay with you until Mack can come or at least until I get there?"

"No," she mumbled, "I haven't even told her yet."

"No way she doesn't already know. You understand that, right?"

"I'm hoping that maybe the news will be delayed ever-so-slightly. At least until I have better control of myself."

"That's a good point." There was an announcement in the background, and he relayed, "They're calling for my plane, so I should be in Kelowna in an hour. I hope to be at your place twenty minutes after that. Got it?"

"Yes," she whispered, "I've got it."

"Hold tight. I'll be there soon."

"The cavalry to the rescue?"

At the odd note of sarcasm in her tone, he laughed. "Only this time, *you* need rescuing."

With that, he disconnected.

Chapter 3

DOREEN SAT HERE for what seemed to be endless hours. Chances were, probably almost an hour since she'd spoken to Nick. Not sure what to expect, she kept looking at the clock and realized that, if nothing else, Nick would be here soon. Hearing a vehicle outside, she bolted to her feet and raced to the front door. Just as she went to open it, somebody pounded on the other side.

The stranger now screamed, "Open the door, you stupid woman. Let me in!"

She froze and stared. Mugs was barking like crazy at the man outside, and she didn't dare try to shush him; she didn't want anybody to know that she was even inside. The angry man again pounded and pounded at her door, until she heard her neighbor, Richard, shouting at him.

"Stop it. She's not even home."

"Go inside, old man," her angry visitor threatened, "or I'll come over there and visit you next."

At that, Richard would have gone inside, but whether he phoned the police, she didn't know. Had Richard also heard the news? Maybe he wouldn't do anything but think this was her retribution. She shook her head, trembling inside, as

Mugs still barked, now jumping up against the door.

The impatient man pounded once more and yelled, "You've got something of mine, you stupid woman. I want it back, and I want it back now. I'll return to get it, don't you worry. You better have it ready for me."

At that, she heard another vehicle, and the angry man swore under his breath. She watched through the corner of the window as the man raced down the stairs and stormed over to a small vehicle parked at the bottom of her lawn. He hopped inside just as a rental vehicle pulled up into her driveway. The angry stranger watched as Nick got out, and then the unknown man tore off.

She waited until Nick came up to the front steps, and he saw her in the window. He looked from her to the direction of the other vehicle and then said, "Doreen, let me in."

She quickly unbolted the door and opened it for him, throwing herself into his arms.

He held her close and whispered, "Are you okay?"

She shook her head. "Not as okay as I would like to be," she muttered.

"Was that man bothering you?"

She snorted. "Is that the word for it? I did have the foresight to record some of it," she shared and quickly played the little bit of a video that she'd gotten from a slit in her drapes.

He stared at her phone, watching the replay, and shook his head. "The good news is," he replied, looking between her and the phone's screen, "it could go a long way toward clearing your name. On the other hand, do you have any idea who he was?"

She shook her head.

"Do you know what he was after?"

She shook her head again.

"Do you know of anything that he thinks you may have that might be his?"

She shook her head.

"*Great*," he muttered, running his hands through his hair. "Let me in at least."

"Sorry." She hurriedly stepped back, tripping all over the animals wrapped around her ankles. Mugs had already given Nick a happy greeting, and Goliath seemed to just want to stare at him with that unblinking-cat look.

As Nick came inside and shut the front door, Doreen sat down on the nearest living room chair and looked up at him. "I don't know what just happened to my life, but it's completely flipped."

He nodded. "I can see that. The question is whether it's a good flip or a bad one."

"I don't know," she admitted, "but, so far, it feels bad."

"Of course it does," he agreed gently. He sat down beside her, picked up her hand, and held it gently in his. "Have you talked to Mack?"

She shook her head. "No, and I keep waiting, expecting him to call."

"I suspect that he's fighting on your behalf."

"What do you mean?"

Nick took a deep breath. "I contacted him as soon as I landed at the airport, so he knows I'm here. He's fighting to stay on the case, but it doesn't seem that he'll be successful."

She straightened. "But, if Mack's not there to look after me, nobody else will."

"Now don't assume that. You've done a lot of good by the captain and everybody else in that department."

She nodded slowly. "Sure, but why won't they let Mack take the lead?" As she said it out loud, the rational thought process part of her brain—apparently shut down by the shock of the events—suddenly lit up. "Oh," she muttered, "right. … His association with me." Then her shoulders slumped.

"Yes, and you'll obviously be the number one suspect," Nick pointed out, "but you also must realize that Mack himself would be number two on that suspect list."

She stared at him in shock. "What?"

"He is the one who wants you free," Nick stated. "He's made no bones about how he felt about Mathew. Mack arrested that man how many times, for God's sake?"

"Of course, but then Mathew has been very difficult to deal with. It certainly doesn't mean that … Besides, the manner of death, that is *so* not the way Mack would kill Mathew."

Nick stared at her intently. "What do you mean?"

"Mack might punch him out, and, if Mathew had a glass jaw or something, that would do the deed, but Mack wouldn't deliberately kill Mathew. And it would definitely be a hands-on deal if he had done it."

"I concur—"

"And Mack certainly wouldn't leave Mathew in a flower bush for me of all people to find," she declared in disgust. "He knew I was picking up Chinese food, so absolutely no way Mack would have dumped the body there."

"Ha. Right, that makes sense," Nick agreed, with a nod and a chuckle. "I'm glad you understand Mack so well."

She gave him a wry smile. "Understanding Mack is pretty easy. His needs are simple, his wants pretty universal. He wants me free, and he wants Mathew to go away. This is one method, but it wouldn't be Mack's. He would care too much about the end result and would never compromise his own standards."

Nick smiled, almost beaming, as if she were his star pupil. "That's very true, and that's what you have to hang on to through this." He looked back at the front door. "I wonder just when your visitor will return."

She nodded. "I don't know what he's looking for or what he thinks I have. I guess I should have talked to him, but I just wasn't up to it."

"That's fine. It's probably for the best," Nick noted.

"Why?"

"I just think it's better if you sit tight and wait."

"I've got to talk to someone at some point. Otherwise I won't know anything," she complained, looking at him wide-eyed. She stared around the living room, as if seeing it for the first time in a long while. "I've just been sitting here, waiting for my world to collapse."

"Guess what? You're still here, and it hasn't collapsed at all."

She gave him a ghost of a smile. "You're right, but that collapse is still looming."

"Maybe, but that doesn't mean it'll ever happen," Nick argued. "I can understand why you would feel that way, and I can see why it would be hard and painful for you to sit here and wait for everybody to get back to you with some answers as to what's going on. Yet, in the end, you must be patient."

She burst out into a maniacal laughter at that bit of advice.

He winced. "Patience isn't your strong suit."

Unable to help herself, she burst out laughing again, but this time closer to a real laugh. "No, it's not. I really don't wait well at all," she muttered, coming to an understanding. "Yet I didn't do it, and I want to go out and find out who did."

"Can you tell me why?"

Surprised at the question, she frowned at him. "What do you mean?"

"I guess I'm trying to gauge how you feel about Mathew at this point."

"Sad, upset, and grieving. Yet not so much for him but for what he could have been. For what we could have had, if he had been somebody else," she shared, lost in her thoughts. "Am I mourning him?" She contemplated that. "I don't know, but he was a large part of my life for many years. For both the good and the bad. I don't think one can just get rid of emotions because he's dead."

"True."

"I think it will be a process to get there," she added. "Maybe I will wake up tomorrow and feel relief. I just wanted to get the divorce all over with for so long, and now I feel horribly guilty because of that."

"Guilt?" he asked in a questioning tone.

"Yeah, guilt because I wanted it over with. The divorce, all the nonsense. I didn't want him dead, but I wanted all the drama to stop."

"Of course," he agreed.

She stared at him. "You don't think I did it, do you?"

He laughed. "No, absolutely not. You didn't do it. I am a little concerned about how you're handling all this though. It's a lot to process."

"I can't believe that, right after Robin's death, he would die as well," she pointed out, staring at Nick, looking bewildered. "I know terrible things happen to people all the time, but I've never seen the likes of it since I moved here."

"Yet those things were happening here all the time, not

only during the last few months since you moved here but before that," he pointed out. "Probably a lot of that focus on the terrible things happening has been brought about because of the cold cases you dug up."

"That's very true." She massaged the back of her neck. Then, closing her eyes, she stretched as she rotated her neck. "Thank you for not asking if I killed him."

"No, but you did ask if you needed a criminal lawyer."

"Yes, because I might get charged, and, if I do, I have no idea how to defend myself. I need a strategy in place before anything else happens."

"That's what the lawyer is for," he agreed, with a nod.

She gave him a wry smile. "Hence the question."

"Let's not go there just yet," Nick suggested. "The authorities must have some proof, some evidence, that you had something to do with it, before they can charge you. And, if they do charge you, it could be more or less to keep you at home and safe, while they continue the investigation."

"That would be a terrible decision because I'm the best person to go out there and solve this," she muttered.

"That's not exactly true," Nick offered. "You haven't been dealing with current cases or not anywhere near the volume that Mack does."

"I understand that, and, of course, it's much better if Mack stays on the case, but I can understand why the captain might want to remove him."

"More than that, it's not even so much about the captain, but this murder case involves a joint task force with Kelowna working with Vancouver because Mathew lived there."

"Maybe, but that doesn't mean that the killer wasn't up here."

"The crime scene jurisdiction is here, yes, but the two departments will work together," Nick added.

"Of course they will," she muttered, then stared at him. "I really didn't kill him."

"I know that," Nick stated, "and anybody who knows you will know that as well."

"But the other people—those who don't want to know who I am or haven't had the chance—they'll believe it, not to mention all the people who hate me."

"That's not our problem right now. You can only show people who you are and go from there. For the record, they don't hate you. Well, not all of them."

She slowly nodded. With a sigh, she looked around. "I feel as if I've been frozen in this chair in this living room for hours now."

"You probably have been," he stated, with a bright smile.

"I need coffee," she announced.

"Of course you do," he replied in a dry tone, smiling.

She looked at him suspiciously, but he wiped away the smile. "What's wrong with coffee?" she asked, frowning.

"Nothing, it's always your drink of choice …"

Astonished, she asked, "Isn't it yours? Isn't it everybody's?"

"No, and, believe it or not, lots of people out there don't drink coffee at all."

She glared at him suspiciously. "I don't know if I could trust somebody who doesn't drink coffee."

With that, he couldn't contain himself and burst out laughing.

She felt a grin tug on her lips. "I know, … a bit foolish, isn't it?"

"Certainly it's foolish, but, right now, you're allowed to

get away with it."

She shrugged, then bolted to her feet and snagged Goliath, who was right in her way. "These animals obviously know something's up. They've been wrapped around me since I got home."

"Of course they know," Nick concurred. "You hold on to that guy and tell me how to make your coffee."

With that, she quickly gave Nick instructions, and he headed to the pot, where he put on what she hoped would be a decent pot. She watched him, as she cuddled Goliath. Meanwhile Thaddeus was tucked up against her neck, muttering against her skin.

"Is that bird talking to you?" he asked, looking at her.

She nodded. "I wish I could understand what he was trying to say."

"I would rather imagine he's telling you that it'll be okay."

"Maybe," she conceded. "He could also be telling me to ensure I have somebody to look after him, while I'm in the slammer."

At that, Nick burst out laughing. "Oh my, I hadn't thought of that. You could very well be right."

She smiled. "I don't know what he's saying, but he's rubbing against my neck, so I'm pretty sure he's just trying to comfort me."

"I agree," he said gently. "You definitely could use a little more comfort."

"What I want to do is talk to Mack."

"As soon as he can, he will be here."

She nodded. "I know that—at least I want to believe it—but I also know that things can get very harried at the station."

"He's probably down there at Mr. Woo's, while they process the crime scene," Nick pointed out. "Even if Mack can't be part of it, that doesn't mean he won't stay involved, as much as he's allowed. He'll want to see as much of the evidence as he can."

"Of course," she muttered.

He looked at her. "Any idea how Mathew died?"

She stared at him. "No, I don't have a clue. Do you?"

He shrugged. "No, I don't. I was asking you."

"Wondering if I had a look at him?"

"You did have a look at him," he stated. "So the question is, did you see anything?"

At that, she nodded. "I get what you're saying, but the answer really is no. I didn't get a chance to see anything."

"Too bad," he muttered.

"I presume that Mack will give us as much information as he can."

Nick shook his head. "Not likely, Doreen. You and he are the chief suspects. He won't be allowed to know much about the case. So, it would be good to have somebody else on this. You don't happen to know a private eye in town, do you?"

She stared at him in surprise and then slowly nodded. "Actually I do. He might help, although there will be a cost."

"Of course there's a cost," he said, with a wave of his hand. "There's always a cost."

"I know. I'm still adjusting to that," she muttered, with an eye roll.

He grinned. "But remember that you have money coming from the antiques auction."

"Yeah, I have that money coming," she repeated. "That seems to be this constant reply from everybody. It's like hearing people say, *the check is in the mail*, yet meaning that it'll never come."

"Oh, the antiques auction money is coming all right," Nick confirmed. "Though I'm not at all sure what happens to the divorce now, in terms of what you'll get from Mathew, but you also have Robin's money too. You did get that reward money from Bernard, so, with any luck, you'll be okay for a bit, while all this sorts out."

"Not if we start paying for a private eye," she cried out. "That's expensive." He glared at her, and she sat back. "Right, but staying in jail is expensive too." Then she stopped, looked at him, and gasped. "Do I have to pay for being in there?"

His lips twitched. "No. And, if you work in jail, you get paid."

"Oh, that's good." Then she laughed. "Watch, just watch. When I finally get my first real job, I'll be in jail." She shook her head. "What a mess."

"Go sit outside, and I'll bring the coffee," he suggested.

She nodded and went outside, walking to the fence to study the roses. When a man jumped over the fence and accidentally clipped her, she cried out. He was unperturbed and started taking pictures with his camera. She held Goliath up in front of her face and cried out, "Get out of here. Get out of here."

He was laughing. "Hey, look at that. Our famous local sleuth kills her ex-husband. Man, will this make good copy."

At that, Nick stepped out and took a picture of him, and declared, "You print that, young man, and we will have everything you own."

The guy looked at him in shock. "What do you mean?" he asked belligerently.

"You're trespassing and in the act of committing yet another crime," Nick explained, "so I suggest you put that camera down right now, and then we won't have to go any further."

The intruder snorted. "No way, old man. No way I'm doing that. Go ahead. Do what you want. You can't stop me from printing this."

"Maybe not," Nick acknowledged, "but I can guarantee it will be the last thing you ever do when it comes to printing photos that you gain illegally. You can wind up in jail yourself for this one."

"No way, my daddy will fix this."

At that comment, Doreen studied him, and his features clicked in the back of her mind. "Is Bernard your father, by any chance?"

He stared at her. "You know him too, do you? Are you one of his sleepover babes?"

"No, I assure you, I am not." Pulling out her phone, she took a picture of him herself, then sent it to Bernard, with a text that asked, **Is this your son?**

An affirmative response came back, then her phone rang. "Hey, what about my son? He was due back here for dinner."

"He's trespassing in my backyard, trying to take pictures of me to post on blogs, saying I murdered my ex-husband," she stated bluntly.

After a moment of silence, Bernard started roaring through the phone.

She held her phone up, looked at the kid, and said, "Your daddy wants to talk to you."

He stared at her, the color draining from his face. "That's not fair. I should get to have a life without him."

"Absolutely you do," Nick declared in a hard tone, "but you also get to have a life where you pay for the consequences of your actions. I already told you that. So, if you plan on printing any of that stuff, you can bet there'll be all kinds of fines and prison time to pay."

At that, Bernard spoke in Doreen's ear, "Keep him there. I'll be at your place in a second."

She looked over at the kid. "What's your name anyway?"

He stared at her. "It doesn't matter to you. Do you know what it's like growing up under that man?"

"No, I sure don't," she admitted, "but I do know that you got a chance to grow up, so it can't be all that bad."

He snorted at that. "He's got money. He's done everything. Been everywhere. Everybody respects him, *blah, blah, blah*," he muttered. "You can't even be your own person in this town, without everybody knowing who you are."

"Oh, I get it. I'm sorry about that. However, how many people will understand your life, as it seems to be a poor little rich kid lament?" Doreen was not willing to pull any punches on this one.

He just snorted at her. "That is not funny."

"Maybe not, but you could do something useful for a change."

He glared at her. "You don't know anything about me. You're just some dumb woman who's in trouble right now and looking for somebody to help you out. I'll make a few bucks off you. Count on it."

"Yeah, you can, and your father will even be more ashamed of you."

He stared at her. "Why? What are you talking about? He'll be proud of me. I got a good score on this one," he declared. "You can't have my camera, and you can't stop me from using this. Even if I don't sell them to a newspaper, I can still post them on blogs."

"Not without my permission," she stated. "You think you just get to post whatever you want, and nobody cares? There is such a thing as libel, you know."

He shrugged. "You're nobody. You're not a public figure. I can post whatever I want."

"And you think your daddy will be proud of that?" she asked, frowning. "Is that what this is all about? Proving to him that you're somebody? That you can do something?"

"I *can* do something," he snapped. "And you don't know the first thing about it."

"No, I don't," she agreed. "After all, you're the one assuming I murdered my ex-husband, so what do you care?"

"That's right," he declared. "I heard the news, and I came running."

"So, you are trespassing right now," she noted. "You illegally entered my backyard in order to accost me."

"That's not true," he stated. "I never touched you."

"Actually you did. Remember when you jumped down? That was me who you hit."

He glared at her. "That was an accident."

"I don't care whether it was an accident or not," she said, staring at him. "You don't know anything about this case, and all you care about is trying to prove to your dad that you're somebody. You don't care that your pictures will potentially turn people against me—people who could be on a jury one day. You could affect the outcome of my case, not to mention hurt innocent people along the way."

"Why do I care? You're nothing but a murderer!" he bellowed.

Just then Bernard let loose as he came around the corner,

yelling in a way she had never seen. "You did not just say that about Doreen!" Bernard frowned in horror, as he raced to her side. He bent down and hugged her. "Hey, I just heard the news."

"Hey," she muttered, returning the hug and smiling up at him, relieved to know that he believed in her.

"What? You know her too?" the young man asked in disgust.

"Remember my ring and the woman who solved the case? That was Doreen."

At that, the kid looked hesitantly toward her.

She nodded. "Yeah, just think. Solving that case was a good thing for you too. Otherwise you could have had a stepmom the same age as you."

Bernard winced. "Okay, that wasn't necessary."

She laughed. "I swear, she would have been a little bit younger than him. I'm sure of it."

"Fine. Okay, have your laugh. Believe me when I say that I changed my tune on all those women anyway."

"Yeah, Dad, sure you have," the kid muttered.

She looked over at Bernard. "He jumped into my yard, hitting me on the arm on his way down, then started taking photos that he plans to post on some blogs, letting the town know about me, stating I murdered my husband."

Bernard straightened to his full height, glaring at his son. "Seriously?"

The kid pulled back sheepishly.

Bernard continued. "Already you're trespassing, which is a crime. You've taken photos without consent and now plan to post them, proclaiming her guilty of a terrible crime, without even knowing if the story is true?" Bernard's voice rose in shock.

"Truth is a thing he considers to be mutable," Doreen stated. "After all, who cares about the truth, if he can get money off it? He figures he can prove to his daddy that he's somebody for having scored on this one."

At that, Bernard popped up in a rage.

She reached out a hand, patted his arm gently, and added, "So, let's not prove to him how wrong he is right now. I do want that camera, and he's been put on notice that there will be a lawsuit if he publishes anything. I have my attorney right here. So you better tell your son all this too because that is yet something else he considers of absolutely no consequence."

At that, Bernard snorted. "I'll probably charge him myself for that."

"What are you talking about?" the kid asked. "Why would you do that? Isn't there anything I can ever do to make you trust me?"

"I don't know." Bernard asked his son, "*Is* there anything you ever do that I can trust you for?" Bernard shook his head. "Doreen doesn't deserve this treatment."

"So what? What do I care if she deserves it or not? Since when do you care about what anyone deserves or doesn't anyway?" the kid asked in disgust. "You've been in business all your life, and you're the one who keeps telling me how you must be ruthless."

"Yeah, I do. In a *business* sense, that is true. But there are limits to what lines you can cross and as to what standards for behavior one must meet."

"What do you even mean? Forget it," the kid muttered, and he looked toward the river. "I'm posting these pictures, and there is absolutely nothing you guys can do about it!" And, with that, he booked it, heading down to the river and disappearing so fast that none of the older group could even begin to stop him.

She looked over at Bernard.

"I'll fix it," he declared. "I promise." And, with that, he disappeared.

She looked up at Nick. "Please tell me the coffee is ready."

He smiled. "And what if it isn't?"

"If it isn't, I'll wait. But, if it is, please just inject it into my arm, so I can get through this day, then collapse."

"So, if that's the case, you don't want any caffeine," he countered, with a smile. "Otherwise you might stay up even later."

"I just can't believe what's going on," she muttered. "Between the kid, the guy pounding at the front door, Mathew's death, my standing on the suspect list, even Mack too, plus whatever else is coming, it's all too much."

Just then she heard one loud knock, and the front door popped open behind them, followed by Mack's huge frame filling the open kitchen doorway. She raced toward him, as he spread his arms wide. Throwing herself into them, she sank against him in relief, as Mack closed his arms around her and held on tight.

Chapter 4

"HEY," MACK MUTTERED, holding her gently and rocking them in place. "Thanks for getting here so fast, Nick."

Nick shook his head. "Still not quite fast enough," he said. "You have no idea what's happened, even in the short time I've been here." And, with that, he related the last hour or so. Mack stilled under her. He stepped back and looked down at her face. "Somebody pounded on the door and threatened you?"

She nodded. "He seems to think I have something."

"Oh, not this again," Mack muttered, closing his eyes.

"Exactly, but I don't know whether it's this case or another case."

He nodded. "That compounds it, of course. If anybody else were in a situation like this, we would assume it was this case. However, in your situation, not so much."

She shrugged. "Not my fault."

"No, it's not, but then it really is."

She smiled. "Nice to see you. I've been waiting all day."

"I know, and I'm sorry I couldn't get here earlier. Didn't Nick tell you that we had talked?"

"He did, and he mentioned you were fighting to stay on the case."

"Yeah, and I lost that fight."

"What?" She gasped in horror, looking up at him. "Why?" She was beside herself. "Why would the captain do that?"

"Mostly because he's trying to keep the integrity of the case. Let's face it. I'm too close to it. I won't be allowed to work it, but I haven't been suspended or restricted in any way. I will at least be where I can see the information coming and going."

She stared at him. "So, is that good news or bad news?"

He smiled at her. "It's as good as we can expect for the moment."

"I'll consider that as bad news then."

He burst out laughing. "The captain knows you didn't kill anybody, as do the men we have worked with all this time," Mack pointed out. "Believe me that everybody wants to solve this as fast as possible. They know what Mathew was like, so they certainly know that any number of people had motive to kill him."

"Oh, you're not kidding there," Doreen muttered, "motive by the droves."

He nodded. "That is a concern, trying to figure out what went down and how. We'll have to get your statement, but I can't be the one to take it."

She winced. "*Great.* So who will it be?"

"One of our new detectives."

"So, somebody who doesn't know me?"

"Yes," he replied, with a concerning frown in his tone.

"You don't like this new detective either," Doreen noted.

At that, his eyebrow shot up. "I didn't say that," he protested.

"You didn't have to," she declared.

At that, somebody cleared their throat from behind Mack.

Doreen looked under Mack's arm and saw a woman standing there, frowning at her. "Oh, you brought somebody?"

"Yeah," he replied in a dry tone. "Doreen, meet the new detective." Doreen winced, as Mack stepped aside and introduced her. "This is Detective Insley Mogamon. She's only recently joined our division."

"Hi," Doreen said. When the other woman frowned at her, Doreen frowned right back. "See? I can do that too."

At that, the other woman's eyebrows shot up. "Pardon?"

Doreen sighed. "Never mind. It's okay. Come on in and join the party."

"I hardly think a party is appropriate, especially right now," she stated stiffly.

Doreen stared at her. "So, you have no humor and can't detect sarcasm. Duly noted. I gather you're here to interview me."

"I would like to take your statement, yes," she replied, keenly studying her, "unless you want to go down to the station."

"Not particularly," Doreen replied. "Depends on if the captain wants me to go down there."

"No, I don't think the captain would have any concerns either way," she replied, looking from Mack back to Doreen.

Mack stepped aside. "I'll go get coffee."

"Good," Doreen muttered. "You can refill mine while you're at it."

He smiled. "Depends on how many cups you've already

had."

"Not enough," she declared, sending him a dark look. Doreen looked back at the woman and asked, "Do you want to sit out here?"

"Sure." She stepped outside and looked at the property. "Is this on the river?"

"Yes, it is. It's my grandmother's place."

"Ah, so you don't own it then." And she started to write down notes.

Doreen frowned at her again. "Actually I do." But then she stopped, turned to Nick, and asked, "If the name change went through properly."

He frowned at her. "Have you gotten the paperwork?"

"I don't know," she replied. "Nan told me that she was putting it in my name, but I don't know how far that got."

"Remind me to follow up on that. I can check."

All through that exchange, the detective seemed to be writing notes. When Doreen leaned forward, Insley pulled back her notebook ever-so-slightly. Doreen frowned at her, and the other woman frowned right back. She shrugged. "So, what do you want to know?"

"Tell me exactly what happened."

"Sure. I went to pick up Chinese food for me and Mack and …"

"Mack?" Insley interrupted, staring at Doreen.

"Yes, *Mack*. He was coming for lunch."

"You pick up Chinese when you have somebody over for lunch?" Insley asked in a deceptively quiet tone, filled with criticism.

Doreen's back bristled, as she narrowed her gaze. "What does that have to do with Mathew's murder?"

Insley replied, "Continue."

Doreen nodded. "I thought it would be a treat, but apparently you don't agree with that, but that's all right, to each his own," she stated, with a wave of her hand. In the kitchen doorway, she caught Mack's frown and glared at him. "That's what happens when I try to do something nice for you," she stated. "I guess it just means I'm not supposed to do that."

He sighed and replied, "Back to the matter at hand, Doreen."

Doreen quickly told the rest and added, "Then I called Mack."

The new detective asked, "Between the time that Mack was on his way and you were standing there, what happened?"

"Nothing," she stated. "I just stood there, waiting, trying to figure out if what I'd just seen was for real."

"Why wouldn't it be real?"

She stared at her again. "No reason for it *not* to be real. Yet I couldn't quite comprehend that it had even happened."

"Why not?" Insley asked. "After all, you're in an ugly divorce battle."

"No, we're not in an ugly divorce battle."

"You're not now, I guess, because he's dead," Insley declared.

Doreen swallowed, stared at Insley, and clarified, "We were *never* in an ugly divorce battle. Nick here is my divorce lawyer, so you can talk to him about it."

At that, Insley turned and asked him, "What's your last name?" He quickly gave his name, and she frowned. "Moreau? Nick Moreau?"

He nodded. "Yes, Mack's my brother."

The detective sighed. "So, does everybody here know

each other and is related to everybody?"

"Pretty much," Doreen said. "We don't have any secrets from each other either."

"Okay, good. So did you kill your ex?"

She stared at her in shock. "No. I didn't kill my ex, and I shouldn't have to remind you that I am deemed innocent until proven guilty. So I really don't appreciate your assuming that I did. You don't know anything about me, so you'd better get your facts straight before you start jumping to conclusions."

"I don't care to get to know you," she stated flatly. "I'm here to solve a case."

"Bully for you," Doreen stated. "Let me know how that works out."

Insley just stared at her.

"Doreen, behave yourself," Mack said.

She glared at him. "Don't start, Mack."

Almost on cue, he held out a cup of coffee and sighed. "Right, so this mood means you probably haven't had nearly enough for today, have you?"

"I haven't had enough for the week apparently," she declared. "Interesting people you bring along with you." Doreen turned and looked at the detective. "What department were you in before?"

"That's none of your business."

"Yet it is," she declared. "Under the constitution, I am allowed to question the veracity of the person interviewing me."

Insley frowned at Doreen. "I'm the one doing the interview, so I'm the one asking the questions."

Doreen pulled out her notepad, grabbed a pen, and started writing her own notes.

"What are you doing?" Insley snapped.

"Obviously writing my own notes," she replied, giving her a glare for glare.

Insley stiffened. "If you don't cooperate with the police, things will be much more difficult."

"Refusal to answer legitimate concerns and now threats of retaliation? What would the captain think?" Doreen noted. "I've had a heck of a day already, so we might as well get this over with." She looked up at Mack to see him staring at her, a worried look in his gaze. "I'm not doing anything I'm not entitled to, Mack," Doreen declared.

"I know, but that still doesn't mean it'll help your case."

"I didn't kill Mathew," Doreen repeated, "so providing the *new* detective here knows what she's doing and didn't come from the speeding and parking infraction department, we should get to the truth just fine."

At that, Nick seemingly coughed and spewed coffee all over his lap. He bolted to his feet, apologizing.

She waved her hand. "Seeing as you'll be staying here, take your bag up to the guest room and get changed, if you want." Doreen sighed, feeling the fatigue hitting her again. "As far as dinner goes, we'll get something, but definitely not Chinese."

Nick stopped and frowned. "Oh boy, I just remembered. You don't cook, do you?" he asked, with a note of humor.

She eyed him cautiously and asked, "Do you?"

He nodded slowly.

"Oh, then it's a good deal for me," she replied, rubbing her hands together. "What are you cooking for dinner?"

He smirked, shook his head, and mumbled, "I am *so* not ready for this." Then he quickly excused himself and walked inside.

Doreen returned her attention to the new detective, staring at her. "Anything else, *Detective*? Otherwise I'll ask you to leave, so I can sit down and entertain my guest."

Insley hesitated, but, getting no support from Mack, she nodded. "I'm done, … for the moment."

"Good," Doreen declared. "Please let me know when you find the guy who killed my ex."

"You don't seem to think I can do that," Insley stated.

"Even if you *could*," Doreen declared, "I just don't know if you *would*."

On that note, Insley got up and quickly walked out, sending Mack a hard look as she left.

"This will be a disaster," Mack muttered.

Chapter 5

"YOU REALLY DO need to get along with people," Mack began. "She didn't do anything to deliberately upset you."

"Did you not hear her questions? She had nothing but attitude. Seeing as she is the new kid on the block, she's not trying to get along. She's trying to bully her way through her first big case—or her first case ever—all puffed up on her newfound power. So she was a dog catcher or a meter maid or something before this new position, right? Did she come from Vancouver, maybe?"

Mach sighed, knowing not to engage with Doreen right now.

"*Insley* did deliberately provoke me with her attitude and her assumptions. She thinks that I murdered my husband. She's not looking anywhere else. She was not forthcoming with her professional history nor in any way was she open-minded. What happened to *innocent until proven guilty*? Exactly how *new* is this new detective? Is she fresh off the turnip truck? She came here not liking that you already had me in your arms, when you first arrived."

"I can see where that might have been a bit of a problem

for her," Mack noted. "Just keep in mind that she also doesn't know you and doesn't know our history."

"Exactly, and that was *her* problem." Doreen's shoulders slowly slumped, and she pinched the back of her neck.

"Are you okay?"

"Let's just say, it's been a heck of a day. I didn't even tell her about being threatened at my front door or being accosted in my backyard."

"No, and I noticed that. Any particular reason?"

"Yeah, I forgot," she stated simply. "It's been a pretty shocking day. Plus, after meeting her, I don't think she particularly cared about anything I had to say anyway."

"I've already contacted the captain and told him about her approach to interviewing," Mack shared.

Doreen snorted. "Finally you stick up for me. Yet you were criticizing me in front of her, not just once either. Why couldn't you criticize her in front of me?"

Mack sighed. "It's been a rough day. Still, you can expect her back again at some point, with further questions as the investigation proceeds."

"*Great*," she muttered. "Where did she come from?"

"She was transferred up from the coast," he said.

Doreen nodded. "Does she have anything to do with my ex? Did she know Mathew?"

"I don't think so. Why?"

She shrugged. "She's in his general area, and she's a beautiful woman, and Mathew has been known to attract multiple women, until he screws them over. It's just one of those things that makes me wonder."

"What do you mean? Do you think she's the one who killed him and somehow got herself assigned to the case in order to ensure it looked as if you did it?"

She stared at him. "Can she do that? Then, yes."

Chapter 6

Saturday Morning ...

WHEN DOREEN WOKE up the next morning, she smiled as she looked around her bedroom, surrounded by her animals. Then the memories hit her, and her smile fell away, tears welling up in her eyes. She didn't even know why she was crying. It's not that she mourned the loss of Mathew, but she mourned the promise of what he could have done and been, if he had made different choices in his life and if he hadn't been murdered.

Of course she was assuming that he'd been murdered. She didn't even know that much. She hadn't asked Mack, and she should have. She'd caught him and Nick talking privately in her kitchen last night, and neither would budge when she'd asked what they were talking about. She finally walked away from them, frustrated and in tears, but she understood that they wouldn't let her in on everything. Clearly she would have to do some investigating herself.

On that note, when her phone buzzed just now, she took a look at the text. Nan was asking if Doreen was okay. She quickly phoned her grandmother. "Hey, Nan. I'm still in bed."

"I'm not surprised," Nan replied, her tone worried. "I did talk to Mack last night, and he suggested that I give you a little bit longer to deal with the fallout."

"I don't think even time will help me deal with this fallout," she admitted. "I had Bernard's son here yesterday, taking pictures of me to post and to sell. He wanted to be sure people knew all about the local sleuth who learned enough to murder her own husband," she shared bitterly.

"Oh my," Nan said in horror. "Will Bernard stop him?"

"He told me that he would, but I don't know. I'm scared to even look at the news or anything."

"I haven't heard anything yet," Nan shared. "Obviously we'd heard about somebody found dead, and then Richie heard about who had died."

"Yeah, he probably heard it from Darren. And did you know that Mack's been taken off the case, and it's headed by some new detective?" Doreen asked in disgust. "A new female detective who doesn't like me."

At that, Nan replied in a soft tone, "Come on now. You probably don't like her either."

"She certainly isn't the same as talking to any of the regular detectives," Doreen muttered. "She thinks that I did kill Mathew and how I must have had plenty of reasons to. She was taking all kinds of notes."

"Well, dear, you have to put your faith in the captain and Mack. I'm sure they won't let this investigation become a farce or otherwise allow you to get railroaded right into prison," Nan stated firmly.

"Maybe not," Doreen murmured, "but it won't be an easy time for me, waiting while they figure it all out."

"No, of course not," Nan agreed. "Even though you didn't want to be married to Mathew anymore, that doesn't mean that you wanted him dead. Yet a lot of people in your situation would have wanted him dead—but that doesn't mean you would do anything about it."

"Definitely not. But nobody wants to believe that."

"No, of course not." Nan asked cheerfully, "How about breakfast? I'm sure we can come up with something for breakfast."

"I don't dare step foot out of my house without people taking pictures, yelling how I killed my husband," Doreen muttered. "I'm feeling pretty … I guess *raw* is the word I would use."

"How about I come up a little bit later then, with a little treat basket?"

Doreen laughed. "I'm eating, Nan, and Nick is staying here at my house."

"Nick, not Mack?" she questioned.

"Yeah, Nick." Doreen hesitated, then added, "I also had a man come to the front door, threatening me and telling me to give him what he wanted, that he knew I had something of his."

"Oh my," Nan noted, "you did have a full day."

"It was a terrible day," Doreen muttered. Mugs rolled over and snuffled beside her. "The animals have been doing their best to keep me sane," she shared.

"Of course they have. That's what animals are good for. You just stay the course and trust," Nan shared. "Remember that, even though Mack may not be on the case, he won't let them railroad you into something terrible."

"Maybe not," Doreen agreed, "but the new detective is out of control, so it all feels pretty terrible right now."

"Get up, have a shower, get some coffee," Nan stated firmly, "and I'll come up in a little bit." With that, her grandmother ended the call.

Doreen pulled a protesting Goliath into her arms and gave him a big hug and a cuddle, then did the same with Mugs. Next she got up and walked into her bathroom and had a hot shower. By the time she was dressed, Thaddeus was awake and staring at her with that unblinking gaze.

She whispered, "Love you, Thaddeus," and he dropped his head against her cheek.

"Thaddeus loves Doreen. Thaddeus loves Doreen."

With tears pricking her eyes, she picked him up carefully, placed him on her shoulder, and replied, "And Doreen loves Thaddeus."

She crept downstairs, not wanting to wake Nick, if he was sound asleep, but instead found the kitchen back door wide open and him sitting outside, his papers all over the place and his laptop out. He looked up when she stepped outside.

"There you are." Nick smiled. "I wasn't sure when you would get up, but I was getting a mighty craving for coffee. I tried avoiding the stuff, but…"

"You didn't make any?" she asked.

"No, I figured that I shouldn't steal any of your coffee."

"It's not stealing," she replied. "You're a guest. Besides, I was secretly hoping you would have it ready," she admitted, giving him a fat grin.

"Go put some on then, and it will be ready before you know it," he suggested. He looked up at the animals and shook his head. "I can't imagine living with a bird."

"It's a very special experience," she murmured. She put Thaddeus on the patio table and said, "I'll be right back." Goliath and Mugs had stepped out into the garden and were busy sniffing out the morning smells. She put on the coffee and then stepped back out again. "Do you always work this early in the morning?"

"Yes, especially when I'm not at home," Nick explained. "I'll be here for a little bit this morning, and then I'm heading over to visit my mother."

"Oh, good, that would make her very happy."

He nodded. "She keeps asking when I'm moving here, but it's just that much harder to move here when I've got so much else going on."

"Eventually, instead of flying up here, you'll be flying down there, until that becomes less and less."

"That's what I was thinking," Nick agreed. "You certainly are stirring things up around here."

"Of course I am, and apparently that's what I do." She plunked down on the chair beside him, looking at the paperwork, and sighed. "I don't like paperwork."

"Really?" he asked. "I wonder why. You certainly generate enough for other people to deal with."

She laughed. "Now you've been talking to Mack."

He flashed her a bright grin and agreed. "I also talked to Mathew's lawyer this morning," he shared.

She stiffened and nodded. "Is it the same lawyer who handled the divorce?"

"It is. He was handling both, and he told me that he knows you."

She looked at him. "Was that Roger?"

He nodded. "Yes. What do you know about Roger?"

"Not a whole lot. During our marriage, he was there at the house quite a bit," she shared, thinking back. "I was the ghost in the hallway."

Nick smiled and nodded. "Roger mentioned that you were the nicest of Mathew's lady friends and that he's waiting to hear from the police. They also want to know the contents of the will."

"*Right*. Did he tell you?"

"Only that he will get back to me this afternoon, as soon as he has the chance."

"What does Mathew's death do to our divorce?" she asked.

"Mathew did not sign off on the paperwork. I did talk to Roger about that, and he shared that Mathew was really struggling with the whole finality of it and had told him recently that he'd made a mistake with you and never should have let you walk away."

She slowly sagged in her chair. "*Seriously?*"

Nick nodded. "Still, I'm not sure how that affects you right now."

"It's not that it affects me," she clarified, "but it just adds to that whole confusion of emotions."

"I agree. The good news is that you will have a little bit of time to process it all."

"Maybe, but maybe not."

"Of course what does confuse the issue is whether you had anything to do with his murder."

"And you already know I did not."

"Exactly, but Mathew's lawyer doesn't know that."

She sighed. "I suppose if I did have something to do with it, I'm not allowed any inheritance, right?"

"Exactly," Nick confirmed, with the briefest of smiles. "However, that doesn't stop people from murdering each other."

"No, but I do wonder why though."

"If they're not caught and not charged, then they get to inherit anyway. There is only trouble if you're found guilty."

"*Great*, so even if I am charged, none of this gets solved until I end up in court."

"Which won't happen," Nick declared.

"I didn't kill him, so …"

"I hear you, and, in this case, that's a good thing, and maybe it's a good thing he had a change of heart about you at the end."

"Why is that?" Doreen asked.

"It depends on what the will looks like," he replied, "but I don't think he took you out of it."

She shrugged. "I was never in it, as far as I know."

"He did put you in, but that doesn't mean a whole lot at this point."

"Right. Have you heard from Mack yet?"

Nick shook his head. "No, he did go to work this morning, and that's all I've heard."

"Good enough," she muttered. "I was wondering about taking a hand at this myself."

"Doreen, that's not a good idea."

"No, probably not," she agreed, "but I'm not really feeling very comfortable about letting *that woman* handle it."

"*That woman* is a detective and should do a good job. Plus she won't be working alone. The rest of the team is there to work with her."

"Yeah, but not Mack," Doreen pointed out, "and Mack would have my best interests at heart."

"He does, yes, which is also why he's not on the case," Nick added, with a note of humor.

She sighed, her shoulders slumping. "Okay, so what do we even know?"

"I can tell you one thing. Mathew was shot."

She stared at him in shock. "What?"

He nodded. "Mack told me last night."

"Good Lord," she muttered, then stopped. "With his own gun?"

He looked up at her. "He had a weapon?"

"Yeah, sure," she shared, "at least one, if not two. They were usually in the safe in his office."

"Okay. Can you tell me anything else about that?"

"He was a good shot, and he told me that he kept them at home for protection."

"Did he ever need it?"

"Oh, yeah," she confirmed. "He had all kinds of business deals going on at any given time. According to how that was going, he sometimes owed people money but didn't have it, and people wouldn't take no for an answer."

"Right, and that was another part of why the killer could be anybody who was after him."

"That's just the thing. It's pretty hard to know who out of many would have wanted to kill him. As you mentioned, there are probably an awful lot in the running."

"As long as it's not you," he said.

"We still have to find an avenue the authorities can go after," she declared. "Otherwise they'll continue to assume it's me—or Mack—and keep coming back, asking stupid questions, wasting time."

He stared at her. "I sure hope not, because that would mean they aren't doing their jobs."

"They'll do what's easy," she stated. "And, in *this woman*'s case, I don't know what to think, but she's bound to be trying to prove herself to the department."

"Maybe so," Nick agreed, "but just because she's new to the department doesn't mean she's new to this work."

"Maybe not, but she sure didn't like my questions and

was defensive when I asked about her prior experience."

"Of course, because she was trying to be the one in control in an uncomfortable situation, where she was up against the girlfriend of one of her coworkers and the girlfriend's lawyer, who happens to be her coworker's brother."

"*She* was the one who was uncomfortable?" Doreen shook her head and snorted.

"Can we at least agree that her discomfort was making her a little more abrasive, and that set you off?"

She stared at him and frowned. "So, does that mean I'm in the wrong? I would really hate having to apologize to her."

He burst out laughing. "I won't say that you were in the wrong. I'm just saying that maybe you could try to understand where she was coming from and understand she wasn't in an easy place."

"Or *maybe* she should consider the position I'm in and not be so rude. This isn't exactly an easy place for me to be in either. I'm sitting here with a possible murder rap on my head, which she is determined to pin on me."

"Which won't happen," he declared.

She smiled at him. "I'm really glad I have your vote of confidence on that."

"You do absolutely," he murmured. "So remember that and stay strong, and it will all work out."

Just then her phone rang. She looked down at the screen. "Hello, Bernard. Did you stop him?"

"I did," he confirmed, "but I don't know where he's getting all this from. He seems to think that he's fully justified because you did murder the man."

"How would he know who is the murderer?" she asked.

"That's the part I'm not sure about. He says he saw you."

She put her cell on Speakerphone, then looked over at Nick. "Saw me when?"

"Saw you at the Chinese food place, where the body was."

"Yeah, that's because I found the body," she replied.

"Oh, you did?"

"Yes, I did. I went to order Chinese food and was waiting to bring it back here to have with Mack. Goliath raced into the shrubbery, the yellow bushes, after the tomcat, although I didn't know another tomcat was there at the time. There was a bunch of howling and yelling, so I headed in there to ensure Goliath was okay. He came out with a plastic card in his mouth, and the tomcat took off. I headed around the corner to see what else might have been there, in case somebody's wallet or something was there, and instead found Mathew."

"That explains it then," Bernard said, with relief. "He saw you coming out from the yellow brush and figured that's when you conked him."

"He wasn't *conked*. He was shot. I don't even know when he died," she replied in exasperation, "but I'm the one who found him, and I'm the one who reported it."

"I am sorry," Bernard muttered. "You do appear to be the one who's always on the spot."

"Unfortunately on the spot, and not in a good way," she muttered. "So maybe you'll want to explain that to your son, before he completely crucifies me on the internet and convinces everybody I'm guilty."

"I've taken the camera away from him."

"But, if his phone and his camera were linked, which they probably were, then he'll already have those photos uploaded and possibly even posted." She looked over at

Nick. "In which case, should it show up on the internet or elsewhere, I will be forced to take him to the cleaners."

"I'm working on it," Bernard said hurriedly. "I'll get back to you." With that, he disconnected.

Doreen stared at the phone in her hand. She shook her head. "I didn't think I was vengeful, but the thought of that little snot putting pictures and headlines on the internet, saying that I killed my ex, just makes me really angry."

"That's because it's an injustice," Nick stated gently. "Now, the fact of the matter is, I'm waiting to hear when Mathew … died," he reported, "and hopefully that will help a lot with getting you away from the spotlight."

She nodded.

"Did you touch the body?"

"No, it was obvious he was dead."

"When you say *obvious*, what do you mean?"

"His face was turned up to the sky, and his eyes weren't moving, and some debris was on his face—maybe from the cats, I don't know—plus a pinkish tinge around his lips." She stared at him. "Oh my, I wonder if that was from cyanide."

"Or drinking strawberry Kool-Aid," Nick quipped.

Then she stopped and added, "But you mentioned Mathew was shot."

Nick nodded. "Mathew was shot in the chest, and it exited out his back."

"The ground would have soaked up any blood, but I didn't even see a bullet hole or blood on his clothes," she muttered, frowning, considering the scene. "But again, maybe the cats did something so the jacket flipped one way or the other."

Nick suggested, "The other thing is, because of the way

he was positioned on the ground, you may not have seen any of the blood anyway. One bullet that went straight through? It could have been a small hole."

"Right," she muttered. "We always think of these big damaging holes, don't we?"

"And yet it isn't always," Nick said, "or the exit wound is bigger."

She just nodded, not knowing what to say. "It would be helpful to know when he died though, wouldn't it?"

"They're waiting for the autopsy now," Nick shared.

"Right, and what are we doing about that lovely guy who came to my doorway?"

"I did contact Corey, your private eye referral. He'd already heard the news and has volunteered to help you out."

"What? He doesn't want payment?" Then her gaze narrowed, as she stared at Nick suspiciously. "Why would he do that?"

"Because he says that you've done a lot for this town, and it's time that somebody helped you out for a change."

"A lot of people have helped me out in many ways, you included," she shared, then motioned to the deck. "This deck is just another example."

Nick nodded. "I do remember all the work that went into this deck." He smiled, as he looked around. "And that's a good example to hold on to. Have faith that people are not deserting you and that they will get to the bottom of it."

She smiled. "I'm really glad to hear that, because some of this stuff is just a little too hard to believe."

"It is, indeed."

"So, Corey and you talked? Now what?"

"He wants to talk to you."

"Right," she muttered, then groaned. "In other words,

he's coming today, isn't he?"

"Yeah, he'll be here soon."

"It would be nice if he came and left before my grandmother gets here. Otherwise he'll be in for a heck of a talking to."

Nick laughed. "I'll tell him to speed it up." And, with that, he brought out his phone and sent off a series of texts. "If your nan's coming, I want to be out of here before then too."

She nodded. "I would think so," she muttered, with a weak smile. "She won't be very happy to find I am still under enough scrutiny to warrant my attorney being on hand to this extent."

"I understand that, but, hey, that's what family is all about."

"Maybe so," she admitted, "but there's family, and then there's the situation when you only have each other. That's a whole different level of family."

"Meaning that your grandmother will be terrorizing everybody until this is resolved?"

"Oh, I would imagine so." Doreen smiled. "Part of her will look forward to it and will enjoy it, while the other part will be terrified that she'll do something wrong and get me convicted."

At that, he burst out laughing. "It's not that easy to get convicted in these kinds of crimes."

"I don't know about that. It sure seems to be pretty easy in some cases."

"I can see why you would think that, with your cold-case history. Yet we have to stay strong and take this one day at a time."

"Oh, I've heard that message already … in spades," she

muttered.

After that, they sat here quietly and had coffee. When the doorbell rang about twenty minutes later, she looked at him and asked, "Is that Corey, or do you think it's our unfortunate previous visitor?"

Nick hopped up and said, "Let's go find out."

Together they walked to the front door, and, sure enough, it was Corey. He stepped inside, saw her, and gave her a big fat grin. When Goliath took a liking to him, he picked up the huge cat, giving him some loving.

Doreen was happy to see the interaction and wondered why Goliath was drawn to Corey. He was a stranger to Goliath, plus the cat didn't warm up to many people.

Corey greeted her. "This time, it's you on the hot seat."

"Right. Whoever would have thought?"

"Hey, it happens." He shrugged. "We'll sort it out."

"Sooner rather than later, I trust," she muttered. "I can't say I'm terribly comfortable being on this side of it."

He burst out laughing at that. "I don't know anybody who's ever comfortable on this side of it," he muttered. "However, it's a really good experience and good empathy training for you, if you'll keep doing these cases."

"I was trying to stick to cold cases," she muttered, "but, every once in a while, I get caught up in some of the current ones."

"Every once in a while?" he repeated, with an eye roll. "I'm pretty sure you're stepping on the toes of the local detectives all the time."

"But not on purpose," she stated defensively. Mugs came over to settle by her feet, as if to calm her down. She reached out to pet him, thankful to have her animals.

He grinned at her. "Maybe not on purpose, but that

doesn't make it any more appealing to them."

She sighed. "Come on in. I was just about to make another pot of coffee."

"Good, though I don't have a whole lot of time. So let's get as much of this information down as we can, and we'll go from there."

And, with fresh coffee, they sat outside, and she prepared to go over the whole thing again. "This time I'm recording it," she stated, "so then maybe I won't have to tell everybody over and over again."

"Good idea," he replied. "Now, what is going on with this kid with the camera?" She then explained about Bernard and his son. Corey shook his head. "Man, we don't need guys like that getting in our way. Do you believe Bernard will keep a lid on him?"

"Oh, I'm hoping so," she replied, "but the kid's pretty slippery. He's young and trying to prove himself, and that motivation tends to complicate things."

"I can see about a restraining order," Nick suggested, "but we must have proof that he's doing something."

"He was definitely trespassing," she muttered. "Surely that's good for something."

"It is, particularly the way his threats have been flying around, and the fact that we don't really know who and where they're coming from," Corey noted, looking at Nick. "Considering that his visit was very close to the same time as the angry guy was at your front door, it's always possible the kid was just here to rattle you, so the other guy can come back and steal whatever he wants."

"That's a theory I hadn't considered," she muttered, frowning.

"So, if they could be in cahoots, you'll have a much easier time getting the kid and his camera in trouble."

"I just want him in trouble for being the idiot he is," she stated. "I don't need to make it worse than it is, and I'm sincerely hoping Bernard can stop him. But, if he doesn't, we'll deal with the fallout, I guess," she muttered. "I'm far more concerned about the unknown guy at my front door."

Corey nodded, then asked, "On the day that you found Mathew's body, did your ex meet you? Or say anything? Text? Phone?"

"No," she stated. "He didn't come around here much …" She stopped and corrected herself. "More accurately, he did not come here recently. Earlier, there were times of him coming around, asking me to reduce what I was asking for in the divorce."

"You talked?"

"A few times. I tried to do exactly what my lawyer told me every time, trying not to speak to Mathew, whether on the phone or in person," she explained, with an eye roll. "I did fail a couple times."

"Why is that?" Corey asked.

"I didn't do it on purpose. I did open the front door without checking who it was all the time," she admitted. "Sometimes I didn't realize who was on the other end of the phone. Maybe Mathew had a new phone number or had called from a different number. While I wouldn't say those calls were amiable, they weren't angry either. Typically I said, *You need to talk to my lawyer. I'm not allowed to talk to you anymore.* That kind of conversation. Same thing if he suddenly showed up at my door. Ask Mack about those times."

"Good," Corey noted. "Did that upset Mathew? Did he get violent?"

She frowned at him. "You do know Mathew was an angry, violent man, right?"

He shrugged. "I don't know that. I only know what you're telling me."

"He was known to hit me, and, for the record—in case you were wondering—no, I didn't kill him."

"I'm not wondering," Corey replied. "I know you didn't kill him."

"Thanks for that," she muttered. "I wish everybody else knew that."

"Don't worry about it," he said, with a wave of his hand. "Everybody will have their opinions, and they'll all be wondering what's going on. That's why we have to solve this as quickly as we can."

"Sounds good to me. Yet I don't know how Mathew got into town because no vehicle was parked at the Chinese restaurant, not one that he would be seen driving," she shared. "Mathew always rented these big green Jaguars, and Mack had something set up to be alerted when Mathew came into town."

"Why is that?"

"Because Mathew got difficult one day, grabbing me, trying to force his way inside my house, and thankfully Mack drove up just then and was a witness to this event himself. So we had to get a court order to keep him away from me."

"Okay, so that means Mathew got very difficult."

"Yes, he did at times, and then, at some point, he calmed down, and the divorce proceedings were going forward, and he seemed to be okay. Obviously the time period after his girlfriend Robin got murdered was very difficult for him, and people were looking at Mathew for that as well."

Corey stared at her. "Do you think Mathew had anything to do with Robin's death?"

"Oh no," Doreen clarified. "We solved that one, and Mathew didn't do it. He was pretty upset about the whole thing, but he was done with Robin at the time."

"Right," Corey replied. "because *being done with* people is something your ex does, right?"

She stared at him, not comprehending. "I'm sure that may make sense to you, but I don't really get it."

"Okay, let me try again. He's the person who has something to do with people, until he has nothing further to get from them. So, when he'd done, he's really done, and then they just don't matter anymore."

"Oh, yes, that's it exactly," she agreed. "That's a pretty good analysis."

"So, that's the kind of guy Mathew was," Corey muttered. He looked over at Nick. "Did you have any personal dealings with him?"

Nick shook his head. "No, not a whole lot. We had the divorce proceedings pending, but I am Doreen's lawyer, so I dealt with Mathew's lawyer, rather than with Mathew directly."

"Right, and that's a nice way to keep everything separate, isn't it?"

"It keeps business clean that way," Nick noted. "In this instance, his lawyer and I had an open channel. I did speak with him today because he had been handling the divorce, though things have come to a stop right now."

"How far did they get?" Corey asked.

"Mathew was supposed to have signed the final paperwork a few days ago. He told Doreen that he'd signed, but, when I contacted his lawyer, he realized that Mathew had missed a couple signatures. So the paperwork wasn't complete. You saw him back then, didn't you?"

She nodded. "Yes, Mathew told me too that he'd signed them and was just trying to get on with his life."

"Good, but, in fact, he'd had missed a couple spots, is that it?" Corey asked her.

She nodded. "That is my understanding from Nick here, but I don't know that myself. I didn't see any paperwork he'd signed. I don't even know what amount I'm settling for."

At that, Corey lifted his eyebrows and stared at her. "What? What do you mean, you don't know how much your divorce settlement is for?"

"I don't know how much it's for," she repeated. "I didn't care."

Corey turned and looked at Nick, who nodded. "Yes, that quite true. She never did get any actual figures as to what she was getting in the divorce."

Corey sat back, stumped. "That's very uncommon, to the point that it makes it hard to believe."

"I can't help that, but maybe I can explain it. We had differences, fundamental differences, as to what *wealth* meant, as to what *money* meant, or *decent money* meant. I didn't want to break Mathew nor cause him any hardship. Nick wanted me to get what I was entitled to, after fourteen years of marriage," she explained.

"When I realized we weren't really getting anywhere and were hung up on what that dollar figure should be, I told Nick to go ahead and to do what was fair and to not stress over little bits. My priority was to have enough to be comfortable here and to have the whole divorce process finished. I just wanted to be free of Mathew."

At that, Nick concurred.

Corey asked Nick, "At no point in time did she have any understanding of how much money was in the agreement?"

"That's right."

"Is the amount substantial?"

"Of course it's substantial," Nick confirmed, "and it still wasn't half of the marital assets, but it was enough that I was satisfied that Doreen would be okay, and it was enough under half that I thought Mathew would be more likely to sign and to be done with it."

"Okay," Corey replied, "so, do you know what happens now that he hasn't signed?"

"That all depends on who's in Mathew's will," Nick shared, "and how the will is set up."

"Right." Corey looked over at Doreen. "Are you in the will?"

"I don't know why I would be. He told me to leave, and he moved on with Robin."

"On the other hand," Nick interjected, explaining the conversation he had had with Mathew's attorney this morning—about Mathew being sad and upset about the pathway that he'd chosen, making a mistake with Doreen.

"*Great*," Corey muttered, "so maybe that was why he didn't sign. Maybe those missing signatures were on purpose. He was dragging his feet and wondering if there was another way."

"That's what I'm thinking," Nick agreed, with a nod.

"That still doesn't tell us who killed him," Doreen reminded them.

"No," Nick agreed, "and we need to find out who else might inherit and who might have inherited more, if Doreen were no longer in the picture."

"More important, Doreen," the PI stated gravely, "we've

got to ensure that whoever the angry stranger is who is after you—or whatever it is that he's after—doesn't get a chance to hurt you." Then he turned back to Nick. "You must ensure her safety."

"Mack is in charge of keeping her physically safe." Then Nick looked over at her. "Do you have a will in place?"

She frowned and then slowly shook her head. "No, I don't."

At that, Nick sucked back his breath. "Guess what we're doing today?" he asked, his tone tight. "That is something that needs to be resolved fast."

She shook her head. "Why? What's the urgency?"

Nick looked at her and smiled. "Depending on Mathew's will, you could get all his money. That makes you a target of greedy people. Even without Mathew's money," Nick explained, an odd note in his tone, "you will be a wealthy woman just because of the antiques, and maybe Robin's estate and everything else happening in your life over the next few months. So, we need to get a proper will for you locked down."

She shook her head. "I only have Nan and Mack in my life."

Nick nodded. "And I'm sure you would much rather have either of those two get your money than the other options, such as the government, for example."

She winced at that. "I'm not sure anybody likes to see the government take their money," she began, with a small smile. "On the other hand, somebody has to pay for schools and roads."

He chuckled. "Very true, but what if two people inherit Mathew's estate? You don't want the other person to take you out so they get the whole pie, do you? Especially not without a will in place. At least with a will, if you die, your share of Mathew's estate goes to Nan."

"Oh my." She nodded slowly. "Since I seem to still be married to Mathew, my own life is the problem, isn't it?"

Nick nodded. "As long as you remain married to Mathew, as his legal wife, you stand to gain everything, yes."

"I don't think Mathew would have killed me, but I could have been wrong. Maybe that's why he was taken out. Maybe he was here trying to do me in, and someone else knew about it and stopped him." She frowned, with a sad smile. "We won't know now."

"Not unless the police find anything or if Mathew's lawyer has anything on file to be given to you in the event of Mathew's death."

Her eyes widened at that. "Oh, good Lord," she muttered. "That is possible. Mathew's father did that very thing."

"What do you mean?" Nick asked, Corey frowning now.

"When Mathew's father died, he left Mathew a note. I remember he was pretty emotional about it."

"These things can be very emotional. When you think about it, … it's your last communication from somebody who cares about you," Nick suggested. "But I'm serious. Right after this, today even, we'll draft a will for you. We do need to sort out some things first though, like as to whether your marital home was in your name or not."

She nodded slowly. "A will won't be difficult. Basically everything goes to Nan."

"Good, except given her age, you need to have other options listed as well." Nick replied. "At least if we make that happen, then, in the event of anything, your estate would go to her. You can always change it later."

"Right, but that will be down the road though."

"Exactly," he said, with a gentle smile. "Let's just keep you safe, both physically and financially."

She stared at him. "Only Mathew would have benefitted if I died, since we are legally married still, so now I'm safe because he's gone first."

Corey shook his head. "But the question needs to be asked, did he leave you anything or did Mathew divide his estate among several people? The man beating on your door was looking for something."

"But I don't have anything for him or Mathew or whoever," she stated, looking between the two men helplessly. "I don't know where he would have gotten the idea that I did."

"If Mathew was tortured first, maybe he thought he could save himself by saying something of the sort."

She stared at him. "But that would mean he was knowingly sending someone like that to me."

"Quite true, but when people are in a tight spot, where they're trying to save their own life, in those moments, most people would say and do anything to make it happen."

"You're right," she murmured, "and I couldn't really blame them. Apparently Mathew was shot. I don't know if there was evidence of torture. We probably need to mention that to Mack."

Both men picked up their phones and started sending text messages.

Moments later, Doreen heard a woman calling her from the river. She looked out, and there was Nan, walking toward her. "Here's my grandmother," she announced.

Both men got up hurriedly, Corey saying, "I'll check in with you later. Keep me updated on what the cops do and find and on anything else you may need me to be on the lookout for." Then he left through the front door. By then, Nick was already on his way out the fence gate. He called back to Nan with a wave and told Doreen, "I'll talk to you later."

Nan just lifted a hand, and he disappeared. When Nan got closer, she noted, "It used to be that the men would stick around to see me. Lately it seems they can't wait to be gone before I arrive."

"I don't think that is it at all," Doreen countered, with a smile, as she walked over and gave Nan a hug.

"I know it isn't, dear. How are you holding up?" she asked, eyeing her granddaughter intently.

"I'm fine," she murmured.

"You're not fine, but you'll pretend to be fine, and I understand that too."

Doreen chuckled. "I do have coffee, if you want a cup."

"No, no coffee for me, but I did bring some treats, so maybe a cup of tea?" She looked at her granddaughter hopefully.

Doreen chuckled. "Tea it is." And she headed inside to put on the teakettle. When she came back out, Nan was sitting at the table, looking at her notes.

"What are these for?" Nan asked.

"Oh, just the conversation I had with the new detective who's handling this case," she muttered. "I didn't like her much, and the feeling was pretty mutual."

Nan frowned at her. "You don't want to piss off the law," she said cautiously. "Certainly not right now."

"No, I don't want to piss her off, Yet she wasn't being, … I guess she wasn't treating me the way that everybody else in the department always treats me. She had me pegged for Mathew's murder before she even began to ask me questions."

"Oh dear," Nan muttered, "and, of course, that would upset you right away."

Doreen gave her a wry look. "It certainly didn't endear her to me, put it that way."

"No, of course not. I've decided that I don't like her either."

"Why don't you like her?" Doreen asked.

"If she'll treat you that way, I certainly won't like her."

"It's not always that simple."

"It's not always much harder either," Nan declared.

With the two of them sitting outside, Nan patted Doreen's hand and asked, "So, where do we start?" When Doreen looked at her in surprise, Nan raised an eyebrow. "Surely you won't sit here and let everybody else handle this one, will you?" she asked.

Doreen smiled. "That's exactly what I needed." She leaned over and brushed Nan's cheek with a kiss. "I needed somebody to put me on the right pathway."

"I would think so," Nan declared, "particularly if you don't like this new detective or whatever she is. Nobody will look after you quite the same way as you will."

"Except Mack," Doreen added, with a smile.

"I'm glad you recognize his value," Nan stated, with a bright smile, "but it seems he'll have his hands full keeping this new woman corralled. So, while he's doing that, you need to get on to solving this murder." Nan eyed her shrewdly. "If nothing else, at least you would know you'd done right by Mathew."

"I'm surprised to hear you say that," she said, looking over at her grandmother.

"I fully recognize the mix of feelings you must be going

through right now. Mathew wasn't for you, and, in many ways, he was the absolute worst thing any woman could have encountered. But you don't have a mean bone in your body, and I can see you're struggling emotionally with his death."

"I'm not struggling with the loss of him," Doreen explained cautiously. "I think it's more the sadness that he didn't get a chance to live and to become the man he could have been." Nan almost snorted at that. Doreen glared at her. "I know. I know, but, hey, anybody can change," she added, holding up her hand.

"Just because I don't like the man, and he hurt you, I am well aware of the mix of feelings because I'm dealing with some of it myself," Nan murmured. "But the bottom line is, this is the hand we've been dealt, and this is what we have going forward. So, we need to figure out how to make the best of this and to ensure it gets correctly solved, first and foremost."

"I agree."

"We don't want the wrong person going to jail, but we also want to ensure that absolutely no suspicion falls on you."

"And Mack," she added automatically.

Nan smiled and then slowly nodded. "Or on Mack, good call, because he'll obviously be looked at pretty carefully as well."

"I think he has an alibi, but again we don't even know when Mathew died."

"Do we know how he died?" Nan asked rather delicately. Doreen filled her in on what she knew, which wasn't very much. Nan nodded. "So, we have to retrace his steps, to find out who he met, where he was at, and what happened to him. If he flew, we need to find out how and when. If he drove, we need to find his vehicle."

"Corey's helping on a lot of that. He and I and Nick were just now discussing this. I don't know where Mathew's rental car is, and, even if he did fly, Mathew was never without his green Jags. I certainly didn't see one at the restaurant."

"No, of course not, and those aren't exactly something you pick up at the airport."

"He would have rented or leased that on a private arrangement with someone or with one of the luxury car companies," Doreen murmured, with a nod. "Maybe we should find out from them too. ... I also don't want to get snarled up with this other detective. If she thinks I'm interfering in her investigation, it'll only make things worse," Doreen shared cautiously.

At that, Nan spun on her and asked, "Why not? If you don't trust her, you must do whatever you need to do to ensure that you're safe and in the clear on all this."

Everything Nan said was correct, but somehow Doreen didn't think dealing with this *Insley* woman would be quite the same as dealing with Mack. "I'm also trying to keep the captain out of trouble as well," she shared.

Nan studied her. "In all of that, you still want to see that everyone gets what they need, and it all shows you come from the heart, ... but this is one of those times when you must look after yourself," she stated with finality. "If you don't, you could find yourself up on a murder charge."

Doreen swallowed hard and nodded. "Why is it so much harder for me to defend myself versus going to bat for somebody else?"

"Ironically, because of Mathew," Nan declared. "He wore down your self-confidence and your self-esteem, and, deep down, you don't think you're worth it. You'll do everything for everybody else, but you won't do anything for yourself. This is a really good time to turn that around and to show me and the rest of the world that Mathew has been put in his place once and for all."

Taking a hard look at her granddaughter, Nan continued. "You don't need to let him control anything anymore, and he definitely shouldn't be allowed to control this scenario from the grave." Doreen stared at her grandmother for a moment. Nan added, "You know I'm right."

With a shrug of her shoulders, Doreen nodded, conceding the point.

The thing was, she did know it. Her grandmother had described the scenario perfectly, as only she could.

Chapter 7

NOTHING LIKE HAVING the truth shown to you in such a way that it freed you from all the strings you've somehow been wound up in and tied up in knots over. Doreen felt as if the burden had been lifted from her, and Nan was right. Doreen had given away far too much of her power to that husband of hers, and now that he was gone, the best thing she could do to say a concrete goodbye would be to solve this mystery, clearing her name and Mack's. Then everybody could move forward, without Mathew's shadow hanging around like a dark cloud.

She was sorry Mathew was gone for his sake, but not for her own, and even being able to freely admit that was shockingly healing as well.

As soon as Nan was gone, Doreen grabbed her notebook, headed down to the river, and sat there with the animals, trying to figure out a plan of attack. She needed to go to the crime scene again, assuming it had been cleared up enough that she was allowed to get near it. She presumed at this point in time it had been. She figured Corey would trace Mathew's movements from the time he arrived in Kelowna to the time he was murdered. That wouldn't be quite so easy.

So Doreen would take another approach. Mathew had a *man of affairs*, as he used to call him, a male secretary, business manager, or something along that line. She remembered him as Reggie, during their marriage.

She pulled out her phone, checked to see if she happened to still have his number. When she found it, on impulse, she called it. When Reggie answered, she identified herself, afraid there would be an immediate hang-up, but instead he perked right up.

"Doreen, it's so lovely to hear from you," he said.

She sighed in relief. "Here I was thinking you wouldn't even talk to me."

"You wouldn't have killed him," he stated, his tone sad. "He was a difficult man to be around. I know that, but I also know that your heart is good and kind. I'm glad you've moved on."

"Not only have I moved on, I've formed an odd hobby."

He laughed. "I do believe I've heard about this, as Mathew himself told me about your penchant for solving mysteries." Then he stopped. "Are you working on Mathew's case?" he asked curiously.

"It's certainly something I need to do. I have to ensure that I don't end up on the hook for this one," she shared.

"Of course. Sadly the police always look to the spouse—or, in this case, ex-spouse—and you are the perfect suspect, being in the middle of a divorce, as well. Yet he did sign the papers," Reggie noted.

"Apparently he missed a couple signatures, so they aren't signed and sealed," she stated in frustration. "So, what should have been a closed, over, done deal apparently isn't quite so clear-cut anymore."

"Oh dear." He hesitated and then mentioned, "He did

tell me that he was reconsidering his options."

"Ah, I don't know who he reconsidered them with, but I'm guessing somebody didn't like the new choices he was making."

"No, and he certainly did have some, … shall we say, rather unsavory friends?"

"Yes, I know. Although a lot of that I would think happened when I wasn't around."

"He never did let you in on the business side of his life, did he?"

"No, absolutely not. As you well know, anytime I walked into the room, you guys clammed up. I wasn't given anything but papers to sign, if and when he needed me to, and beyond that? … I didn't have anything to do with his business life."

"Maybe that's for the best," he murmured. "When you think about it, it leaves you in a much better position right now."

"Only if the police believe me when I tell them that I didn't kill Mathew," she stated. "And honestly, they're not too cooperative at the moment."

"Right, given the circumstances, I don't imagine they'll be terribly cooperative with anybody."

"Have they contacted you yet?" she asked.

"Not yet, but I am expecting them."

"Yes, you should be. Obviously anybody connected to this mess will be part and parcel of it."

"Of course, and I will cooperate fully."

"I appreciate that. Do you have any idea what he was even doing here?" she asked curiously. "He didn't contact me, which is odd."

"He didn't?" Reggie asked.

"No, the first I saw him was when I found him, unfortunately."

"Oh dear, did you actually find him?"

"Yes, at the Chinese food place," she shared. "That's what I don't really understand. Why he was even there?"

After a moment's hesitation, Reggie admitted, "He did ask me for a list of your favorite hunting grounds."

She stopped and stared at the phone. "Oh, good Lord," she muttered. "Did you tell him of this place?"

"I do remember you used to complain that you couldn't get Chinese food whenever you wanted it, which was such an odd thing, considering the amount of money you have."

"You mean, the amount of money *my ex* had," she corrected.

"Sorry, I forgot. He didn't believe that Chinese was good for you, as I recall."

"Not good for me, not good for my waistline, not for anything," she replied in a dry tone. "So you told him that I would be at a Chinese food restaurant?"

"No, no, not at all. I didn't know where you were or where you might have gone, but I did remind him that you had this penchant for Chinese food."

"*Huh,*" she muttered. "It seems a little too much of a coincidence for him to have gone there, then me to have shown up as well."

"I do know that he may have … I don't even know if I should be saying this."

"You might as well because, if we don't start speaking up, none of us will get any answers. Not to mention I can be on the hook for this."

"Fine. He may have hired somebody to follow you."

Her breath let out in a single gush. "Wow." She could

hardly formulate the words in her brain. "That's so him, isn't it?"

"Unfortunately, yes," Reggie said apologetically. "When he wanted to know something, he didn't waste time and energy. He just went right to the source."

She sighed. "Do you know who he hired?"

"Somebody he's used off and on, and they are from down here."

"Okay, that's good to know," she said. "Did he tell you why he wanted to see me?"

"I think he was hoping for one last-ditch effort to charm you back into his life again."

"But he knew that wasn't possible," she stated. "I made that very clear the last time."

"He mentioned how he got you to go out for dinner with him, and he thought that maybe he could get you to ditch your country boyfriend and come back to him."

"I don't think he thought that at all," she declared. "I'm not sure where his brain was at, so I don't know what he thought would have supported that idea to begin with." Another long moment of silence came from the other end, and she just waited. Reggie was definitely a poker player. He could generally outlast the rest of them, and it was always her that broke. Not this time though.

"He hadn't stopped caring," Reggie shared, with difficulty. Then he gave her the name of the person Mathew had hired to follow her.

When he gave her the name, she wrote it down, then stared at it. "It's not somebody I know," she murmured. She would look him up online, so she had a face to go with the name. Plus she would have to remember to share this with Corey.

"No, it's a newer one," Reggie noted. "Mathew's made a lot of changes lately."

"Was he worried about something?" she asked him.

Reggie hesitated and then, with a sigh, replied, "I guess it doesn't matter now, and, if it helps solves this, I'll tell you. Although I'm sure I should be speaking to the police."

With a note of humor, she reassured him, "They'll be getting in touch with you soon enough, don't worry. But, hey, anything you can tell me would give me a jump on them."

"Should you be getting a jump on them?" he asked.

"Maybe, maybe not," she admitted, "but I'll end up sharing everything with them anyway. If my friend was handling the case, it wouldn't be an issue, but, because he's been deemed too close to the situation, it's all become far more difficult."

"Of course," Reggie said. "We always want to keep our friends close and our enemies closer. The problem is, with this case, I'm not sure who is who."

"I understand, and I am sorry, Reggie. I know that the two of you were very close."

"We were, but a lot of times I didn't like who he was and what he was doing," he admitted, with a heavy sigh. "I threatened to quit on two occasions and was prepared to see it through."

"Oh my, I didn't know that."

"After he hit you the first time, … and again after he hit you the second time."

She sat back and sighed. "You mean, the first and the second time that *you* knew about."

There was silence at the other end. "Yes, I guess that is true. He swore to me that he wouldn't do it again. Abusing women, the one thing I couldn't tolerate."

"Yet Mathew told me the one thing he couldn't tolerate was my being disobedient," she shared, blindly staring off into the distance. "I had no idea you even talked to him about it."

"That was also one of the things about him—complete and utter silence was the rule, remember?"

"Yes, *loyalty*, that was everything to him." She sighed. "It's too bad he ended up in such a mess at the end."

"It's too bad he didn't stick with what was good and honest and treat it right. Although I will say that, after Robin died, he went through a time of rethinking his life—and you were a part of that."

She heard the smile in his tone when he spoke those words. "Not that I ever aspired to be considered a *rethink*," she noted in a dry tone, "I am glad that something good may have come from Robin's death after all."

"That was a pretty rough one here too."

"I'm sure it was."

Reggie said, "It seems you've been through a lot these last few months."

"Too much," she replied, "though at least I didn't have to resort to eating dog food."

A shocked gasp came on the other end. "No. Surely he gave you money to live on, didn't he?"

She snorted. "You should know. You handled the books for him."

"No," he corrected, "only the household accounts. He has an accountant for the books." He waited a minute and asked again, "Did he not give you anything?"

"No, he let me have my old car, which was mine before we married, and I took Mugs, and that was it, whatever I could fit in my car, whatever he didn't withhold from me," she explained. "He was supposed to pay for the hotel, while I got a job and better situated, but, of course, he didn't do as he said about that either."

"Oh, good Lord," he whispered, shocked.

"Apparently you didn't know him quite so well either, *huh?*"

"Not about that, no," he whispered. "And, of course, he wouldn't have told me because he knew how much I already disapproved of the way he treated you."

"I'm really glad to hear that," she shared. "More because I didn't know anybody cared about what happened. It's nice to know that you at least cared a little bit," she murmured. "Though somehow it feels very wrong to even be having this conversation over his dead body right now."

"I understand."

"Have you contacted Roger, his lawyer, at all?"

"No. He usually contacts me, when needed. Roger knows I'm here, and I'm to continue maintaining the house, until somebody can sort out what we're supposed to do," Reggie replied.

"Do you have enough saved up for a pension? Do you have a place to go?"

"It all depends on if I'm mentioned in the will. ... I would like to think so, but I don't know that for sure."

"No. Unfortunately none of us do, do we?" she noted. "I don't know what'll happen now with me either, since he hadn't completely signed the actual divorce document. I thought it was all done and taken care of, but apparently it wasn't."

"So intent was there, and yet I'm not so sure," Reggie pointed out. "Remember that part about doing a major rethink?"

"Yes, but he still had to have my agreement for that re-think to go through, so to speak," she argued. "And I had already made it abundantly clear to Mathew that I'd had all I could stomach of him and his antics. I wouldn't put myself within range of his fist anymore."

"I am so sorry about that. I had no idea how often that happened."

"I wouldn't have known that you cared either," she added, "but enough of that. I'm free and clear, and I'm a heck of a lot happier now."

By the time she finished talking with him, she had a bunch of names, including the private detective Mathew had hired and an idea of where he'd gone and why, but that still didn't explain everything. Just before she disconnected, she asked Reggie one more time, "Did you have any idea what was going on in his world? Something that could result in this?"

"For sure? No," Reggie replied. "The lawyer might know. They were friends. His accountant might know. They were friends too. But I think the bottom line was, he got himself into trouble and had no way to get out."

"So, not divorcing me would have helped his problem? Because wanting me back could only be about money."

Reggie hesitated, then spoke. "Unfortunately, I think so."

"So, it *was* money based?" She was shocked.

"Knowing Mathew, I would assume so, but I don't know for sure," he murmured. "If you find out anything, please let me know."

"Ditto," she said. "We will get to the bottom of this."

Chapter 8

AFTER DOREEN'S CALL to Reggie, Mathew's *man of affairs*, she sent off an update in a text to Corey. There was just so much to digest. She sat here at the river, her notebook in hand, writing down the gist of that conversation. She picked up several sticks and threw them for Mugs. He half-heartedly retrieved them, only to get sidelined by a squirrel, dashing into the water. At least that made him happy. She smiled at the dog's antics, as he splashed himself and everybody else around him.

When he raced to her, she braced herself. Sure enough, he stopped right beside her and shook all the water droplets onto her. She protested, hugging the notebook to her chest, but Mugs ignored her and shook again and again.

Groaning, she smiled as she cuddled him, looking down at her soaked shirt. "What made you think I needed that?" Of course he didn't seem to care. But then why would he? She was many things, but definitely not somebody who cared about getting wet, or had to dress a certain way, or always had to be perfect.

As a matter of fact, she was very comfortable with who she was now, and that was a very strange feeling. Also a very good thing and a definite improvement. She absolutely loved the sense of discovery she felt, as she figured out who this new Doreen person was. The personal freedom she had slowly recovered with Mathew out of her life had gradually changed her. His death, while unfortunate, made that process complete in a way, and she was feeling quite overwhelmed. She felt a glimmer of joy at the start of what would appear to be a completely joyful experience.

As Nan had pointed out, Doreen should do one thing, and that was put this all to rest. With her phone out, she quickly looked up the name of Mathew's newest private detective. Seeing the contact info and the guy's photo, she added his name and number to her notepad. She was tempted to call him, but she figured Corey would do that. Then she phoned Mack.

When he answered, his tone was very calm, quiet, and gentle. "Are you okay, Doreen?"

"I'm fine," she replied briskly. "Look. I talked to Reggie. He is the *man of affairs* for Mathew, and apparently Mathew had sent a private detective up here, who tracked down where I was likely to be. I'll text you his name and number. Now, whether he was following me or whether he accidentally saw me, I don't know, but it seems to be one huge coincidence about Mathew being at the Chinese food place. He may have been there for me."

"What?"

"I also spoke to Reggie in regard to anything going on in Mathew's world, and Reggie indicated that Mathew had gotten himself into trouble, and he was reconsidering his options with me. Reggie doesn't think it was a coincidence that Mathew was here that day. The fact that he didn't fully sign the divorce papers was most likely intentional because he knew that, if he didn't have to liquidate his assets for me, he could probably get out of the trouble he was in." With all that rushing out in a blur, she took a deep breath and relaxed a little bit.

After a few moments of silence, she continued. "You should also talk to the accountant who handled Mathew's books," she noted, then followed up with the contact information. "His *man of affairs* is Reggie, who I just spoke to …" Then she gave him the phone number as well as the name of the private eye he'd sent to Kelowna.

"Wow," Mack said briskly. "Apparently you've woken up."

"Woken up and realized that, whether Mathew intended it or not, he has given me a huge gift."

"And what is that?" Mack asked.

"The gift of his no longer being an issue for me," she stated, with a note of humor. "I get that's probably not the nicest thing I could say, but the perfect way for me to move on from this is to have it all go by the wayside once and for all."

"I would really like that very much."

"You're doing okay with this?"

"Yes."

"I'm not happy to hear that he could have solved this problem by the divorce not happening."

"Yet, either way, if he's dealing with those kind of people, he was probably in way too far, and nothing would have fixed it for very long. Once those guys get their hooks into someone, they have a way of hanging on."

She added, "It was also very enlightening to hear from Reggie that he had fought on my behalf after"—she struggled to get it out—"after Mathew hit me. Reggie didn't know about all of it. He just knew about a couple times, and apparently he went to bat for me, which was nice to find out that I had a benevolent uncle looking after me, or trying to."

"Of course," Mack agreed. "This is really good information, Doreen. We'll contact Reggie and Mathew's PI and Mathew's attorney too, get their statements."

"Absolutely," she confirmed, with a smile. "Now there were other people in Mathew's world than just these three."

"We know of a couple because of Robin's case."

"Exactly. I also need to contact the lawyer, Roger. I'm hoping that Reggie has been taken care of in Mathew's will. Otherwise I'm not sure Reggie has enough to live on either. He's at an age where finding a job will be almost impossible."

"Will you let us handle it, please?" Mack stated, not asking for her permission.

She snorted. "*Sure.*"

"*Doreen,*" he said, with a note of warning.

"You think I don't know that the new detective doesn't care about me?" she argued. "I'm just a case. I'm just a name, a number, and, if she can close it and make herself look good, she won't be particularly bothered as to whether she finds the true killer. She's looking to pin it all on me and carry on."

"That's not fair," he protested.

"Maybe not, but I did not get a vote of confidence from her. I've become quite used to working with your department and hadn't realized to what extent I had become so comfortable," she shared. "I can see it's a problem."

"A problem in what way?" he asked in alarm.

"Just that I trusted it, the system, you know? I trusted that things would be okay and that people would have my back. I guess that's one of the first laws of business, or life really, that nobody has your back but you."

"No, that's not true," Mack argued. "You're supposed to be surrounded by people you trust."

"That's all fine and dandy, until something shifts, and then you're taken off the case, and they put a stranger on it."

"That's different. You can't blame the captain for that, and you know it. I didn't like being taken off the case, but I do understand it. It does no good to arrest someone for murder if some slick lawyer will set them free because I was part of the investigation."

"Are you really a suspect?" she asked.

"No. I've got an alibi for the time of death now, approximately two hours before you found him."

"Interesting," she murmured.

"You don't have an alibi, do you?"

"Of course not," she snapped. "I talked to Nan that morning, but I could have been calling from anywhere. I was at home with the animals, as always. Now Mugs can do a great job at trying to talk, but he's not that good a conversationist."

"No, he sure isn't, but Thaddeus certainly can talk."

"I know, but we weren't there at Mr. Woo's at the time of Mathew's death. We were at home," she declared.

"And I suppose you never spoke to Richard or nobody came by or anything, right?"

"No, and I wasn't down at Nan's, and Nan wasn't up here with me," she added. "It was a nice, calm, relaxing day—until it wasn't. You were coming for lunch, and I walked out to get Chinese as a treat."

"Which I very much appreciate," he noted, with a heavy sigh.

"Apparently I'm not supposed to do things like that. Look what kind of trouble it got us into. Two hours, *huh*? So at least you have an alibi."

"Luckily I do. I was at work with everybody else, so I'm more or less off the hook at this point."

"More or less?"

"There's always the suspicion that I hired somebody," he shared on a dry note.

"Oh, good Lord. Absolutely no way that would happen. As I told your brother, if you had killed Mathew, it would be more of a bare-knuckle affair, since it would be all about what Mathew did to me. You would never hire anybody else to do your dirty work."

An odd silence followed on the other end, before he finally spoke. "Thank you, I think?"

She burst out laughing. "No, it's definitely a thank-you moment," she declared. "Now we just have to clear me, and the only way to do that is to find out who decided to take out my dearly beloved ex, and the answer to that won't be quite so clear-cut. He's got way more enemies than anybody deserves to have."

"Seems he earned them, to be honest."

"Yes, he was often a very tough businessman, and, because of that alone, we'll find no shortage of people who didn't appreciate his methods, or the fact that he had money and they didn't."

"He also didn't care about who had money and who didn't, as long as it involved something he wanted. Such as you."

"Exactly, and the fact that he was reconsidering his options in that regard doesn't mean that he would have succeeded. Remember that," she murmured.

"Hey, I didn't say that."

"That's good, but I don't want you thinking it either."

"Deal," he said, now laughing. "You're right. We will get to the bottom of this. Just go easy on your detective work, will you?"

"*Sure*," she snapped, with a sniff. "If she stays away from me, we'll get along just fine."

"You're the prime murder suspect. Remember that?" he asked, deepening his tone.

At that, she snorted. "Which means she's not doing her job. I won't even deign to listen to that nonsense. I've got things to do that are far more productive."

"Wait, wait, wait," he wailed.

However, she ended the call then, with a big fat smile on her face. Now she was starting to feel better. She was starting to feel like herself. Hopping to her feet, she walked up to the house, calling the animals, "Come on, guys. It's time to start shaking up this town a little bit. Somebody is trying to make it look like we did something wrong, and that'll never go over well. Particularly when it comes to my ex."

Chapter 9

NOW DETERMINED, DOREEN walked into the kitchen, grabbed the leashes, and put both Goliath and Mugs on a leash, even though Goliath gave her a look of disdain. She shook her head. "Either you're staying at home or you're coming on a leash."

At that, he submitted, as if he completely understood. She figured what he understood was her tone of voice. She meant business, and every one of them understood that much. As soon as she got her animals and then herself in the car, she headed down to the Chinese food place.

She could have walked, and maybe she should have, but, at the moment, it seemed a whole lot easier to figure out exactly what was going on with wheels, since she would have multiple stops, she was sure.

As she arrived at the Chinese restaurant, she stepped inside, the animals on the leash. Mr. Woo, the owner, came out, took one look and started scolding her.

She raised both hands. "I know. I didn't pick up the Chinese food from my previous order, and I'm sorry." He just glared at her. "I also didn't kill him." The look of astonishment on his face made her smile. "Yeah, because I found him and because he's my ex-husband, a lot of people think I might have killed him."

Immediately he shook his head, then shook his finger at her.

"No, I know. I wouldn't have done it either," she murmured. "Yes, I would still like my Chinese food, but I need to pay for that today and for what I didn't pick up yesterday." She winced at that though, talk about a waste of money. Not to mention a waste of good food. Yet her fault for not having gone into the restaurant and gotten it.

"Food gone," Mr. Woo said. "You had bad day. I had bad day. We make bad day go away. I give you hot food. You pay half price."

Considering what they'd both been through, and probably the state of business that he hadn't been able to conduct because of the mess going on, she thought that was very fair of him. "Okay, but I'm here to ask you a bunch of questions though."

He stared at her, his eyebrows going up. "You police?"

"No, of course I'm not police," she stated, giving him a look. "But you also know that I do an awful lot of work solving the mysteries of the cold cases."

He nodded slowly.

"Have the police been here? Did they ask you about whether another man was hanging around?"

He nodded again.

"And was he?"

He shook his head.

She sighed in exasperation. "Mathew was killed two hours before I came to pick up the food."

His jaw dropped. "Two hours?"

She nodded. "Yes, so he was here sometime before, so

somebody must have seen something."

"I was in kitchen, cooking."

"I get that. Did anybody come in during that time?"

He shook his head. "No. We just open when you come. That's why you come then."

"That's true," she stated. For once the Chinese restaurant in town didn't wait until three o'clock to open. Thankfully this one opened at noon, so she'd ordered early to beat the rush. "Did you go out for supplies? Did anybody come in? Did you get any deliveries?"

He stared at her, and she could see him trying to think. He frowned, his face cleared, then he frowned again, and then he slowly shook his head. "No, I do prep work in the kitchen. No one came."

She nodded. "So somebody was sitting around outside your place for two hours, and you didn't know?"

He nodded slowly. "I didn't know."

"Right." She sighed and tucked a strand of hair back behind her ear. "Okay, do you have any cameras?"

He shook his head. "No cameras."

"That's not helpful either."

"No cameras, no see nobody. You want Chinese now?"

She shook her head. "I'll be back though." She looked at her watch and frowned. "Give me about an hour and a half."

He nodded. "Ready in ninety minutes. You be here this time."

"I will, provided there is no other dead body."

At that, he gave her a look.

She nodded. "Yeah, that's about how I feel right now myself. I really don't want any more dead bodies."

And, with a small smile, she turned, left, and headed outside to the back of the restaurant. There, she noted that the crime scene tape was put away. Maybe for that reason alone, she felt a little bit more comfortable about walking around, but still the place had an odd feel to it, an odd smell. Blood was like that.

As she walked toward the site, Mugs's nose was low to the ground all around. The crime scene people had made a horrific mess. All the yellow yarrow flowers were trampled to the ground. The whole area was dirty, and some garbage was on the ground. She sighed, as she stared at it.

"Nothing pretty about the after effects of a murder," she murmured. "Absolutely nothing is here that makes me happy." Of course nobody would care about making her happy at this point. It was all about making the guilty party pay.

Now, if only she had the answers on how to make that happen.

Chapter 10

DOREEN HEADED DOWNTOWN and parked at the police station. Not leaving her car, she phoned Mack and asked, "Can you check the street cameras outside the Chinese food place?"

"Yes, my colleagues already requested access to the traffic cams this morning," he shared. "Where are you?"

"I'm just outside the police station. I'll take a walk around."

"Outside here?" he asked.

"Yeah," she confirmed.

"Why?"

"I don't know," she muttered. "I guess I don't really have an answer to that."

"*Doreen*," he said, with a note of warning.

"I know. I don't even understand what this impulse is about. Still, I'm here, but I don't know why. Anyway, I talked to the owner, Mr. Woo, from the Chinese food restaurant. He didn't see anything, didn't hear anything, doesn't know anything."

With a note of humor, Mack shared, "Someone has already spoken to him, and yes, that's what he told us too."

"Right," she muttered. "I don't understand how everybody can be so blind as to what goes on around them. I'm not certain I believe him."

"Yes, you can understand that. It's happened to you a couple times."

"Maybe so," she muttered. "That doesn't make me feel any better, and I'm not altogether certain I appreciate your bringing it up."

He chuckled. "Maybe not, yet whatever is happening right now, we're on it."

"I know, but not fast enough. I would like very much to know where Mathew was and how he came in."

"Someone checked with a couple rental agencies, but they don't have green Jags."

"No? I bet Bernard would know."

"I don't know about that," Mack countered, "and do you really want to get involved with him, when his son's out there, gunning for your mug shots?"

"I wish I knew what his son was up to, or if he is still being difficult."

"Why don't you just leave Bernard to handle his son?"

"I was planning on it," she replied, "but Bernard would definitely know where to rent a green Jag privately." And, with that, she ended her call with Mack and quickly phoned Bernard.

"Doreen," he greeted her in a jovial tone. "Are you coming for coffee?"

"Ha. Afraid I might kill you while you're making it?"

He snorted. "No, not in my dreams or my nightmares. Come on over. Come have coffee."

"I wondered if you knew where somebody could rent a green Jag on a private or commercial level, for when they're in town."

He hesitated. "Why are you asking?"

"Because my ex only traveled with green Jags. Always."

"What?"

"Yeah, that was his favorite vehicle, and, if he could get it, that's always what he got."

"Okay. Weird."

"He's had them here in the past," she shared. "I don't know whether he drove up this last time or flew in and rented here, but, in either case, where is his vehicle?"

"The police should find out if he flew in, and, if he did, they could also access cameras at the airport to verify if he was picked up in a green Jag."

"Yes, well, I'm jumping right ahead to assuming a green Jag, just because I know Mathew," she stated. "I've also determined that he was coming up to talk to me, trying to make me change my mind on the divorce."

"Really? I thought you had a done deal?"

"It was done for me, but I've since learned that Mathew was in dire straits and needed money. The divorce would put him in over-the-top, so he was likely wondering if he could get me to hold off on the divorce for a bit or go back to him long enough that he could get out of trouble."

"Wow. And I thought I was low."

"I know, right? Anyway, I never even saw him, so I don't know what was on his mind for sure. However, if that's the case, he would have been heading to me. However, after his run-ins with the local authorities, he was sidestepping my house, I guess. He had sent a private detective here to track my movements, so apparently that's where he learned I would likely be at the Chinese food place that day."

"So it seems."

"There's a good chance they were listening in from my backyard—or had my phone bugged," she suggested, now staring down at her phone, "which I'm just now realizing is potentially still a problem."

"Get a new phone," Bernard suggested.

"Yeah, I think I will. At the same time, it's quite possible that I was being followed."

"Yeah, absolutely," Bernard agreed. "But how would they have known you would be there ahead of time?"

"I did talk to Nan on my phone, and I probably did mention that I might go down for Chinese food."

"There you go. Definitely get a new phone, and hand yours over to the police."

"Right, I'm at the police station right now, but I don't have another one."

"I've got one you can use," he offered. "Go drop off your phone, then come down here, and we'll have a cup of coffee together. I'll get lunch ready, and we'll talk about what you can do next. I'm finding this very exciting."

She snorted. "I would ask what the update was on your son."

"Let's just say he likes his allowance."

"Yeah, ya think? Maybe you could put him to work doing something useful."

"Oh, do you need something?"

"My lawyer has hired a PI to look into things for me as well, but your son could always get a job doing stuff like that, if he wanted to, or something along that line."

"Ha, I never even thought of that. It's still kind of sleazy …"

"No better than selling photos to some rag, yelling, *She killed her husband?* Still, maybe he could benefit by learning to do it right, without breaking the law."

He snorted at that. "I tell you, give kids an inch, they'll take ten feet and smile at you while they do it."

"I don't have any kids, so I shouldn't be giving you any advice. Just pass it off as I'm having a bad week," she noted, with a chuckle, "but I will take you up on that offer for a phone. I'll pop over and hand this one in." She stared down at it.

"Go on, then drive straight here." With that, he ended the call.

She got out, sent Mack a text to meet her outside, then walked up to the station door. She waited outside for him to show up. She'd only been here a moment, when he came barreling out front.

Looking at her, he frowned. "What's the matter?"

"I was talking to Bernard, and we decided that the only way the private detective or anybody else might have known I was going for Chinese food is because I talked to Nan about it that morning. I had told her I would go pick it up."

His eyebrows shot up. "So, do you think somebody had a listening device in the house?"

"Or on my phone," she added, holding it out to him.

He took it and nodded. "What will you do for a phone then?"

"You check that one for listening devices. Meanwhile, I'll go have coffee with Bernard, and he has a phone I can borrow. I guess they call them burner phones?"

He nodded slowly, then looked at her. "It's just a phone that you put SIM cards into, when you want to make an untraceable phone call."

"That also means nobody could call me."

"Except if you call me first, then I would have your

number in my call history."

"Good enough," she said. "I will do that for a couple key people. Then, beyond that, don't be surprised to see that new number."

"Right, I'll get the techs to look at this one, and, if it's clear, you'll have it back pretty soon."

"Perfect," she said. "And, if it's not clear, maybe we can use it to set a trap."

He stared at her, a slow smile twitching up the corner of his lips. "As I mentioned before," he repeated cheerfully, "you would make a great cop."

She gave him a dark look. "And, as I recall, that's becoming an insult."

"Not an insult at all, and you're just judging by one person."

"Yeah, I don't like her."

"Any idea why?" he asked, staring at her, because he didn't really have a problem with his new colleague.

"She was rude to me. She thinks I killed Mathew," Doreen replied.

"If you were a real criminal, it would have been much worse."

"If I was a real criminal, I might have been geared for it, but I'm not. I just didn't like her attitude. Is this her first ever detective position?"

Mack avoided her question, giving her a hug, then saying, "Say hi to Bernard for me."

"Will do." She walked back to her car, and, with the animals now settling down, clearly irritated at not being able to greet Mack, she drove to Bernard's.

As she pulled into the big fancy driveway, the gate opened in front of her, and she pulled up to the front entrance. With the animals out and sniffing around, generally more interested in their next set of journeys, Bernard stepped out of the house and opened up the big front doors.

"Come in, come in," he greeted her. "It's a terrible state of affairs."

"It's a pain in the butt," she declared.

"And yet," he replied, waggling his eyebrows, "a somewhat convenient one."

She sighed. "That just makes me feel worse," she muttered.

"Do you still care for Mathew?"

"No," she declared, "but he represents a stage of my life that I can't easily walk away from."

He listened to her and nodded. "That's very true. Grief doesn't end just because the relationship did."

"Exactly. Even if the relationship had been a good thing and was over, one would have feelings about it. In my case, the marriage was not a good thing at all, and now hearing that he planned to try to change my mind again doesn't make me feel any better."

"Especially considering that he was only trying to make you change your mind to make his life easier."

"Yeah, but that was him," she stated, with a wry look. "As much as I hate to admit it, nothing seems to have changed in terms of who he was."

"Why would it?" Bernard asked, with a shrug. "He was happy with who he was. He was just in a spot and needed a way out. That's what we all do."

Again, no real way to argue with that because it was true.

Bernard led her into the big drawing room, and she smiled as she entered. "I do love this room, Bernard. I love the space, the openness."

"It is my favorite room too," he agreed. "Although it tends to give off more of a chilly feeling in the evenings when it's cold, it's absolutely lovely during the day, especially nice sunny ones like today. Now sit down and relax. I've got coffee coming, and I have arranged for lunch."

"Good," she said, giving him a fat grin. "I can always eat."

He burst out laughing. "You're one of the few women who really enjoys their groceries and isn't afraid to say so."

"Are you kidding? I absolutely adore groceries, especially yours."

He gave her an affectionate smile. "Set the animals free. They can't do any damage here."

She snorted at that. "You're kidding, right?"

"It's fine. They'll be totally okay, and, if we do have messes to clean up, I have housekeepers."

She burst out laughing. "I had forgotten," she muttered.

"Which is strange because you lived this life before, did you not?"

"I did," she confirmed cheerfully, "but I would be totally okay to never go back to it."

"That surprises me."

"That's because I didn't really get to live it. I existed in it, but it wasn't my lifestyle. It wasn't me or even any aspect of me that I recognized. It was more like pretending to be that quiet and perfect china doll that Mathew wanted."

Bernard shook his head at that. "Quiet? He didn't know what he was missing out on."

"No, and now he'll never find out either," she reminded him.

He nodded, giving her points for that. "And you'll still try to solve this case, *huh*? Even though he was who he was?"

"Yes. It's a good way to bring closure, not only to the case but for me."

"I can understand that, but you certainly do stretch tolerance and affability. Not sure he deserved it."

"Not sure he did either," she agreed, "but it doesn't matter because this is the mess that faces me, and I want to put it behind me as quickly as possible."

"What's next? You've been waiting for this divorce to go through, as I understand."

She nodded. "I have been."

"Then what? Will you be putting poor Mack out of his misery?"

She shot him a look. "What do you know about poor Mack's misery?" she asked in a dry tone.

"Hey, I can see a man in love, having been there and having loved every aspect of that process," Bernard shared, with a big grin on his face. "I can definitely sympathize with him."

She sighed. "He is really not having such a hard time."

"No, but he is not totally sure where he stands either." He glanced at her. "Did you tell him where you were headed today?"

"Yeah, I sure did. He says hi."

Bernard nodded. "You know he really cares for you, right?"

"Of course I do, and, yes, I am planning on *putting him out of his misery*," she admitted, with an eye roll. "Whatever that means."

He just laughed. "Whatever it turns out to mean, have some fun, explore it, and dive on in. You may have existed in your previous relationship, but don't do that to Mack. Be there 100 percent, and you'll be surprised at the good it does for both of you."

Chapter 11

DOREEN WAS ON her way home, with a new phone in her hand, realizing that she'd forgotten to text the number to Mack. She headed to the Chinese food place, so Mr. Woo wouldn't be angry. Still, knowing that this order would go cold before she ate again, she would have it for dinner, and that would be just fine. As she pulled up in front of the Chinese food place, her gaze once again went to the yarrow patch, as sadness overwhelmed her for a moment. Trying to ignore it and to escape unscathed, she raced inside, quickly paid for the food, then picking up her parcel, gave Mr. Woo a smile. She noticed he appeared to be unhappier than he had been earlier that day.

She asked him, "Have you had a lot of flak from the media?"

He shook his head, his gaze darting everywhere but at her. Frowning, she took the food and headed home, wondering what was going on. But, hey, he was probably having just as much trouble dealing with what had happened as she was. She put the bag on the table and texted Mack, adding him as a new contact. **I got my new phone.**

When her phone buzzed. She answered it.

"Good thing you got a new phone."

Silence then it hit her and she gasped. "Did you check my phone?"

He sighed. "Yeah, it's got a tracking device in it."

She frowned, a little shocked to hear it. "Oh my God," she muttered in a strangled voice. "I knew it was possible, but I guess I didn't really want to believe it."

"It's there," he murmured.

"Can you trace it?"

"Nope."

"Can I have my phone back?"

"Not at the moment. We're wondering how best to take advantage of the fact that we've found it, before he finds out."

"To set a trap?"

"Maybe. At the moment, I'll hang on to it. You've got your new phone, so we can communicate this way, but we don't want the word to get out, so keep it quiet."

"Right," she agreed, then brightened. "Surely that also helps prove that I'm not guilty."

"Nobody said you were guilty," Mack replied in a testy tone of voice.

"*That woman* thinks I killed my husband," she declared.

"Okay, that's probably true. Anyway, the tracker on the phone does help you, but it doesn't completely clear you from the suspects' list."

"Right, of course not," she muttered. "Anyway, I did pick up Chinese, and it's sitting here."

"I thought you would have lunch at Bernard's."

"I did, but, before I spoke to Bernard, I'd stopped by the Chinese place because I felt bad because I didn't pick up my previous order when I found the body," she explained. "So I went back to apologize and pay him, and we made a deal and split this order so we were both happy," she said, with a note of humor.

"That's fair."

"Yeah, except today, when I went to pick it up, after eating at Bernard's, Mr. Woo seemed a little off somehow."

"Off how?"

"I don't know. It's hard to say, just off, compared to how he'd been earlier. He didn't seem very comfortable with my being there."

"He may have gotten some interest that made his job a little more difficult, which isn't uncommon in these situations."

"I know, and I did ask him about it a little bit, but he really didn't want to talk to me. As a matter of fact, he seemed to want me to disappear."

At that, Mack laughed. "Not the first time you've had that reaction."

"I know," she grumbled, "but I wasn't expecting it from him."

"Maybe not, just stay the course and see what comes up."

"That's what I thought too," she admitted. "I will do a bit of searching online into Mathew's detective. Did you get in touch with him?"

"No, but someone did get in touch with Reggie, and contacted Mathew's lawyer, Roger. We're making progress. Slow, but progress just the same."

"Did Mathew fly in or drive? I never did talk to anybody over that rental."

"Bernard didn't give you a name?"

"No, he mentioned that a couple companies were in

town, but he didn't know them personally. I guess he doesn't rent Jags."

Mack laughed. "And Bernard wouldn't be renting them in town because he lives here," he reminded her.

"That's true," she conceded. "I could make some phone calls."

"And Mathew did fly in," Mack shared. "We do know that. He was on the eight a.m. flight that morning."

"Wow, so he comes into town, meets with his PI, finds out where I'm expected to be, but doesn't have a time frame. So he's there for two hours waiting? Yet I saw no sign of a Jag there."

"No rental car? Nothing with a sticker advertising the rental company?"

"No cars at all were right around the Chinese food restaurant. Maybe Mathew got dropped off, in which case his driver would be the last person to have seen him alive and could potentially be our murderer."

"True, but we can't jump to conclusions."

"No, of course not," she muttered in a dry tone. "That would be a terrible thing to do. Tell that to *Insley*."

He sighed. "Remember how we want this case founded on evidence and then become a locked-in case and not something that'll get thrown out on a technicality."

"I agree with you," she said. "It's just always so slow."

"It seems slow, until the avalanche happens. When we get the one vital piece of missing information—as you know yourself—everything blows up and moves very quickly," he explained. "Meanwhile we need to keep you safe. Somebody has targeted you, either trying to set you up or setting you up so your ex could find you."

"And Mathew had already been warned to stay away

from me and the house. Plus Richard probably would have seen him, and that would have made things ugly too."

"Exactly. So, Mathew wanted a more public place, though Mr. Woo's is a strange choice."

"But there is a bench outside, and I have been known to sit there and just enjoy watching the world go by. So maybe Mathew thought that we would sit there and talk."

"Would you have talked to him?"

"Maybe," she replied. "You guys wouldn't have been happy about it, but I probably would have heard him out. I don't know what he wanted to talk about, but I do understand now that, whatever his trouble was, it must have been more serious than I realized. The divorce was causing more stress than I would have expected."

"Not your problem," Mack noted.

"Maybe not, but it doesn't feel very good to know that I'm sitting here, wondering about it, and he's dead. Probably all because of money, some deal gone wrong. One of the instructions I gave to Nick was to ensure that I wouldn't get too much money."

"And yet do you really think it was too much?"

"I don't know because I have no idea how much it was." There was silence at the other end. "I get that it's something that really doesn't make sense to people, but it wasn't real money to me."

"What was it, monopoly money?" he asked, with a note of humor.

"It wasn't real because it wasn't in my hand. You've got to remember what my marriage was like. I never had money or a checkbook or a personal bank account. If I needed something, I told somebody, and they got it for me. I rarely went shopping for myself because Mathew had a particular sense of style, and nothing else was good enough. So Mathew went shopping, usually without me. Then he would have a seamstress come to the house and tailor items, per Mathew's directions, not mine. The only time I didn't get what I asked for was usually about food. Anything that Mathew thought could make me fat, then I couldn't have it, like pasta and potatoes and bread.

"So, as long as the divorce was still being negotiated, there wasn't anything in my hand that I could count on. Therefore, I didn't want to know because I didn't want to get my hopes up. Now maybe his death is not my fault," she shared. "Yet somehow it doesn't feel that I'm completely blameless either." She heard Mack's heavy sigh through the phone.

"We'll table this discussion for now. Anyway, we know how he got here."

"True. So, if he flew in, he must have had a rental or a ride of some sort, so if you could check the cameras at or around the airport, we could—"

"I know that, Doreen," he declared, his tone measured.

She chuckled. "Fine, I wasn't trying to insult you or to get into your business. I get it. I really do."

"I'm glad to hear that," he replied, with a note of humor. "Now, will you go home and stay home?"

"I'm home now," she confirmed. "The Chinese food is on the kitchen table. It's all good."

"Oh, will you be sharing?"

"I don't really know how much Mr. Woo gave me," she said, with a chuckle. "I'm walking into the kitchen now to take a look." She opened up the bag. "Wow, a lot. … Three boxes are here, so, yes, I'm sharing."

"Good to know, but I'll be a few hours yet."

"That's fine," she murmured. "Since I ate lunch with Bernard, I'll just make a pot of tea and relax for a bit."

"That sounds like a good idea. Chances are, Nan will be on you. As soon as you mention teatime, all I do is think of her."

"Maybe I should just walk down there and see that she's okay too. I'm sure everybody will be on her case, one way or another."

"Maybe. That would probably make you feel better too."

"She was up here earlier, delivering stuff, so I don't really want her to get bugged too much by all the hateful gossip," she murmured.

"You look after you," Mack reminded her. "That's the bottom line." And, with that, he said goodbye, promising to come by for Chinese, as soon as he was done with work.

She put on the teakettle and then stepped outside, looking around. She was full for the moment because Bernard had put on quite a spread. She really appreciated it, and yet, outside of the fact that he could do something like that whenever he wanted to, she didn't miss that life at all. And that was the part she knew neither Mack nor Bernard understood. She just didn't have any good memories of that.

As she sat here, she wondered what else she could possibly do, when her phone rang again. Sighing, she picked it up but didn't recognize the number. With a shrug, she answered it.

"Hey," Nick said.

"Oh, hi," she murmured. "Did you get this number from Mack?"

"Yeah, though it would have been nice if you'd thought to share it with me."

"I haven't even been home five minutes," she muttered.

"There's been no time to think of anything."

"Good point. Sorry, I didn't mean to snap at you. I've been talking to lawyers all day."

"Yeah, I can't see how you would even want to get into that business," she shared, with a heavy sigh.

"It's not for everybody, that's for sure," he stated cheerfully. "Anyway, it appears the murder investigation is moving forward."

"It's moving, I just don't know how well," she muttered. "You may know more than I do though."

"I doubt it." He chuckled. "I'm sure you're on Mack's case constantly."

"I just got off the phone with him, and I had found out bits and pieces earlier, though I don't know that any of it has much value."

"Maybe not, but you should trust that, at some moment in the future, all those little pieces will align, resulting in a big break in the case."

"Did Roger say anything about Mathew's will?"

"Yes, and you are mentioned in the will, but it's still not terribly clear where we're going. There's been no reading of the will as yet. They're waiting for the investigation report."

"We know that Mathew was murdered," she stated in exasperation. "I don't know how long they can wait for something like that."

"I think Roger's hoping that you'll get cleared, which would make his job a lot easier."

"Maybe, but I really want to hear that Mathew thought of Reggie."

"Reggie?" Nick asked.

"Mathew called Reggie his *man of affairs*. His man-about-town guy, the one who handled the house and the staff, overseeing the groceries, messages, laundries, all that stuff. Reggie has worked for Mathew for a very long time and apparently stood up for me, after Mathew raised a hand against me."

"It's nice to know that you had some champions," Nick noted. "Too bad it wasn't enough."

"Guys like that, it's never enough, but that doesn't change the fact that we're still here, and Mathew's not."

"Good point," he agreed. "So, what's this about your phone?" She filled him in on the details. "That's very interesting," he murmured.

"And it should go a long way toward proving I didn't have anything to do with this."

"That would be the hope," Nick concurred, "but leave it to them—remember that."

"I am, though I'm out of sorts."

"I'm over at my mom's, if you want to come and do some work in her gardens. Believe me that there's plenty to do," he shared. "I feel guilty and should be out there doing it myself, I suppose."

"If you do that," she replied, with a note of humor, "then I don't get paid."

He burst out laughing. "You still feel like you need to get paid, don't you?"

"How else will I put food on the table? It's easy for you guys, but I haven't got any of these paydays everyone keeps talking about. Outside of the reward money, which is what I'm currently living on, I don't have anything else."

"Right. Then my mother would love to see you, so why don't you come over and do what you normally do? It'll make her happy."

"As long as it doesn't make you feel that I'm there trying

to get money," she added, now worried she'd spoken out of turn.

He sighed. "That would be the last thing on my mind. Come and sit in the garden with Mom, weed, do whatever. Mom's fussing over something," he muttered, clearly in misery. "Nettles or some such thing that I know nothing about."

"Has she got stinging nettles in there?" Doreen asked in horror. "She better not touch those. You either."

"Why not?" he asked.

"They can give you a nasty stinging burn. I'll bring gloves and take care of them," she stated. "Tell your mother to leave them be."

He laughed. "Yeah, she's almost as stubborn as you are."

"Almost?" she cried out. "I must be slipping." And, with a big smile on her face, she ended the call.

"Okay, guys, we're going to Millicent's," she called out. "If nothing else, the exercise will be good for me." And, with that, she clipped the animals onto leashes and announced, "Let's go."

Although everybody was already a little bit tired, the walk would do them all good. It took her a little bit longer to get to Millicent's. By the time she arrived, Millicent sat on the deck, almost bouncing in excitement.

Doreen couldn't help but smile. "You seem to be a happy camper."

"Nick's here," Millicent cried out, obviously not realizing that Doreen already knew.

"Aha," Doreen said, as Nick stepped out onto the deck. "Finally the prodigal son returns home."

He glared at her. "Don't you start too," he muttered.

She snickered. "Why not? Your mom wants you home."

"Sure, but that doesn't mean the job allows for that."

"No, surely not, especially when you keep taking on clients who don't pay."

At that, he looked at her and then burst out laughing. "There is that," he agreed, his grin wide. "Somebody needs to finally deal with all this, and then I can take on paying jobs."

"Yeah," she agreed, "I've got the same problem. I don't get paid for any of the cold-case stuff I do either."

He nodded. "Another aspect to your life that most of us don't consider, do we?"

She shrugged. "If I have enough food for me and my animals, and all the bills are paid, ... I don't really care. So maybe I can still do these cold cases, once that money train comes in. But, if it doesn't, I'm still looking for that proverbial job."

"One job you can get at," he muttered, "is the nettles."

At that, Millicent perked up and looked over at Doreen. "Oh my, Doreen, you've got to see this. There's a whole clump of stinging nettles over here."

"A whole clump?" Doreen asked, her gaze wide. "They seriously decided to come to your house when I wasn't looking?"

At that, Millicent bounded to her feet, with an energy Doreen hadn't seen in her for some time. "Oh my." Obviously Millicent was thrilled to have Nick around. As they headed down the steps, Doreen muttered to Nick, "See how much more energy she has when you're here?" When he glared at her, she just grinned.

Then Millicent stopped, made a big presentation. "Look!"

Nick bent down to take a look, frowning. Doreen studied it from where she stood, trying hard to hide a grin. "Yeah, that's a stinging nettle, all right," she declared. Donning her gloves, she bent down with a shovel and carefully dug it up. She held it out to show Nick.

He just nodded, as if to say, *What on earth, and why do we care?*

She smiled and explained, "This sucker would reproduce everywhere, and, if you touch them, they'll burn you and make you very uncomfortable for a while."

"Get rid of it. Get rid of it," Millicent cried out.

"I am, don't worry. I am." And she walked over to the compost bin and carefully dropped it inside. Then she turned to Millicent and asked, "Was that the only clump?"

"Yes, but wasn't that enough?" she cried out in horror. "You know how fast those things grow."

Doreen laughed. "Absolutely I do, but good news. You're safe now."

After a visit with Millicent and doing a bunch of her yardwork, Doreen gathered her animals and said goodbye.

"Wait," Nick said, as he raced behind her.

She stopped and asked, "What's up?"

"I just wanted to ensure you're okay."

She sighed. "I feel weird, disassociated from everything," she murmured. "Am I fine? Yes. Will I be okay? Absolutely. It's just a weird space to be in right now."

"I can understand that," he replied. "Are you and Mack okay?"

She nodded. "As far as I know, we are, other than fighting over that *Insley* woman. She rubs me the wrong way, and Mack sticking up for her also rubs me the wrong way." She narrowed her gaze at Nick. "Unless you know something I don't."

He shook his head. "No, I sure don't," he muttered, "but I wish I did. I wish I knew something."

"Yeah, you and me both," she muttered. "It's frustrating that they get to hold back on information that would really go a long way in helping me."

"But would it though?" he asked, his gaze twinkling. "You seem to do pretty well on your own."

"Yeah, out of necessity," she grumbled. "It would be nice if a little more sharing was going on."

"You know they can't."

"I know. I know," she muttered, with a wave of her hand. "I get that, but I don't have to like it."

At that, he burst out laughing. "No, I'm sure you don't," he agreed, with a snicker.

She smiled at him. "You're a nice man, Nick."

He rolled his eyes. "That is definitely not what a guy wants to hear."

She burst out laughing. "Maybe not, but it's true. At the end of the day, it's what every girl really wants," she explained. "They just don't always know it. Everybody may go through that stage where she wants that dashing bad boy on the surface, but the reality is, when the nights are cold and long and painful," she shared, looking anywhere but at him, "they want somebody with staying power. Somebody who'll be there through good times and bad," she stated, a small smile crossing her face, "and you're definitely one of those."

He nodded. "That I am, but, since you don't have any sisters, don't try to sell me on myself anymore," he muttered.

"You and Mack both have bad records with relationships," she noted, staring at him. "What's up with that?"

"It's not that we have *bad* records," he clarified, "but we both had relationships right out of the gate when we were really young. Neither of them were particularly successful, and that made us both gun-shy. So since then, there have been some relationships but not the best in the world," he admitted, with a cocky grin. "We're just waiting for the right one."

"*Great*, though I'm not sure waiting is a good answer."

"Maybe not, but it worked for Mack." And he gave her a big hug and quickly left.

She groaned and called back to him, "Dirty trick."

He burst out laughing and added, "Whatever works."

And, with that, she gathered up the animals and headed home.

Chapter 12

D OREEN DIDN'T EVEN touch the Chinese food again, until she heard Mack at the front door, then noted the clock—dinnertime. She bolted to her feet, just in time to see him walking in the front door. Something was just tired and worn out about him tonight. She stopped and whispered, "Are you okay?"

He nodded. "Yeah, are you?"

She smiled back. "I'm fine, but just for a moment there, you appeared … defeated somehow."

"No, not defeated," he countered cheerfully, "but definitely some times are easier than others, and today has been a bit of a whirlwind."

"But we're getting somewhere, right?"

He chuckled. "We are, and, if I could just keep you out of trouble, we might get to the home stretch on this one."

"That sounds good," she replied, "but you can't blame me for investigating it though."

"Of course not," he quipped, with an eye roll. "Yet somehow it feels very much that I should be able to."

She snorted at that. "Wishful thinking isn't allowed."

He burst out laughing, then walked over, pulled her into

his arms, and gave her a big hug. As he stepped back, he smiled and added, "I needed that."

"Anytime." She looked up at him and grinned. "Dinner, however, will be microwaved."

He shrugged. "I can live with that, especially on days like today. Not cooking a meal is a gift right there."

"Sometimes it's just hard to come up with ideas, wondering what I want to eat, isn't it? I had never realized what a challenge that was."

"That's because you've never really been in a position where it was your job to do it."

"No, and I'm not sure I would ever sign up for that job either," she replied, with a shudder. "Do you know how hard that would be?"

He chuckled. "Housewives the world over do it all the time."

"I'm not housewife material," she admitted candidly. "You do know that, right?"

"Know what?"

"That I would make a terrible one."

His lips twitched. "Are you warning me about that?"

"Oh, I probably should, since everybody seems to think that I'm supposed to put you out of your misery, now that Mathew is gone."

His eyes widened. "Do I look miserable?" he asked cautiously.

"It's not so much that you're miserable, as much as you're waiting. At least that's the word on the street."

"Wow, who is it that has me waiting?"

She winced at that. "I guess I did do that, didn't I? But—okay, fine—I didn't really mean to put you on a waiting list. I was just trying to find closure in my own way."

"I get that," Mack noted. "You didn't see me pushing, did you?"

"Well …"

He eyed her and held up his thumb and forefinger, almost touching. "Maybe just a tiny bit," he replied, his chuckle infectious.

She walked over to the bag of Chinese food and asked, "You want to grab a couple plates? We'll serve this up and then just heat up the plates."

He brought out two large plates and asked, "What are we having?"

"I don't even know," she said, looking over at him. "So that could be a bit of a problem."

He shrugged. "I'm hungry enough to eat cardboard, so it really won't matter to me."

"You like all Chinese food anyway, don't you?"

"I do," he muttered. He opened up the first container and nodded. "This one is a noodles dish, so I'm good with that," he said, rubbing his stomach. He served up half of the noodles on his plate, filling more than half of it.

She frowned. "Wow, that's a lot of noodles."

"Mr. Woo's been very generous. Next time I want Chinese food, maybe I should order in your name."

She snickered. "I don't think it would do you much good."

"Why? Did you save his grandmother or something?" he muttered.

"No, I don't think so. I don't think I've had anything to do with any cases involving him or anything related to him."

"Maybe not," Mack stated, "but it sure seems he's grateful for something."

"I don't know if he's got any business after this whole

Mathew deal," she shared. "I did feel bad because I couldn't even go back to pick up what I'd first ordered, and that made me feel terrible."

"I'm sure he wasn't too bothered."

She shrugged. "He didn't seem to be very happy about it, but I think he got over it."

"I'm sure he did. You can't always worry about everybody else."

"I can't, or I shouldn't? And, besides, it's easy to say but hard to do."

"Ah, I get that," he agreed, with a sigh. "You're always trying to help out the underdog."

"Isn't that why you became a cop?" she asked. That grin of his flashed again, reminding her just how cute his mannerisms were and how it had been such a rough day that she hadn't had a chance to see much of him. She handed him the next box. "Let's open this one."

"It appears to be chow mein or something, filled with loads and loads of veggies."

She smiled at that. "Now that's my kind of a dish."

Generously he put half of the container on her plate, making it quite full. She gasped. "He really has given us lots this time, hasn't he?"

"Absolutely." Mack pointed at the third one. "What's in there?"

"I don't know, so let's find out," she muttered. She opened it up and froze, then looked up at him, her eyes wide. "*Uh-oh.*"

"*Uh-oh?* No room for *uh-oh*s today. Today is not the day for it," he declared, sounding stressed.

She flipped around the container, which held a chicken omelet dish, but on top of, spelled out in strips of some vegetable, was a clear *SOS*.

"*SOS*?" he repeated, staring at her. "What's going on?"

She shook her head. "I don't know," she whispered, "but it can't be good."

He closed his eyes and whispered, "The trouble is, what time did you get this?"

At that, she realized what he meant. "Oh no." She raced for her car keys.

"No, wait, wait, wait. You're coming with me."

And she realized that of course he was coming; she wasn't alone this time. "We have to go, and we have to go fast. Oh, why didn't I look at this earlier?" she cried out.

"Because you'd just eaten at Bernard's, so obviously you wouldn't have seen it earlier," he stated. "Let's just go down, nice and calm, and see what's going on." He led the way outside, and she automatically grabbed the animals and brought them along. He stared at her, then at the animals, "Really?"

"Stop. Let's just go. We don't have time to argue." He didn't say a word afterward but hopped in the driver's seat, as she loaded the animals into his truck, and they all drove to the restaurant.

"What time were you there?" he asked her.

She pondered that for a moment. "Somewhere just after Bernard's, so two-thirty or three p.m."

He glanced at the digital clock on the dashboard and saw it was already five.

"Oh my God, if something's happened to him, it'll be all my fault," Doreen wailed.

"No, it isn't," Mack disagreed. "If something's happened to him, it'll be because of whoever did something to him. You had nothing to do with it."

"It seems to be my fault," she stated, staring at him.

"I know, but that doesn't mean it is."

Yet she wasn't so easily appeased.

By the time they pulled up in front of the restaurant, she frowned at it. "It's quiet."

"He's closed," Mack suggested.

"He's never closed."

"Mr. Woo has to close sometime." Mack hopped out, looked at her, and ordered, "Stay here."

She glared at him. "I'm not a puppy dog."

"Good. Then I won't have to tell you to go home or *sit* right now," he said, with a note of humor. "Just behave yourself for a minute and let me check this out." Then he quickly raced up to the door and opened it. She watched as Mack disappeared inside, feeling a sense of relief because it hadn't been locked. So, maybe Mr. Woo was okay.

Mack came out a little bit later, but a frown was on his face. He came over to the vehicle. "Nobody is there."

"What?" she cried out, bolting out the door. "He's always there. Did you check the kitchen?"

"Of course I checked the kitchen," he replied, with a note of exasperation.

"Mr. Woo has to be in there. He just has to." She raced inside, Mugs and Goliath racing with her.

When she got to the counter, nobody was there. She walked around and pushed her way through the swinging doors into the back. All the stoves were turned off, but food was still out everywhere, as if he'd just literally stepped outside but didn't return. She stared for a long moment, then turned to face Mack. "Oh my God," she whispered, "something's happened to him."

Mack nodded, his face grim. "I've called forensics."

She nodded slowly. "I'll check out the back."

"Wait, dang it," Mack said.

Yet she was already out the back door, racing into the alleyway. She stopped when she got out here, looking for a sign of anyone. Despite the awkward relationship they had at times, Mr. Woo was a good man. She really hoped nothing had happened to him, but obviously something had. Now she had to solve it before something seriously bad happened to him. Still, for all she knew, they were already too late.

Feeling horribly guilty because she hadn't checked out her food and found the SOS in the first place, she ran up and down the alleyway with the animals, looking to see if Mugs picked up on anything, but he didn't appear to.

Finally she returned to the kitchen, where Mack searched, looking for clues. As she stepped inside, Mack said, "Don't touch anything."

She nodded. "I won't," she whispered. "But no sign of him out back, no sign of him in the alleyway anywhere."

His face was grim, as he nodded. "Yeah, I got that message." He took a deep breath. "I'm looking for information as to where he lives."

She stared at him, then pointed straight up. "He lives upstairs."

"Really?"

She nodded. "At least I assume so. An apartment is up there." With that, they looked around for an internal staircase. Spying one door that may have led to a pantry, she opened it up and cried out, "Here, Mack, here."

She bolted up the stairs, calling out, "Mr. Woo, Mr. Woo, are you up there?"

No answer came. She opened the door at the top of the stairs and stepped into a small apartment. It was clean, neat, and very sparsely furnished, but obviously very well kept. Everything looked neat and tidy, except for one thing—a bloodstain in the middle of the floor. She raced to it, and, as she came around the corner of the small couch, she found Mr. Woo, lying in a pool of blood. She dropped beside him, her fingers immediately going to his neck. "Mack," she cried out.

"I'm right here," he replied. He checked out Mr. Woo's pulse and said, "He's alive." He phoned for emergency assistance.

"He's awfully pale," she noted, frantically looking up at Mack.

"He's survived this long. Let's just hope he stays strong."

She nodded. "Oh my gosh," she whispered, trying to hold back the tears. "Why would anybody hurt him?" she asked.

"It could be what's behind all this," he murmured. "Somebody obviously thinks he saw too much or heard too much in connection to Mathew's death."

Doreen frowned and muttered, "Saw too much. They probably didn't realize he was in the store when they killed Mathew."

Mack nodded grimly. "That would be my take on it too."

"So whether he knows anything or not, it'll put him in danger. And if anybody realizes he's still alive—"

"I know. We're on it."

Chapter 13

AS DOREEN SAT here, Mack might say he had everything under control, but she didn't think so, not when she desperately tried to bring Mr. Woo around, but he remained unconscious. There was a slow bleed from the back of his head.

"The bleeding has slowed down," Mack murmured at her side. "That's a good sign."

She shook her head. "I don't think you and I share the same concept of what's a *good sign*," she murmured.

He smiled at her. "We're getting there."

"No. This just means that whoever is out there is feeling pressured, probably made worse when I came and talked to Mr. Woo today, asking him exactly the same questions somebody was probably afraid I would ask."

"You think this is about you?" Mack asked. He'd pulled a blanket off the couch and covered up Mr. Woo to try and keep him warm.

In her mind, that seemed to be the least of Mr. Woo's worries. She nodded. "I did talk to him."

"Did you see anybody here?"

"No, I didn't see anyone at all." She stopped and asked,

"I guess that's a problem, isn't it?"

He shrugged. "It does mean that theoretically you may have passed by whoever killed Mathew and maybe attacked Mr. Woo."

"Can't say I saw anyone." She pondered it. "I did say hi to an older guy walking a dog, but nobody else was necessarily right here though."

"Not that they would have to be. Think about it. Sometimes what we see isn't what we really see. It's just a little bit of what was there."

She pondered that. "I don't know that Mr. Woo would be anybody to be concerned about. He looked to be pretty old."

Mack nodded. "What about anybody else? Or anything out of place?"

She frowned at that and thought back to everything and everyone who she had seen, but still she came up with nothing. She shook her head. "Nothing I can remember."

"Okay. What about when you came here earlier?"

"When I came here today to place the repeat order? I walked out of Mr. Woo's place pretty quickly."

He nodded. "Yes, maybe somebody saw you coming out, maybe you were racing to go talk to Bernard, or maybe somebody heard you would come back. Maybe *they* came back." He asked her, "Did you come back on time?"

She shook her head. "No, I was a little bit later than I'd told him because of Bernard."

"Right. You didn't see anybody there?"

She shrugged. "Not really, but I wasn't looking," she admitted, with a wince.

"Of course not, and anybody who was here, staking it out, would not want to be seen." He turned and walked to the street-facing window of the apartment.

"Right, that little coffee shop and a health food store are across the street," she noted, "and a pizza place, so they could have been hanging out in this area for a while."

"Maybe not even for a while, maybe they just came back and forth and sat in the vehicle."

"Nobody will notice a vehicle."

At that, he nodded slowly.

"So often people do forget about a vehicle, don't they?" she asked.

"Absolutely," he muttered. Just then they heard the sirens.

"Oh, thank heavens," Doreen muttered.

"Wait here," he ordered, and he raced down to the restaurant. Within minutes, she heard the EMTs coming toward her. She backed away, and they immediately went to work. As she turned around, she saw several cops standing there, talking to Mack, as he gave them a rundown on what happened. When they saw Doreen here, Arnold rolled his eyes.

"You again," he muttered.

"It's got to be connected," she stated boldly.

"In what way and why?" asked the new detective, as she came up the stairs, stopping to look at her. "How come you're always in the midst of the trouble?"

Doreen glared at her. "I'm here to check on Mr. Woo. And lucky that we did."

Insley shrugged. "Sure seems suspicious that, every time I turn around, you're there."

"Get used to it. It's a small town," Doreen declared. "Every time you turn around, we're all here."

At that, Arnold agreed. "I have to admit that Doreen's

got a point there." Insley just stared at him. He shrugged and turned away, but he gave Doreen a wink.

She felt better at that. At least not everybody thought she was a murderer.

As she headed down ahead of Mr. Woo, now strapped to a gurney, Insley stopped her. "I need to hear your side of the story."

"Sure, but can we do it downstairs?"

"Why?" she asked, looking around. "This is where you found him."

"Yes, it's where we found him, but we're in his private space, and I would prefer to not invade his privacy any more than necessary." The detective frowned at her. Doreen just shrugged. "I can feel the pain that he's gone through, the same as I have," she muttered. "Surely, it's not a big ask to take it downstairs."

Insley shrugged. "I don't care." With that, she walked downstairs with Doreen.

"Now, if you think this space isn't *too* personal," Insley stated, with an eye roll, "tell me what happened."

Doreen snapped at her, "You need some empathy when dealing with your investigations. Remember how we are all deemed innocent, until you find some *credible* evidence?" Not allowing Insley time to reply, Doreen explained about coming back and apologizing for the order that had gone awry, when she'd found Mathew's body and hadn't been allowed back due to the proximity to where the body was found. So when she'd returned to talk to Mr. Woo, she'd reordered with a promise to come and pick it up in an hour and a half.

"Why an hour and a half?" Insley asked.

"Because I was going to see Bernard, then would pick up

the Chinese food afterward."

"Who's Bernard?"

It was much harder to talk to people who didn't know who you were talking about. Doreen frowned, then explained who Bernard was.

"Why would he have an extra phone?"

"I don't know why he has phones," she declared, frowning at her. "You'll have to ask him that. But since I had already spoken to Mack and knew that my phone wouldn't be returned right away, I was quite willing to pick up a phone I could use in the meantime." She pulled it out of her pocket and waved it in the woman's face.

"So, you went to Bernard's and what took you so long before you came back?"

"Because we had lunch."

"What time was this?" she barked.

Doreen gave her the information, wondering why she was as cranky as she was. Maybe just a case of being thorough. While Doreen gave Insley the benefit of the doubt, Doreen described her visit at Bernard's house.

"Fine, so you were having lunch with your boyfriend."

"Bernard is a *friend*." Doreen stared at her. "I didn't say he was my boyfriend, and you would do well to stick to the facts," Doreen declared. "Unless you want to upset a coworker of yours as well as your interviewees."

Insley's lips twitched, but she kept her gaze flat.

"I suggest you should always record your interviews, since you have a hearing problem or just a really short memory." Getting the evil eye from the new detective made Doreen smile. With a curt nod, she continued. "What I *did* say was I went to see Bernard, a *friend*, and he'd had a lunch prepared for us, so I joined him. I had planned on bringing the Chinese food home to have later in the evening anyway. I knew Mack would be over, and I figured that I could give our plans to have a Chinese dinner a second try."

At that, Insley asked Doreen, "Where's the Chinese food now?"

"At home in my kitchen."

"Yet you didn't open it in the meantime?"

"I'd already eaten and intended it for dinner, after Mack got off work, so why would I open it?" she asked, glaring at the woman. "Obviously you would leave it packaged in the bag, until you need it."

Insley contemplated that and then shrugged. "Then what?"

"What do you mean, *then what*?"

"You brought the takeout home and then what?"

"I went over to Millicent's, Mack's mom, to do some gardening. I saw Nick there as well. I came back home again. When Mack arrived, we opened up the Chinese food, and that's when we found the SOS."

"Sure, but you could have put that there anytime during the day."

Doreen stared at her. "*Right.* So now I'm making SOS signals in the Chinese food so that we go check on Mr. Woo and *not* find him in the restaurant?" Doreen asked, shaking her head and frowning at Insley. "What possible reason would I have for doing that?"

Insley just stared at her.

"Of course a reason doesn't really matter to you, does it?" Doreen asked, just starting to warm up. "I don't know why you have such trouble believing me," she began. "I think your concern should be more about what happened to Mr. Woo."

"It is," Insley replied. "We only have your word for it that you picked up this food today, and I don't even know that you did. For all I know, you knocked him over the head upstairs, snagged somebody else's lunch, then came home and stuck the letters in there to appear that somebody else had."

"Why would I do that?" Doreen asked in bewilderment.

Insley shrugged yet again. "I don't know. I still haven't figured out how your brain works."

"If you ever figure that out," Mack called out with a snort, "you can tell the rest of us."

After hearing chuckles all around, Doreen glared at him and pointed at Insley. "Do you hear what she's suggesting?"

"She's just hypothesizing," he suggested in a soothing tone.

She glared at him. "You and I are about to have a problem. I won't take any verbal or physical abuse anymore, not after Mathew. Just so you know upfront, that applies to you and to *her*. And what she just said doesn't sound like much of a *hypothesis* at the moment," Doreen declared. "It sounds a lot more like an accusation. I would suggest that she save her *unsubstantiated theories* for back at the station. Let her share those with the captain too. I would love to hear how that goes."

"Is there anything I should be accusing you of?" Insley asked.

"You already have accused me of anything you wanted," Doreen replied, her voice soft, yet her gaze hard. "It still won't make me your killer."

Chapter 14

Sunday Morning …

DOREEN WOKE THE next morning, her heart heavy. She rolled over, picked up her phone, and called the hospital.

When she got the same nurse on the other end, she repeated, "Doreen, he's fine. He's made it through the night okay."

She sagged back into her bed. "Thank heavens for that."

"You need to get some sleep. Otherwise you'll end up here in the hospital yourself," the nurse scolded.

Doreen smiled. "Just because I called a time or two doesn't mean I didn't sleep," she muttered.

"A time or two? I swear, every time you rolled over in bed, you woke yourself up and called."

Doreen grimaced. She did have some fitful dozing, waking, calling the hospital, rolling over, worrying in the dark, then starting the cycle again. All night long. The nurse was probably frustrated and fed up with Doreen's calls, but she had tolerated them with patience and forbearance, something that Doreen really appreciated. "It just breaks my heart to know that Mr. Woo laid there longer than he should have. If

I would have unpacked that Chinese food, I would have found him sooner."

"You can't know that," the nurse argued. "I haven't heard all of what's going on, but I do know that you can't be responsible for what happens to everybody else."

"No, but it would sure be nice if I could help in some way."

"You did. You got to him and saved him. Why don't we go with that for now?"

Doreen smiled. "Somebody saved him, not sure it was me though." She yawned.

The nurse ordered her, "Okay now, get some sleep. Don't you be calling me again."

Doreen chuckled. "You'll be off shift anyway."

The nurse laughed out loud. "You're right. I will be soon. Now go back to sleep. Mr. Woo made it through the night. He's not conscious yet, but his progress looks decent."

And, with that positive note, Doreen rolled over and went back to sleep. When she woke the next time, the animals all stared at her.

"Oh goodness," she murmured. "Is it that late?" Mugs looked at her and woofed. She nodded. "I'll take that as a yes." He just woofed at her a second time. "Got it. Okay then, I'm getting up, honest." But she didn't move. She found it hard to, considering she was weighed down with a very heavy Goliath parked on her chest. She looked at him and sighed. "If you want me to get up, you'll have to move." He just mewed at her, reached out a big paw, then tapped her gently on the cheek. She felt the tears coming to her eyes. "Guys, I know. It's been a pretty tough day already, hasn't it? … Heck, it's been a pretty tough week or month really. I'll just flat-out call it a year at this point." She gently cuddled Goliath.

"Still, I need to get up, have a cup of coffee, and clear my brain." At that, Mugs barked again, reminding her that he needed to go outside, then to get them some food.

"I know. I know. You're right. I need to get up." She slowly sat up, perched on her elbows, then collapsed back with a groan. "Maybe not," she muttered. "If I were wealthy, I would call for a maid and have coffee delivered. But since there is no such maid in my employ at the moment, I guess that's out." She pushed herself back up, and this time her big Maine coon cat rolled off, then got up himself.

Finally upright, she made her way to the bathroom and turned on the hot shower. By the time she stepped into the water, she was a little bit more aware and awake. She stood under the hot steam for a long minute, then started to scrub down. It had been a bad night.

By the time she stepped out of the shower, she felt a little bit better—and *a little bit* meant a *very little bit*, but, hey, she would take whatever she could get. She got dressed, her body moving sluggishly, as if aware that, with so much going on, her body shouldn't have to move at all.

But, of course, that wasn't in the cards for her. Soon enough she had put the coffee on to drip and set about to feed everybody.

With them all chowing down into their bowls, she opened up the back door to the deck, then stepped outside, yawning. She reached up, twisted her hair into a quick braid, and sat down on the deck steps, her legs felt so heavy and not happy to be mobile.

Almost immediately a head popped over on Richard's side of the fence. He looked at her. "Are you okay?"

"I'm okay." All her animals appeared at once, interested

in who she was talking to.

"How's Mr. Woo?" he asked, his tone worried.

"He made it through the night," she shared. "I got off the phone with the hospital not long ago."

He nodded. "That's good news."

"Is it?" she muttered. "Sometimes I wonder whether we're into the good news or just went straight into *bad*." He stared at her. She shrugged. "Don't worry about me. Life is a bit bleak at the moment."

"You'll get through it," Richard stated. "Your kind always does."

She stared at him. "I have a kind now?"

"Sure you do," he replied. "Always happy, always seeing the sunshine, always there for people. You have one of those gifts that I haven't seen in very many people before, but somehow you can always find the sunshine and roses. Just look at those animals of yours and how you enjoy them." He frowned at the cat, investigating the roses.

"Maybe," she conceded, "yet, at the moment, the sunshine and roses have up and left."

"Not for long, I'm sure of it. You'll get through this rough patch and be fine, all before you know it."

"Maybe." She yawned again. Mugs nudged her with his nose, getting an ear scratch in return.

"You probably didn't get any sleep, did you?"

"Nope, not much. Not after finding Mr. Woo like that."

He frowned at her. "Why am I not surprised that you're the one who found him?"

She winced. "I know. It's not ideal, but I'm certainly glad we found him in time."

"And you found your ex, not that his being dead was any great loss there," Richard declared, with a sniff. "That man was a menace. You do realize I reported him to the cops time and time again?"

She raised her eyebrows at that. "I appreciate that, Richard."

He shrugged. "I'm sure you don't think I do anything," he muttered. "However, I'm not about to let somebody beat up a woman, particularly my neighbor."

"Thank you," she murmured. "Every once in a while, Mathew would lose control, and things could get pretty ugly."

"Oh, I got that message all right," Richard noted, with feeling. "I didn't see any police at your place though."

"No, I'm sure they had other things to deal with."

"They shouldn't have," he snapped. "You should get as much support as everybody else."

She was quite surprised at his indignant tone. She smiled at him. "I just want Mr. Woo to wake up and to be okay."

"You and me both," Richard agreed morosely. "Best darn Chinese food in town."

She chuckled. "That's my take on it too, but I haven't tried many others."

Richard waved a hand in the air, dismissing the very idea. "He's the best. He's also the cheapest, and he serves really nice portions."

"Isn't that the truth," she agreed, "although he probably won't be doing too much cooking anytime soon."

He glared at her. "He better be. I don't like the other Chinese food," Richard said, returning to his typical cranky tone. "He needs to get better and to get back to work." When Thaddeus peered out of Doreen's hair and squawked, Richard jumped in surprise.

She just nodded, as Richard's head disappeared over the

top of the fence. She wasn't even sure how to tell him that Mr. Woo might not even survive. The better question was, how did Richard even find out about this so fast? She brought up her phone and saw that the local news was all over it. Sure enough, they had reported the break-in. "Home invasion, one injured at his place of business."

She sighed, thinking it would sure be nice if they left details like addresses out of these reports.

But, since it was a business and a popular one, it made sense because it certainly helped to identify who was attacked and where. Though it didn't make her happy to know that now people on both sides of the law would be trampling all over the Chinese food place, seeking evidence or clues. She was pretty sure Mack hadn't gotten any sleep last night either and sent him a text, asking just that.

When she got a short reply confirming her suspicion, she realized that he was probably still dealing with the issues at hand. **You still can't go home and get some rest?**

He phoned her this time. "No, I sure can't. Not yet anyway."

"Sorry. You must be exhausted," she said. "Anything new to report?"

"Nothing."

She yawned just then.

"Are you okay?"

"Yeah, I'm okay," she murmured. "Just tired. I only slept in fits and starts, tossing and turning. I must have phoned the hospital at least a half-dozen times."

"Yeah, you and me both," he admitted. "At least we care."

"We do."

"It sure would be nice if we heard that he'll pull

through," Mack noted.

"I know. For now, I just want to hear that he's awake," she replied, with a heavy sigh.

"Me too."

"Have you eaten at least?" she asked. "I guess I'm having cold Chinese for breakfast."

"If you don't want the food to go to waste, absolutely," he said. "I don't know if you even noticed, but I sent somebody to your house to collect the Chinese food container with the message in it."

"Oh, I guess that means no chicken omelet or whatever that was for me," she added, with a note of humor.

"Nope. You'll have to wait until Mr. Woo's back on his feet for that."

"I can do that. … I don't think I'll want Chinese for a while anyway." With that, winding up their conversation, she told him, "I hope you have a better day. Try to take care of yourself." Then she ended the call.

She headed inside and grabbed her first coffee of the day. Undoubtedly the first of many. It would be a long day, even if nothing else even happened. Her animals followed behind her, keeping close to her. Frankly just getting out of bed seemed to be quite an accomplishment, so she would take that as a win.

Chapter 15

GETTING UP WAS one thing, but staying up, being productive, and keeping all the worries at bay was a completely different story. Doreen did check on Mr. Woo's condition at eleven this morning. The news was that he was slowly coming around, but he certainly wasn't able to talk to anybody. Only family was allowed to visit, so that put a stop to Doreen's hope that she could go by and talk to him.

Of course she wouldn't be allowed to talk to him; only the cops were. No matter how much she butted into their investigations, Doreen still wasn't a cop. As she had mentioned to Mack, it wasn't a lifestyle that would suit her, but that didn't mean it wasn't fine for him. Some things were better left to others, and being a cop was one of them. She could do her investigating another way, even if it was frustrating at times.

When Bernard called a short time later, he asked her, "I presume you were involved in that somehow?"

She snorted. "It doesn't say much about my reputation when you automatically assume I'm involved in something like this."

"No, it sure doesn't," he agreed cheerfully. "However,

my little birds have told me that you were seen down there."

"I'm the one who found Mr. Woo, and Mack was with me," she explained. "Hopefully Mr. Woo will be okay, but it's too early to say that he's completely out of the woods."

"At least you found him when you did."

"Yet I feel horribly guilty," she muttered, tears coming to her eyes.

"Why?" he asked. She told him about the Chinese food and not opening it until Mack came by. "Good Lord," he muttered. "I can see why you feel that way, but honestly nobody opens their dinner before it's time to eat."

"Yet a lot of people probably would have."

"They might have taken the things out of the bag to put it in the fridge maybe," he argued, "but they wouldn't have opened up each of the containers, and, even if they had, no guarantee they would have noticed."

"But it was right atop one of the dishes," she noted, with a sigh. "So it's not likely they could have missed it."

"Which also means Mr. Woo had somebody in his store at the time."

"That's what we figured," she muttered. "And I have absolutely no proof one way or the other and saw nothing to go on to solve it either."

"No, of course not," he muttered. "It is a fascinating life you're living, Doreen."

"No, it isn't," she muttered. "I keep hoping for peace and quiet, and, just as I thought I was getting there, *boom*, somebody goes and kills Mathew."

"Did you ever find his Jag?"

"No, and I even have a local PI on it too. The police are checking security cameras to see who may have picked up Mathew from the airport, plus checking for any street cameras around the restaurant. Yet I didn't see any. However, we do know that my phone was tapped, so it's likely Mathew was sitting near the restaurant a couple of hours before I showed up."

"So, whoever shot him was obviously the last person to see him, and we still don't know if anybody saw him before then."

"Exactly, and that's the problem. We don't know who may or may not have seen him sitting there."

"Why would anybody care if he was?" he asked her.

"That's true. Why would anybody care? He's just sitting there, as it would seem to any casual passerby. Unless somebody was out walking a dog, bored, waiting for their animal to lift a leg or something, it's not at the top of anybody's thought process."

"Maybe not," Bernard agreed, "but people do stop and talk. People do notice. Particularly since Mathew's not a local, so somebody may have seen something."

"That's always the problem," she muttered. "Somebody always sees something, but nobody ever says anything."

He sighed. "I can hear the frustration in your tone, and I'm really sorry there isn't anything more I can do."

"Hey, you've already been great," she replied, "and thank you for the phone. It's keeping me in the loop, while the police use my phone for whatever they're doing."

"I hope they can find something useful in yours," he replied. "The fact that we know it was tapped also means that you need to consider how they got a hold of it to make that happen."

"I was considering that, but, if I can't come up with an answer, it makes me look guilty again, especially to that new detective. She's convinced I killed Mathew and tried to kill

Mr. Woo too. She's infuriating."

He laughed. "Nobody in their right mind would see you as the guilty party in this. And I've also heard from my little birds how the new detective's trying too hard, thinking she has to be a jerk or act heavy-handed in order to get any respect from her male peers."

"I agree with all that. She thinks I'm the one who's supposed to benefit from Mathew's death."

"If the divorce documents weren't signed," Bernard pointed out, "in a way, that's quite true, but it now depends on what's in his will. For all you know, he didn't leave you a thing."

"Considering who we're talking about, that's quite possible," she declared. "As much as I hate to admit it, I'm not sure he'll even take care of the staff he left behind, even those with him for decades."

"Lots of people don't," Bernard stated. "A lot of people don't consider staff to be anything other than furniture."

"That was Mathew, but he did have a close relationship with Reggie."

"Yet you really only find out what *close* means when somebody is dead and gone, and you see what they put in the will," he reminded her.

"And we can't have anything to do with that at the moment—at least I can't, not until the police talk to the lawyer and move me off the number one position on their suspect list. So nobody will give me anything if there's any suspicion I had something to do with his death."

"True enough, so, in other words, you're right back to the point of having to solve the mystery in order to get out of this mess."

"Oh, that's the easy part," she quipped. "After all, everybody seems to think I've got this."

"I'm sure you do," Bernard confirmed. "You're probably off your game a little bit because you've had a tough time dealing with your ex's demise, and then the attack on Mr. Woo has upset you even more. However, you've got this, Doreen. It'll be good now, and soon enough you'll be cleared and finished with something that's bothered you for a long time. There's your motivation."

"I know, but I'm still looking for that green Jag and whoever Mathew had with him. Mathew would have had a driver, either driving him around town or picking him up from that location."

"Sure, but, as soon as you find out, it would seem to be the killer."

"And he's likely back down in Vancouver by now," she muttered. "Maybe if I find the green Jag," she suggested, "I can find the driver."

"I did pull up the name of somebody I know who has a Jag that he rents out on a private basis."

"Oh, I need to talk to him."

"I spoke to him this morning, once I realized that's what he did, and he told me how he'd rented it out to a man who got off at the airport. Not the first time he'd rented to him, though he said it would be the last."

"Really. Did you ask him why?"

"I did. The car wasn't returned, and, since the insurance on something like that is pretty high, he's quite upset."

"Yeah, I would think so," she muttered. "Did you tell the police?"

"I was about to," he noted, with a chuckle. "Yet I figured you would want to know as well."

"I absolutely do. Thank you."

"Enjoy getting ahead of the new detective again."

Doreen snorted, then asked, "Did your guy have a description of the man?"

"He mentioned there were two men. One drove the Jag, and the other sat in the back."

"Mathew doesn't usually sit in the back," she shared, finding that odd.

"Apparently he had a bunch of paperwork, something about having to do some work."

"Maybe," she murmured, "particularly if he was short on time."

"That was definitely the impression he made. He was supposed to return the Jag at the end of the day, when he was to fly home, after conducting his business."

"But he didn't show up, right?"

"No, he didn't show up."

"So, there is a very good chance it *was* Mathew," she said.

"Wouldn't that be an interesting twist?"

"In what way?"

"The driver with Mathew probably just drove Mathew around and then dumped off the Jag somewhere where it wouldn't easily be found. Then he carried on."

"That would make the most sense," she murmured, "but we still have to find the Jag. And the owner must be looking for it now and will probably report it as stolen."

"I think the guy renting it out is probably being open about it being a rental, and the owner did have it insured for other drivers, so I'm not sure that's a problem, but the owner still really wants the car back."

"Of course he does," she muttered. "And once again we know where Mathew ended up, but we just don't know where he was before that."

"The airport and then to Mr. Woo's. But beyond that, who's to say?"

"Although he is a coffee drinker," she suggested, "so it would make sense that he was somewhere he could get coffee."

"So, we're talking about a coffee shop?"

"Yes, providing he wasn't planning on staying overnight, which he wasn't, since he only rented the Jag for the day."

"And again all good deductions," Bernard pointed out, "but still not helpful."

"No, because, if he wasn't getting a hotel room, there won't be anything we can track."

They both sat in silence for a moment.

She asked, "How does anybody even find the green Jag in a city the size of this?"

"The thing is, we're not such a big city, and cars like that stand out. You would think somebody would have seen it."

"Somebody did see it," she declared, with that wry tone. "They just haven't realized what it means."

"Not everybody knows what a Jag even looks like. Especially the newer models, and that's what this one was."

"There can't be that many places for it to be hidden, or it would have turned up by now," she muttered.

"I don't know," Bernard said. "It could be anywhere."

And he was right. There just weren't any answers for where it ended up. "The police are on the lookout for it, and it will turn up at some point, and, odds are, it will have been cleaned already and devoid of any evidence."

"So," Bernard asked, "who was this man with Mathew? That's what the cops really need to know. They could then follow him around town."

"It doesn't seem that our mystery driver is all that interested in telling the cops, or he would have come forward by now." She paused, frowning. "He's probably a bit on the shady side and can't afford any contact with the police."

"I didn't ask my guy about the driver, but I'm guessing the cops wouldn't get much out of him anyway."

"Of course not." She groaned. "That would be far too easy, wouldn't it?"

He chuckled. "I don't know about that, but, depending on what the driver's history is—"

"Sounds dodgy, if you ask me. And speaking of dodgy, what about this guy he rented the Jag from?"

"I don't know much, just that the guy makes a decent living renting private luxury cars."

"Are they his though, or does he run a long-term lease, then rents them out by the day?"

Bernard snorted. "Wow, I never even considered that."

"You have to wonder how this guy gets a Jag that he then rents out on a daily basis. You can bet he probably gets $500 for the day."

"No clue," Bernard said.

Or was he some parking lot attendant, renting out cars that weren't his? Oh my, she thought.

"I didn't ask him that, but I think I'll call him back and find out." And, with that, Bernard disconnected.

She stared down at the phone, wondering at how quickly everybody else seemed to get on the investigation train, even when they probably shouldn't. However, it wasn't her job to tell Bernard what *not* to do. After all, she wasn't even heeding her own advice, so she couldn't imagine anybody else listening to it. If Bernard *could* find out anything as a friend of this guy, it would be helpful because, in some circles, particularly wealthy ones, the police tended to find doors more often closed than open.

Lawsuits happened, and people grew fearful about talking. Sometimes it took personalities like Bernard and Doreen to make people want to talk. She didn't have to wait long for him to get back to her.

"The other guy was six foot, real thin, balding on the top, and acted like a butler."

She frowned. "Seriously?"

"Yeah, why?"

"It's almost a stereotypical description that you think of about a butler."

"He sounded pretty emphatic about it."

"It is interesting," she muttered, "although I can't say who it could be."

"You don't recognize the description?"

"Not really. Reggie is tall and thin, but, last I saw him, he had a full head of hair. I don't yet know who Mathew's private eye is or anybody else around him these days."

"Interesting," he muttered.

"But we still don't know what's going on and who is involved in this."

"But we will get there, so keep the faith," Bernard added. "I'll keep digging too." And, with that, he was gone again.

She smiled into the phone when it rang right under her finger, poised to make a call.

"You've been a busy girl," Nan stated.

"Not busy enough," she muttered. "I still don't have any answers."

"No, but you will, dear. You'll get them," she declared. "You know that."

"I'm hoping so, but we're not there yet."

"It's just about making progress," Nan suggested, "and we've got everybody here looking and talking, trying to figure out who could have done this."

"Has anybody seen a green Jag and anybody down at Mr. Woo's place on the day of …?"

"I did ask around and got a no to that. Everybody here is really happy with our new cook, who was trying out some fancy Italian dishes," she shared. "So nobody was down there getting Chinese."

"Right. That makes sense. I'm just having a hard time finding answers. I'm not sure the police still see me as a suspect, but I'm not off the hook until I'm completely off the hook."

"You're not off the hook," Nan declared, "until we have the murderer caught. Just because some of us want to give him an award for taking out that ex of yours doesn't change the fact that we must ensure everything on his case is tied up, nice and neat. Otherwise that hint of suspicion will continue to follow you."

"I'm not so concerned about that," Doreen stated, "as much as finding justice."

"There's no justice in this world sometimes," Nan reminded her. "So, we take what we can get. In this case, we need to get that killer."

Doreen chuckled. "I won't argue with you, that's for sure. We do need to find out who did it and what went on. I just don't have any particularly helpful answers yet."

"Not yet, but you will. I have faith." And, with that, Nan rang off too.

Doreen snorted into the phone. "Glad you guys all have the faith," she mumbled to herself, "because I'm not at all sure that I do." With so much going on, she wasn't at all sure if anyone should have faith in her on this one. She was even starting to lose a bit of faith in herself, but she didn't dare because she wasn't at all sure that the new detective, *Insley*, was anybody Doreen could trust to handle the case.

Mack, the captain, and the rest of them? Absolutely, but then she would also be partly in the loop and in there getting her hands dirty. And she was trying in this case, really trying, but, so far, it wasn't working out to her advantage. But since when was that a thing? She'd always had to make things happen in her life, so, hey, that's what she would do this time as well.

Chapter 16

LATER ON, JUST as Doreen sat down to eat a sandwich, Mack called. She snatched up her phone. "What happened?"

"Hi, Doreen," he greeted her, with that calm sense of good humor in his tone. "Nice to hear your voice. Nice to know that everything is good."

"How do you know everything is good?"

"I don't," he replied. "I don't know a thing. You didn't check in today."

"Was I supposed to?" she asked.

He sighed. "No, it wasn't mandatory, but it would just be nice to know that you're okay and not running around town, getting into trouble."

"Even if I *was* running around town and getting into trouble, you would be the last person I would tell because you would just send me home."

"And for good reason," he muttered. "You can't even stay out of trouble picking up Chinese food."

She gasped. "That's not fair. Besides, you're the one who was supposed to eat it with me."

He snorted. "I don't remember eating any of it."

"No," she muttered, "there is that."

"Are you eating it yourself?"

"No, I was about to have a sandwich instead. I'm struggling to get past the fact that the Chinese food came from Mr. Woo while he was in such trouble. He must have been terrified."

"Mr. Woo certainly wouldn't think less of you if you ate it," Mack stated. "He definitely wouldn't want to see it go to waste."

"Maybe not," she agreed, "but I can't get him out of my mind either."

Mack sighed heavily. "Mr. Woo's awake, I hear, so I'm heading down to talk to him."

"That's good news," she said. "I don't suppose I get a chance to talk to him though, do I?"

"No, family only," Mack stated.

"You're not family," she muttered.

"No, but I am a cop, so different story."

"So you guys keep telling me," she muttered. "But, whatever, just keep listening to your self-serving narrative, while the rest of us get our information the old-fashioned way."

He snorted at that. "Yet, with your recent track record, you might get him into even more trouble."

"I would never do anything to hurt him," she declared.

"I know that, but somebody might hurt him now, since it got out to the media that he is alive. That might be something the bad guys are trying to change."

She stared at the phone for a moment. "I hadn't considered that. Do you really think his life is in danger?"

"Somebody went to an awful lot of trouble to silence him."

"But the fact is, they didn't kill him. Maybe they thought that would be enough of a warning or that the head injury would stop him from remembering anything. Until you're able to talk to him, we won't know, but it may have done just that."

"It is possible, yes, but I really hope not," Mack replied. "I'm heading down there now."

"Are you investigating this?"

"Somewhat," he said, with a wry tone. "We do work better as a team here."

"Except when one of the team is a suspect," she snorted.

"Hardly, I have an alibi, remember?"

"Yeah, *great*, thanks for that," she muttered. "Anyway, go talk to him, see what he has to say, and report back," she stated cheerfully. And, with that, she ended the call. For the first time today she felt much better.

She knew it would piss him off, of course, and that was just fine too. Not that she was trying to, but it was a game they played, and it always made her feel better when she had a chance to end a call on him. It made no sense, and she did realize her actions were that of a two-year-old, but, if it made her smile today, she was all for it because, right now, life wasn't exactly going her way.

What she would really like to figure out was how somebody could have tapped her phone. At the moment, she couldn't remember any point in time that somebody had access to it, and that was a concern. Was it sometime when she went outside and left the house open? Possibly. Could somebody have crept in and done it? Absolutely.

Why, though, was a whole different story, and she wasn't sure she could get anybody on board with any of the crazy theories going around in her head. It didn't make any sense why somebody would even care about her activities. Wasn't Mathew's PI supposed to follow her everywhere anyway? So why go to that level of effort, unless they were trying to set her up for Mathew's death? Mack luckily had an ironclad alibi for that, since Mathew died midmorning that day, while Mack was in the station with the other cops. Whereas she did not have an alibi, as usual, and that would cause her more trouble than she had expected.

Still, going down this pathway occupied her because Mack kept uncovering bits and pieces, where she didn't have a chance to get too involved. What she really needed to figure out and to give Mack was an idea of when her phone could have been compromised. Must have been before his death, obviously. Plus she would very much like to talk to this private rental person with the Jaguar, possibly even show him some photos.

She called Bernard back. "I have a few photos of Mathew's staff," she began. "Do you think I could meet up with this Jaguar rental guy and ask him a few questions?"

Bernard hesitated, and a few seconds went by.

"If you went with me?" she asked impulsively.

"Oh, if I went with you, I'm sure it would be fine. But, if you bring the cops, not so much." His good humor was now beaming through the phone.

"Right, so what is he thinking? That he will avoid talking to the cops?"

"*He* thinks so," Bernard said, with a note of humor.

"Then, of course, we better get there before the cops really do figure it out."

"Have you told them about it?"

"No, and I should at least tell Mack," she admitted, "but, the minute I do, he'll tell me to stay away."

"We don't know for sure that the Jaguar guy has any information."

"True," she agreed. "Okay, I'll be at your place in a few minutes."

"Good enough, and bring the animals too. They'll be a good icebreaker."

"Is he an animal lover?"

"I would think so. He's got a big, huge Doberman at the car park."

Only after the call ended did she realize her guess about him working at a car park was quite correct. She thought about that the whole way to Bernard's. When she pulled into the driveway, he was already standing outside, waiting for her. She unloaded the animals and quickly loaded them up into his vehicle. "He really does work at a car park, doesn't he?"

He snickered and nodded. "Yes, and, for that reason, I would never leave my vehicle in such a place."

"I had no idea people would actually do that. It's sounds risky in so many ways."

"Unless you have some tracking system on your rentals, and you keep checking it regularly."

"I can't imagine Mathew liked that system."

"He may not have liked it or even known about it. If he was aware of any GPS tracker on those Jags, Mathew probably wouldn't have rented this guy's Jaguars. Still, that doesn't mean Mathew was above renting other people's vehicles, while this middleman was getting the money. But who knows? Maybe this guy shares the rental money with the owners."

"It's possible, and it would keep him on this side of the law, so that, if anybody found out, then he wouldn't be in quite so much trouble. It would also make him ever-so-slightly less slimy," she muttered.

He chuckled. "That's just your definition," he murmured. "Remember that not everybody has the same qualms and honor system that you do."

"Right," she agreed, "and, according to Mack, it keeps getting me into trouble."

"But please don't change, my dear Doreen. The world needs more people like you."

"Yeah, so everybody says, until it comes down to something like this, and then they all stand back, enjoying the show, while, once again, I'm the one in trouble."

"Everybody prefers and loves it when somebody else gets into trouble, remember?"

"Yep, then they get to cheer about how it's not them." It was true and went back to humanity in general. They can all cheer for somebody else, provided they are off the chopping block.

As they drove up to a parking lot, manned by a person at the gate, she asked Bernard, "Is that him?"

"Yeah, sure is."

He pulled up and parked to the side. With her and the animals in tow, Bernard walked over and greeted the guy in the booth. "Hey, Tony."

Tony looked at him and frowned. "Oh, man, I really would prefer that you didn't come down here in person."

Bernard shrugged. "Maybe not, but Doreen was intent on coming down here and talking to you. So you're much better off this way. You talk to her right now with me here, rather than at another point in time, when she's likely to just barrel into your life and not give a hoot."

"It's not as if I care what you are up to," Doreen protested. "I'm not trying to bust up your business here or anything, but I really need to find out if you know the guys who rented the green Jaguar."

He stared at her. "You're that amateur detective chick, aren't you?"

She winced. "That doesn't sound quite the way I think of it," she murmured.

He shrugged. "You are, aren't you?"

"Yes," she said in exasperation. "I'll say that's a yes."

"Cool," he replied. "Okay, so who is it you want me to look at?" She pulled out her phone, the one she had borrowed from Bernard, then brought up her email, where she'd set up a folder with a group of photos that she had. Then she flipped through them, until she got to the one of Mathew. "Is this the guy who rented the green Jag?"

He looked at it and nodded. "Yeah, that's the guy. He sat in the back seat."

She nodded. Then she went through photos of Reggie and Roger and a couple other staff members she knew. "Were any of these the guy who was with him, who was the driver?"

He shook his head, shook his head, shook his head, and then said, "No, none of those."

"Interesting, so you don't know who it was?"

"Nope."

"Was the rental paid for with Mathew's credit card?"

"No, cash, it's always cash," he stated, turning to look at Bernard hesitantly.

She nodded. "Better to keep your receipts that way, *huh*?"

Tony just shrugged and didn't say anything.

"Did the driver have anything with him, a suitcase, a

backpack, anything?"

"No. Just the guy in the back seat with a briefcase."

"I have no idea who this other guy is then," she muttered. "Mathew had contacted a Vancouver private eye, so all I can think of is it might have been him."

"Somebody from the coast, you said," Bernard added.

"As far as I know, but exactly where he's from is speculation, but that would make sense."

"Okay, so chances are he probably just drove up on his own or flew down a day or so early to follow you around town. So the driver could have rented a car as well."

Doreen frowned. "Did this other guy, the driver, show up here in another car to get the Jag?"

Tony shook his head. "I dropped it off to them at the airport, a small private one."

"And?" Doreen asked.

"And what?"

"Did you see the driver around any other cars at the airport?"

After several seconds of silence, he muttered, "Jeez. I don't know. A small white car was close by. It might have been one of those electric ones. But I don't know that he rented it here. Maybe he drove it here. Still, could he have driven very far on an electric one? Regardless I don't know that it was his."

"They do go quite a distance," she murmured. "So, that's about all I have to ask then." She pondered that for a moment. "I guess if I come up with more pictures, I'll just come by and ask."

"Or you just don't bother," Tony replied in alarm. "You'll kill my business here."

"And, of course, your rental business is one that the

owners of the cars are fully aware of, right?" she asked Tony.

He frowned at her, looked back at Bernard, and replied in a dry tone, "Sure."

She rolled her eyes. "*Right*. So, in other words, I'll be back to check in with you, if I find some more photos or have other questions."

And, with that, he looked over at Bernard. "*Thanks*."

With a shrug, he told Tony, "You keep on the straight and narrow now."

"Sure, like I'll make it in the world if I do that," Tony muttered.

Doreen smiled. "There will always be people like me around, looking to see just who you're renting to."

He shrugged. "They pay, so it doesn't matter. It's a good deal."

"Sure, as long as they're insured and nothing goes wrong. Then everybody's happy," she noted. "But, if the owners of the vehicles don't know about your rental business, that's a whole different story."

"Some of them I have agreements with," he stated. "But some of the others? They aren't really open to agreements. Oh, they want to rent it out, but they want all the money, instead of giving me a share for being the agent in-between."

"Of course. Most people with the money to have vehicles like these are all about the money," she noted, with a smile.

"Hey, not all of us," Bernard protested.

She looked at him and nodded. "Not all, but a good share of them." And, with that, she tried to pull Mugs back over to Bernard's vehicle, but he resisted. She looked at him. "What's the matter, buddy?"

Clearly he wanted to go into the car park. Unsure if he

wanted to just lift his leg or had something else on his mind, she followed behind him, even as Bernard and Tony talked.

As she got farther down the way, she whispered to Mugs, "What's the matter, boy? What are you after?" But his nose was to the ground, and he was sniffing, as if he were a hound dog. Mugs just woofed and kept on walking out of the car park itself. Finally he stopped in front of a vehicle parked just behind the parking lot, in between two dumpsters.

She stared at it.

Then she quickly walked back to the two men, calling out, "Are your vehicles ever parked over there?" She pointed to the two dumpsters.

Tony shook his head. "No, they aren't."

"The Jag that you lent out," she began.

"Rented!" Tony called out. "Rented, a business deal."

"It was due already, right?"

He nodded. "It was due back the same day."

"And nobody ever found it, right?"

He nodded. "Nobody ever found it. What are you getting at?"

"A green Jag is parked between those two dumpsters over here."

"I saw that one earlier," Tony noted. "But it's all dented, and it's got a different license plate."

The two men walked over to join her, as they all checked out the green car. "The one I had here was in much better shape than this."

She looked over at Bernard because Mugs was standing up close to the vehicle, sniffing like crazy. She sighed. "So, do you have a spare set of keys for the one that went missing?"

"Of course," he replied, and he stared at the vehicle and

shook his head. "Man, there's no way. He will kill me if that was his Jag."

She shrugged. "Not sure what you want me to say, but there is an easy way to find out."

He stared at her and asked, "How?"

"Your spare set of keys."

He swore, then turned and raced back. Bernard looked at her, then back at the Jag and winced. "What would happen to him if that is the missing Jag?"

"Obviously," she stated, with an eye roll, "something bad happened to it."

Tony came running up to rejoin them. "Why do you want to get into it?"

"Look at Mugs," she pointed out, who was sniffing at the trunk, then immediately took several steps back.

"Oh no," Tony muttered. "I didn't sign up for that."

"Really? I figured that you thought this was an exciting business venture," Doreen teased.

Tony pointed the fob to the driver's side and hit the button. It unlocked. "No!" he cried out. "It can't be. This one's been out for a joy ride. It's all dented even. The other one was pristine."

She nodded, walked around him, opened the driver's side door, leaned in, and popped open the trunk release.

"Hey, what are you doing?" Tony cried out. "The cops need to see this first."

"Yeah, they sure do," she agreed. "Unfortunately I think they also need to see something else."

"What do you mean?" Tony asked.

She walked to the back of the vehicle, and, while the two men watched, she lifted the lid on the trunk.

Chapter 17

"CLOSE IT! OH God, close it!" Tony shrieked. "Why'd you do that?"

Doreen shut it, then turned to look at the kid and explained, "You needed to get a good-enough look to see if that's the man who was with Mathew."

He nodded slowly. "It was. That's his driver. … Suddenly I don't feel so good."

He did appear to be sick. In fact, a moment later, he raced over a few steps and upchucked onto the gravel.

Doreen already had her phone out, calling Mack. When he answered, she asked, "Remember that comment about how I can't even go pick up takeout without getting into trouble?"

"Yes," he answered hesitantly. "Are you in trouble?"

"Maybe," she muttered. "I think you need to come to the car park downtown." She gave him the address.

"And why is that?" he asked, his tone ominous.

"You'll understand when you get here, but, to save time, you should bring the forensics team and the coroner. And don't bring the new detective. She's useless." And, with that, Doreen disconnected.

Bernard sighed and shook his head. "I don't think a relationship with you would be all that easy."

She looked up at him, gave him half a smile, and nodded. "No, I'm sure that's true. Yet, if you died, you can bet I would chase down every lead, until I found out who did you in."

He stared at her, then grinned. "That's really good to hear. In this day and age, not a whole lot of people you could count on to do that."

"Still, I must insist that you don't die on me," she muttered. "Although, when Mack finds out that you're the one who brought me here, he might try to choke you just a little bit," she added, wearing a big grin on her face.

Bernard's face scrunched up, and he turned a bit pale. "Oh no, now I have to deal with Mack."

"Yeah, you sure do."

At that, Tony started to fidget, looking around in a bit of a panic.

"Oh, no, you don't," Doreen declared. "You don't get to walk away on this one."

"I do. I have to. You don't understand what'll happen to my job."

"Which one? Your real job or your side gig? Because, I've got to tell you, the light is about to shine on that sideline of yours. Then, when Mack finds out, it'll get even uglier."

When Tony turned and faced Bernard, he just held up his hand and added, "I didn't know you were holding bodies here, Tony."

The kid looked as if he wanted to cry.

Doreen pointed out, "Technically he wasn't. The body is not on the parking lot that he's charged with protecting."

At that, Tony nodded frantically. "This has nothing to

do with me," he declared. "I really should just call in sick and go home."

"You could," Doreen conceded, "but that'll just make it seem you're running away. I can't really condone that choice because I've got to tell the authorities who was here, and it'll take them all of five minutes to track you down."

Tony's shoulders sagged. "I knew it was too good to be true."

"What? Renting other people's vehicles out for money?" she asked, with a chuckle. "These easy-money side hustles probably seem great in the moment, but I don't think they're intended to be long-term career paths."

At that, Bernard chuckled. "Oh, I do enjoy your sense of humor."

She grinned at him and noted, "You're in the minority there. An awful lot of people don't think very much of my methods, and we may be meeting some of them in the next few minutes."

At that, Bernard chuckled and nodded. "And I can see why. You're a little hard on everybody's emotions, though you certainly make for an interesting date," he declared, motioning toward the trunk holding the body.

"Hey, we're not on a date," she clarified, with a big smile, "and, so far, I've avoided finding bodies on dates."

"So, what was the most recent result when you and Mack went out for Chinese food?"

She frowned at that. "That was us answering an SOS," she countered. "And, for the record, we didn't find a dead body. We found Mr. Woo, injured, and got him to the hospital in time, we hope." At that, she turned to face Tony. "So, you didn't see this vehicle arrive?"

He shook his head. "No, I don't know when it showed

up. And, since it didn't look to be one of mine—not in its original shape and not being on the car park itself—when I did see it, I didn't give it a thought," he explained, with a shrug. "I only look after the ones I'm paid to look after."

Bernard shared, "You have a rather broad interpretation of 'looking after,' young man."

Tony nodded. "I'll be in so much trouble, won't I?"

Doreen glanced at Bernard, then shrugged. "That depends on how many vehicles you rented out without the owners knowing. That's the bottom line. If you rented them out, and all the owners know, maybe it's not an issue but otherwise? Yeah, it could be a problem."

"Yeah, it'll be a problem," Tony admitted morosely.

She winced. "Then I'll just tell you now that the best thing for you is to confess. Come clean right off the bat and don't make your situation worse by wasting time and making Mack pull the information out of you. That will make him much happier."

"Is a much-happier Mack a better deal?" Tony asked in a bit of a panic, just as they heard sirens coming closer.

"Well, Tony, a pissed-off Mack is like an avalanche, so anything that avoids setting him off is a better deal, and you'll need all the help you can get."

"*Fine*," Tony grumbled, glaring at her. "I hold you responsible for this though."

She frowned. "Why is it that people who are doing something wrong always want to blame me?"

Tony glared at her. "If you hadn't killed your ex-husband, I wouldn't be in this mess."

"Careful, son. I wouldn't go there," Bernard warned him.

"Are you kidding?" Doreen snapped. "How is that even

logical? If I had killed my husband, do you really think I would be here trying to find out what is going on?"

He frowned at her. "You didn't kill him?"

"No, I most certainly did not. But, if ever I had been tempted to do such a thing, you are rapidly working your way to the top of the list."

He just glared at her, while she glared right back.

Bernard put a hand on her shoulder and murmured, "Easy now, Doreen. Not everybody is as accustomed to finding bodies as you are. People react differently, remember?"

She snorted at that. "Yeah, imagine if that was your coveted Jag, and you caught sight of it cruising around town, looking like that."

Bernard winced. "Yeah, I might have killed the guy myself."

"Exactly. So, who knows what brought this on?"

"Maybe the owner of the Jag saw this guy driving it. Maybe it's got nothing to do with Mathew's death at all."

At that, the poor kid shook his head. "The owner's out of town. He doesn't know."

"I'm pretty sure he's about to find out," Bernard said.

When a shout came from behind them, Doreen stepped out from between the dumpsters, so that Mack could see her, then waved him over.

He stormed over, looked at Bernard, then glared at her, at the kid, and then back at her. "Somebody want to tell me what's going on here?"

"First off," Doreen began, "this is where Mathew's rented green Jag came from. Tony here has identified Mathew from my photos, but he didn't recognize any of Mathew's staff I had photos of." With a glance down at the tired and fed-up-looking canine at her feet, she hoped Mack would be softened by his presence. "Mugs brought me over to this vehicle."

Mack frowned at her, then over at the car. "It's a green Jag."

"Yes, it is. Now, Tony here, who works at the car park, didn't think it was *his* car park's green Jag because it's in a lot worse shape than the one he rented out, and the license plate doesn't match. However, he had the spare keys to the one he rented out and found that they opened this one."

"Ah."

"Once we had opened the driver's door, and, based on the behavior exhibited by Mugs, naturally I popped the trunk latch." And, at that, she eyed Mack uncertainly, expecting him to burst out in a fit of warnings or profanity. "At this point, you should probably open the trunk."

He sighed, closed his eyes, pinched the bridge of his nose, then asked, "So, who will I find stuffed in the trunk?"

"The driver," she replied. "The same man who Tony here saw driving off in the Jag, with Mathew in the back seat. Likely Mathew's PI from the coast."

Chapter 18

BERNARD SUGGESTED THEY go for a cup of coffee or something afterward, but Doreen declined, saying she was too tired and knew she had an inquisition coming up. Taking no offense, he'd driven her and the animals back to his home, where she picked up her car.

She wished she hadn't gone with Bernard to the car park, anything to stop the never-ending circle of thoughts running through her head. The fact that she'd found the Jag and the driver was helpful but only to a point, since the man had yet to be identified. She suspected he was Mathew's private eye from Vancouver, and, after the death of Mathew, somebody had decided to terminate his PI, since he probably knew too much.

Anyone around Mathew appeared to be in trouble right now. Of course that meant her own life was potentially hanging in the balance. But, as long as she was useful as the current number one suspect to whomever had set this game in motion, she figured the killer would probably leave her alive to take the fall. If that didn't work, eventually they would take her out.

It worried her that she understood that mind-set, but

frankly, it's exactly what she would do, if she were that kind of a person. The fact that she wasn't didn't exactly help, and, in what seemed to be her typical fashion, her progress was one step forward and ten steps back.

She settled down in the backyard with a cup of tea, knowing that Mack would be a while, and, with Doreen's luck, it wouldn't even be Mack who came to visit her to take her statement. She could sympathize to a degree. Obviously the more that Doreen discovered for Insley—who didn't like her to begin with and was already suspicious of Doreen—just made Doreen look like she was involved even more. She was sure that *Insley* would determine this latest finding to be even more incriminating evidence of Doreen's involvement.

The fact that Doreen had absolutely nothing to do with Mathew's death—or his PI's death—was out of the question, as far as Insley was concerned. If Insley, as the detective assigned to the case, decided to close the murder investigation with Doreen under arrest as the accused, Insley would. Doreen, however, wanted to ensure that the case was closed properly, as Nan had pointed out.

Otherwise, having this rumor around town that Doreen had killed her soon-to-be ex-husband would haunt her forever, and she didn't want that at all.

Solving the case would not only absolve her of all suspicion but it would also bring her some closure regarding Mathew. However, right now, the case was nothing but trouble. Yet it was so important for her not only to clear her name but also to solve the case, for personal, emotional, and legal reasons, which she couldn't argue with. She just wanted to make it happen. She didn't quite know how to make that happen, but she needed to.

As she sat in her backyard, she went back to her notebook, adding more notes and reviewing the previous ones. It wasn't long before Mack called her. "Hey," she said. "Not pretty, *huh?*"

"No, not pretty at all," he confirmed, his tone gaining in strength.

"Not my fault," she blurted out, before he could really blast her.

He snorted. "I know that, … but you're making us look like idiots," he muttered, struggling for control.

"Not you," she pointed out. "You're not even supposed to be on the case."

He stopped, then asked, "Is that what you're trying to do? Make her look like an idiot?"

"No, not at all, although she's doing a bang-up job of that herself," Doreen declared. "Yet it's obvious that she doesn't trust me, like me, or believe anything I say. So, if I have to solve this on my own to clear my name, I'll go ahead, regardless of what she says."

"That'll just make you look worse, you know?"

"How does it make me look worse? I'm out there trying to solve Mathew's death, so I don't get railroaded into a murder charge that I don't deserve, so what else can I do, if *Insley's* not up for the job? Plus it's not as if this is my first time to solve a case. This is my twenty-fifth case … and counting. And *Insley* seems to be getting on-the-job experience. Is this her first-ever homicide case? Her first week on the job as a detective?"

Mack sighed. "You know you won't get charged."

"Nope, I don't know that at all," she declared. "*Insley* made it very clear that I was a suspect—and keeps pointing it out."

"I understand that, but—and I'm *not* defending her, and

I *have* pointed out to the captain how her interrogation of you could be improved—but I think she's just dealing with the fact that she's new. Think about it. … Everybody knows you. She doesn't, and honestly I'm not sure she's all that good with women."

"*Ya think?*" Doreen snorted. "I'm not sure I'm all that good with women either, especially *that* woman."

Mack sighed again. "You still have any Chinese food?" he asked.

Dorren shook her head. He was changing the subject on purpose, but she let him do it this time. "Yeah. Do you have time to stop by?"

"I need to make time, so I'll take an hour. I'll be there in a little bit." And, with that, he ended the call.

She smiled down at the animals. "Look at that," she crowed. "We'll see Mack—and not on the wrong side of the table either." She got up and put on fresh coffee for him, after hearing the fatigue and frustration in his tone. Probably frustrated with her, the case, and the circumstances, which she understood.

She got it; she really did. She wasn't trying to be diffi-cult, although that seemed to be something she was inherently good at. She groaned at that because it shouldn't be that way, and there shouldn't have been this level of frustration with it all, but there definitely was. She tried to relax, as she waited outside for Mack to arrive.

When Richard poked his head over the fence, she looked up at him. "Hello. Mr. Woo is awake. I don't know about talking, but he has survived."

The relief on Richard's face was heartwarming. "Good to know. I was quite worried about it."

"Me too," she muttered. "I didn't want anybody else

getting hurt because of me."

"I get that," he agreed, "but it would be more because of that husband of yours."

"Sure, but everybody wants to blame me for his death too. You know that, right?"

He frowned, considering it, then shrugged. "I guess. Although, to a certain extent at least, it's probably well deserved for you to be a suspect." She glared at him, but he smiled back at her. "You have to admit that you've caused quite a bit of chaos and ruffled a lot of feathers."

"Yes, but only for people who were connected to those murders or cold cases that I've been involved in."

"Yeah, I get that, but the average person doesn't care enough to seek out the actual truth of the matter. That's okay, since you can't control that. Honestly this too will pass."

"It needs to pass," Doreen muttered, "and then I need a nice long break."

"If you stopped looking into cold cases, you might get it," he suggested in a cheerful tone. "So, are you still a suspect?"

She nodded. "I guess, although somebody tapped my phone, and that's how they figured out I was going for Chinese food at some point. So that's why Mathew was there, waiting for me to show."

He stared at her. "Where on earth would you have left your phone so that somebody could have done that?"

"I don't know. The only thing I can think of is when I was outside working," she suggested. "I always have my phone with me, but not always when I'm gardening. Sometimes I leave it on the deck or in the kitchen, when I'm here at home, you know?"

"Or you could have just misplaced it for a time," he offered thoughtfully.

"*Right*. I did that just a few days ago. I couldn't find it and wasn't at all sure where I'd put it, but I knew it had to be here somewhere. I eventually found it upstairs. I guess I'd gotten up and come downstairs without it one morning."

He nodded. "I've done that a time or two myself," he admitted. "So, if somebody was around, and they snagged it, particularly if you were down at the river or something, it would be an easy-enough thing to add in a bug."

"Maybe," she said, "I suppose it wouldn't take them long."

He nodded. "Probably not. I'm thinking maybe ten minutes or something."

"In that case, it could have happened when I misplaced it then. I didn't think anything of it."

"Maybe now you should mention it to Mack, so they can figure out that part at least."

She nodded. "He's on his way over just to grab a few minutes rest and to get a bite to eat, since I keep filling up the morgue."

He stared at her. "What do you mean?" His tone was cautious.

She winced. "I just found Mathew's driver in the trunk of the vehicle Mathew had rented." She quickly explained the little bit she knew.

Richard stared at her, shaking his head.

"I just went down to talk to the kid at the car park, and he said the green Jag hadn't been returned. Mugs got to smelling around and led me to a spot between the dumpsters, and there was a beat-up green Jag. The license plate number was wrong for the one expected back at the car park.

It would have been reported missing by somebody eventually, maybe even today. I just happened to be there."

"*Just happened to be there*? You were out looking for it, so it makes perfect sense that you would be the one to find it."

"That's the thing though. I have a local PI looking into a lot of related items regarding Mathew's death, and the cops were looking for the rental car as well. This car park attendant—who was renting out the vehicles—wasn't looking for it. Yet, since it hadn't been returned, he'd reported it as stolen."

Richard nodded. "It still figures that you would be the one to find it."

"Yeah," she agreed morosely, "that's what I was thinking too."

Just then his mobile rang, and he said, "Got to go." And his head disappeared behind the fence.

She smiled, wondering at how much friendlier Richard was these days, ever since the Roscoe scenario. That was good, and maybe it was time for some of these hardships around town to ease off and to let people be happier. At least she hoped so. It seemed fruitless and sad to have people at odds all the time.

Of course Richard hadn't really been fighting with her. Maybe his crankiness was natural or it had been more about his privacy and space. She didn't know. Thankfully things were better between them.

Other than the oddness of his personality, she had no problem with Richard. Plus it wasn't up to her to determine whether that oddness was good or bad. Richard was Richard. He was who he was, and she was okay with that.

Now all she needed was to be okay with the fact that whatever happened with Mathew, whatever had actually happened, she couldn't do anything about it. However, what she *could* do something about, that was up to her to change, if she could. And, if she couldn't change it, that was where the acceptance part came in. With that, she heard a noise out front. She smiled at the animals. "Is that Mack?"

Mugs raced up to the front door, just as Mack opened it and stepped through. She watched as he bent down to give the dog a royal greeting.

"He just saw you couple of hours ago."

"Yeah, a different scenario though," Mack noted, with a smile. "Hey, big fella, that was a great job you did today." Mack looked over at her. "Did you ever consider putting Mugs into some search and rescue or drug-sniffing training? He already seems to have cadaver-sniffing talents."

She frowned at him. "Are you serious?"

He nodded. "Why not? It could get you involved with the local authorities on that angle too. Plus Mugs obviously has something going for him in that area."

"Yeah, I'm not sure what it is though," she muttered.

He chuckled. "Go easy on him. He's pretty special. After everything else he's already shown himself to be, give him some credit."

She nodded. "Now that I can agree with."

Chapter 19

As Doreen and Mack sat outside with their warmed-up Chinese food, she asked, "Can you tell me anything about the case?"

"Not much," he replied. "You've done pretty well helping us out, but did you get a chance to see the body? Did you recognize him?"

"I didn't recognize him," she confirmed. "I figured it would be the PI who Mathew hired down the coast."

He nodded. "That's exactly who he was. His ID was still on him."

"I don't imagine he thought this job would be particularly dangerous."

"Maybe not, but he had information about your house and a notebook on your whereabouts." She froze and slowly turned her attention from her forkful of food to tilt her head at him. "So, is he the one who tapped my phone?"

"It's very possible," he agreed, with a nod, "and maybe the angry guy at your door too. Anyway that's the premise we're going on for now. Once the coroner confirms the driver's time of death, we'll know better."

She went back to eating. "We really don't understand

people in this world, do we?"

"No, we sure don't," he noted, with a smile.

"And you don't know who's after what. Was Mathew really so worried that I wouldn't talk to him? Sure, I've been warned by you guys to not talk to him, but why go hide by Mr. Woo's for who-knows-how-long, waiting for me to turn up?" she muttered, "And why there?"

"We still had active alerts to detect his presence in town. So, if you think about it, Mr. Woo's location is a bit out of the way. Nobody really sits around that corner, and chances are that Mathew could have gone undetected for quite a while."

"I suppose," she muttered. "It boggles my mind to think about it."

"Why?" he asked curiously.

She shrugged. "Mathew was not really the kind to sit around and wait. I would have expected him to hire a lackey to do it."

Mack pondered that for a moment and nodded. "That's a good point. But who would he have hired?"

"I don't know. I was wondering if the driver, his Vancouver PI, was the one who took out Mathew. Maybe Mathew had arranged for the PI to sit there and wait for me, but then they got into a confrontation that turned ugly, and Mathew was the one who ended up dead."

"Maybe, but where was Mathew while the PI staked out Mr. Woo's? Did Mathew just drive around in the rented Jag, waiting for you to finally show up?"

"Do we have at least an estimated time and day when the PI died? Did he die before or after Mathew?"

Mack shook his head. "The coroner's working on it."

"Maybe Mathew killed the PI, hired another driver, who

then double-crossed Mathew."

"*Huh*, of course in your world, double-crossing people is a common thing, I suppose."

"No, not in *my* world, *his* world," she clarified, enunciating her words very carefully. "Mathew was the one who chose to live in a world where that deceit was prevalent."

"Seems it came back to bite him in the end, didn't it?" Mack muttered.

"It sure did," she whispered.

He frowned at her and asked, "Are you still upset over his death?"

"No, not any worse than I was," she stated carefully. "It's just difficult, knowing that somebody in your life has died in such a terrible way." He nodded but didn't say anything else. "It's not that I'm mourning him or unduly sad or whatever you want to call it," she clarified. "It's just such a waste, you know? It didn't need to happen. I don't know how it went wrong, but this didn't need to happen. Two men dead, and Mr. Woo not out of the woods yet, and for what?"

"I agree with you there," he muttered, "though it seems that death and violence followed Mathew a lot."

"That's the thing. He obviously wasn't expecting a betrayal. He wasn't armed, correct?" She studied Mack with a raised eyebrow.

He nodded, yet frowned. "That's right, but he owned a gun, didn't he?"

"He absolutely owned a gun, though I don't know that he would have tried to fly with it. However, if the private eye was driving up, I can imagine Mathew not bringing his gun along at all—or maybe gave it to the PI to drive it up. Plus the PI would have had his own weapon as well, wouldn't he?"

"You would think so," Mack muttered, as he thought about it. "We didn't find a weapon on either body though. The PI did have a license for one, but we don't know for sure that he had it with him. We do have somebody checking out his apartment right now."

"Which is down on the coast, correct?"

He nodded. "Yep."

"So, Mathew hires him down there, arranges for the guy to drive up—or fly up early—and to do his scouting work on me. Mathew flies in later, never one to take the long road trip if he didn't have to. That is very much him. The PI finds out where I'll be, which is creepy in itself, and somehow Mathew ends up at the spot, although he's there early, some two hours earlier.

"Whether by design or not, Mathew would just have this PI guy wait until I showed up and then come and take his place, which would make more sense to me. But I don't really understand what makes this other guy tick, so who knows? Then they get into an argument, and the PI kills Mathew and takes off. Either the argument or the killing was planned, so the PI tells the other person he's involved with about what happened. Then the PI gets double-crossed, killed, and stuffed in the trunk of the Jag. And nobody knows anything."

Mack shrugged. "That works, if you look at it that way, but we still have an awful lot of open threads."

"No doubt, but I'm not associated with this PI guy, so it should let me off the hook as a suspect a little bit more."

"Except that he had all kinds of information on you."

"Of course he did. He's a private detective and was assigned to track me for some reason."

He smiled at that. "That's true. Yet he was potentially

somebody you knew and that you had provided that information to."

"No. He got that info from the phone bug. Otherwise they wouldn't have found Mathew behind the Chinese restaurant, since he could have just come to my house. If I was part of this, it doesn't make sense to kill him down there, does it?"

"Right, and that's what everybody is still trying to figure out."

She rolled her eyes at that. "Of course they are. Everybody just needs to admit that you don't have any evidence on me because I didn't do anything."

"I don't have a problem with that, but it's not quite that easy for the new detective on the block."

"No, of course not." She raised both her hands and shook her head. "I hope she was hired with a probationary period in her contract. Dealing with this is definitely getting tiring though."

"What, not being able to investigate?"

"Oh, I'm investigating," she muttered. "Obviously so, since I found that body."

"Which is another problem, of course."

"Oh, what now? Did I arrange to kill the PI too?"

At that, he burst out laughing. "There are bound to be people who think you did."

"Sure, people who don't want to put any real work into finding the real killer. Regardless, I didn't kill anybody, so that really shouldn't come into play."

"Maybe not," he agreed, with a smile, "but we know that a third party was in the middle of this and, at some point, that vehicle sustained some damage. What we need to do now is to figure out who else was in that vehicle with the ill-fated PI."

"The city cameras should help with that," she noted. "Hasn't anybody found the vehicle throughout the days in question on any of the street cam videos?"

"Not so far," Mack said.

"And I saw no cameras in the back alley where the Jag was left," she muttered. "I suppose everything was pointed to the lot to catch anybody who might have been stealing cars."

"Exactly." Then Mack looked over at her, and his lips twitched. "I suppose you know all about this kid from the car park?"

She rolled her eyes at that. "I certainly don't know *all* about him, but I do know some things. Like the fact that he's been renting out luxury vehicles, both with or without the concurrence and knowledge of the owners."

"A tip from Bernard then?"

"Sure, but I guess it's been a lucrative business for Tony and for the lucky owners who knew about this side gig and got their cut. However, Tony did admit to me that not all the owners were willing or even informed participants."

"That's an interesting sideline," Mack noted. "It's not the first time we've heard of it happening, although I've not heard of it happening *here* before. It is a problem in the larger areas."

"*Interesting*," she repeated. "I guess wherever there's a criminal element, there'll always be somebody willing to take advantage."

He smiled at her. "Absolutely."

"I still don't really see the point. Why didn't Tony just buy one of those luxury vehicles and rent it out himself?"

"But why?" Mack asked. "Then you have to put out the money for it, and those are not cheap vehicles."

"No, they sure aren't, but, hey, Tony's not my problem."

"Unless …"

"No, not my problem," she stated, with a glare. "It had nothing to do with me."

"You realize that Insley still needs to take your statement, right?"

At that, Doreen rolled her eyes. "Why her?"

"Because she's heading this investigation," he said calmly, "and it definitely can't be me."

"Fine. I guess I need to go down to the station then, *huh*?"

"Or she can come here."

"No, she doesn't need to come here."

At that, he stopped, then looked at her curiously. "I thought you would want her to come here, so you didn't have to go to the station."

"No, not at all," she declared. "If she'll treat me like a suspect, then she can treat me like a suspect in front of everybody. I don't want her in my home. This is my sanctuary, my space, for me and my friends. And, if I have a choice, she doesn't belong in that category, and I don't want her here."

His breath came out in a quick *whoosh*, as he sat back. "You really don't like her, do you?"

She shrugged. "No, I really don't like her. Why do I have to keep repeating that?"

"You don't normally take a sudden dislike to people, so what's going on with this one?"

"I have this funny rule where people who find me capable of killing two men and injuring another man is someone I instantly dislike." He continued to frown, and she continued to ignore him.

"You'll have to tell me sometime."

She looked at him and replied, "No, I really don't."

At that, his frown turned to a glare. "We shouldn't be keeping secrets."

"Considering you keep a lot of secrets from me," she reminded him, pointing her fork his way, "that's hardly fair."

He sighed. "I don't mean about work. I can't let you in on all of that, especially on a current case, and you know it."

"Maybe you can't. Yet it's hardly fair that you get to keep all these secrets, then expect me to tell you everything." He glared at her, and she shrugged. "And now that I have helped as much as I have, surely you would think that *Insley* would have the case solved by now."

"It would be good if you didn't say that in the interview."

"Did you arrange for me to go in?"

He nodded. "I arranged for an interview."

"You weren't going to tell me?"

"I set it up but wanted to talk to you first."

"Why did you set it up at the station?"

He pondered that. "Because I figured that's how you would feel, how you would prefer to do it at the station."

"And you're right," she confirmed, "but I still find it all just very uncomfortable."

Doreen wanted to push it but didn't want to make it worse or to have Mack leave prematurely. As long as they were talking, there was a chance she might get information out of him. Yet he would do his best to protect everything too. Including *her*, and Doreen couldn't really blame him. *Much*.

"Whatever. I'll go down to the station and be interviewed," she declared, with an eye roll. "Maybe I should start writing a book or something? Then I can do a tell-all."

"I would hope not. That would hurt a lot of people in the department."

"Yeah, well, I'm not exactly feeling supported by the people in the department right now." When he turned and glared at her, she shrugged. "I'm not."

"She hasn't treated you like a suspect," he reminded her.

"She told me how she *suspects* that I murdered my husband. She probably added on the PI's death now too, along with Mr. Woo's attack."

Mack raised a hand. "You're still free to do whatever you want. Come to think of it, you haven't even been interrogated."

"That's because nobody has anything on me," she snapped. "I didn't do it, remember?"

"You didn't do it, but we still have to go through the process."

She sat back and left it again, but she wasn't happy. She finished her food, then got up and walked into the kitchen, without saying anything.

He followed quickly behind her. "I really don't want this to cause a rift between us," he muttered.

"Good, because I don't either." Then she turned and looked at him in the eye. "But I *really* don't like her."

"I wish you'd tell me why."

She pondered that for a moment. "Other than her thinking the worst of me? I'll have to think about it. I really don't have an answer at the moment."

"Do that, please, because it would be helpful to know what it is about her that bothers you so I can understand. For all I know it's because she's doing what you would really like to do and aren't."

She stared at him. "You think I'm jealous of her because she's a detective?"

"It's one of the possibilities that's gone through my mind. I'm not saying that's the one. I'm just throwing out suggestions."

"Good, because that would make me sound incredibly small-minded." But he could have a point there. She grimaced.

"I'm not saying that," he said pointedly. "But obviously things are a little on the rougher side with this case, so I'll head out. I'll talk to you tomorrow."

She watched as he walked back out to his vehicle, and, as he was about to drive away, she called out, "Drive safe."

He smiled at her. "Will do."

And that was all the peace-making she could handle for the moment.

Still disgruntled and out of sorts, she finished cleaning up the kitchen and headed up for an early night. Running a hot bath sounded like just what she needed. The perfect thing to help wash away the stench of death once again.

Chapter 20

Monday Morning ...

THE NEXT MORNING Doreen woke up bright and early to the sound of her phone ringing. She groaned and rolled over, reaching for it. "Hello," she asked in a raspy tone.

"Doreen? Doreen, that you?" asked a man, with a deep accent.

"Hey, Mr. Woo," she said, sitting upright in bed. "I'm so glad to hear that you're okay."

"Not okay, much pain."

"Yeah, I'm so sorry about that," she replied. "I feel terrible it took me so long to find your message and to come find you."

"It fine. You came. Thank you. Thank you."

She realized he was calling to thank her. She smiled at that. "I'm just sorry we didn't get there faster. I'm so glad to know you survived this. I was terribly worried."

"It okay."

"Did you tell the police who it was?"

"No."

"You didn't remember?"

"No, no, I didn't tell them."

Something was going on here. "Okay, so do you want to tell me why?"

"They say they kill me."

"*They?*"

"Yes, yes," he said.

"Did you see anything? Why would they say that to you? Why would they threaten you?"

"I not know," he cried out. "They tell me not to say anything, but I not see anything."

"You told them that, and they didn't believe you?"

"Right."

"I'm assuming that they think you saw whoever killed Mathew outside of your place."

"But I not even see him. I see no one."

"They didn't believe you. What I don't understand is why they left you alive."

"One got a phone call, and he ran."

"What about the other one?"

"He cursing, say something. Then … he took off."

"Okay, so the one guy took off first, and then the second one left?"

"Yes."

She thought about it and asked, "Did you see their vehicle?"

"No."

"Would you recognize them?"

"Yes."

"Okay, I'll come to the hospital. I have a couple pictures here," she explained. "So, I'll ask you if it's any of these men."

"Okay. I wait for you. You come now?"

"Yeah," she replied, looking around the room for her clothes. "I'm just getting up though, so give me a minute to get dressed and to get down there."

"No bring animals. No animals in hospital."

"Right, I know," she said. "I'll leave the animals at home."

"Good, good." And, with that, Mr. Woo was gone.

She frowned but phoned Mack. "Normally I wouldn't be calling you, but Mr. Woo contacted me, and he didn't tell you everything."

"What? I just spoke to him yesterday."

"He's scared. They said they'll kill him."

"That doesn't make sense though. He didn't see anything."

"I know. I told him how I had some pictures to show him to see if we can identify the two men from Mathew's staff."

"Two men?"

"Yeah."

"What the heck? He told me that he didn't see anybody," Mack said in exasperation. "Why does everybody keep telling you everything?"

"Probably because he either thinks I'm involved, or he's afraid I'll get hurt too."

Mack sighed at that. "I'll meet you at the hospital."

She hesitated. "I don't know that he'll talk if you're there."

"He darn well better," Mack snapped, "because I've had enough of this. We need to know who attacked him."

"He doesn't know who," she reminded him, "and he didn't see anything when Mathew was killed, but the two bad guys seem to think he did."

"They probably didn't realize he was there until afterward, then got worried."

"Exactly. Yet he's scared. Keep that in mind."

"Scared people do all kinds of stuff. Including throwing you to the wolves."

She snorted. "You can meet me there, but I can't guarantee that he'll talk."

"*Great*," he muttered in a heavy tone. "I just don't understand how police work has gone by the wayside, as everybody wants to talk to you instead."

"I don't know. I guess he trusts me."

"Or he's setting you up."

"Well, in that case, it's good that you'll be there," she snapped. "Certainly something is going on, and we need to find out what."

With that, she quickly got dressed, and, leaving the animals behind after feeding them breakfast, she raced to the hospital. She met Mack there and asked him, "Do you have a picture of the dead man?"

"Why? You didn't take a picture?" he asked, his tone wry, almost sarcastic.

She glared at him. "No, I did not, but to show Mr. Woo would be a good idea."

He nodded, then searched his phone. "This is the one I have." And he held it up for her.

"He definitely looks dead in that photo," she muttered, avoiding his gaze.

"Yeah, well, that's because he was, remember?" And, with that, Mack led the way to Mr. Woo's room.

When she got there, she poked her head around to see him sitting up in his bed, staring out the window. "Mr. Woo," she said gently.

He turned to her and whispered, "You came."

"Yes, of course I came." She walked inside, but then he saw Mack, and fear crossed his face. She quickly walked over to the bed and reached for Mr. Woo's hand, patting it gently. "I had to bring him. No need to be afraid. It's just Mack, and he has a couple pictures that you need to see."

Mr. Woo looked from her to Mack and back. "But he police."

"He is police," she confirmed. "Which is why he needs to know what happened."

Mr. Woo shook his head. "They come back and find me."

At that, Mack stepped forward and held out a picture of the dead man's face. "This man, is he the one you're afraid of?"

He looked at it and nodded. "Yes. That one."

"He's not coming back," Mack declared. "He's dead."

At that, Mr. Woo fell back against the pillow and stared at him in shock.

"So that's one you don't have to worry about," she murmured.

He nodded at her, then looked at Mack. "The other one?" he asked, his tone rising in fear.

"We're looking for him, but we didn't know anything about a second guy because nobody told us," Mack declared, frowning at him.

Mr. Woo had the grace to look ashamed. "They say they kill me."

Mack frowned and added, "I'm surprised they left you alive to begin with."

He nodded. "I tell Doreen. One man got phone call and left. Second man said they be back."

"But," Doreen said, "we found you just in time, so they didn't get the chance to come back."

He nodded.

"I don't know when this guy was killed," she said, looking down at Mack's phone, but the picture was no longer on the screen. "That guy was a PI hired by Mathew. So, to find the second guy, you need to tell Mack everything this time. Every detail you can remember."

Mr. Woo nodded slowly. "You no charge me for lying?" he asked fearfully.

Mack shook his head. "No. I'm not here to put good people in jail, but we need the truth, all of it, and right now, please, before somebody else gets hurt."

Mr. Woo hesitated, then Doreen patted his hand again. "We're trying to stop the second man, so he can't come back for you. That's important, so we have to ensure that nobody can come after you. Now tell Mack everything you know."

Mr. Woo nodded. "Nobody come back. That good. Nobody come back."

She smiled. "That's right, so help us figure out what's going on."

He sighed. "They say something about Mathew, but I not know what."

"They said his name? They actually said the name *Mathew*?" Mack asked.

Mr. Woo nodded. "Something about *Mathew not have it.*"

At that, Mack looked at her. "Did Mathew give you anything?"

"No, of course not. Remember how I didn't see him earlier that day?" she told Mack. Turning to Mr. Woo, she asked, "Did the two bad guys mention my name at all?"

He shook his head. "No, they no say *Doreen*, but they say something about find it before *that woman*."

She nodded. "That's probably me then anyway," she muttered.

At that, Mack glared at her. "So, once again, you're right smack in the middle."

"But this has way too many echoes of Robin's case," she declared, staring at Mack. "So what is it that they were after? … Did you find a briefcase or anything like that with Mathew's body?"

Mack shook his head. "No, nothing."

"And, if the two bad guys had it at that point in time, there was no need to beat up Mr. Woo."

"Exactly."

Mr. Woo said, "No reason anyway, but they came."

"Once they realized your store was open, they were afraid that you'd seen or heard something when Mathew was killed nearby."

"I hear nothing," he cried out. "I hear nothing."

She smiled at him. "And that's a good thing. If you had heard something, they would be even more aggressive."

He shook his head. "I see nothing," he muttered. "That's the rule. See nothing, say nothing."

She sighed. "And yet, this time, that's not the way to go."

He looked at her, frowning.

"Did they say anything else when talking to each other? Did they mention anybody or anything else? Even if you didn't understand. Anything could be helpful," she prodded. "We need to find this other man, before he comes back."

Mr. Woo started to tremble. "They talk. They talk a lot. Something about *business development*. They need something, supposed to get from Mathew, but they not get it. Then they killed him and now have no way to get it."

She nodded.

"Does that make sense to you?" Mack asked, studying her carefully.

"I suppose so, but I don't know exactly what they could have been after. If I were looking for business docs, I would probably go back to the source, and that … Oh no. That means Reggie." She frowned at that and pulled out her phone. "I need to ensure he's okay."

"Wait," Mack said. "Let us talk to him."

She glared at him. "Reggie's a good guy."

"He may be a good guy, and he may not be. It doesn't matter, but let's ensure we don't have any more bad guys out there, coming back after Mr. Woo."

She nodded. "No, I don't want that happening either."

Mack relaxed a little bit, then asked Mr. Woo, "Did they say what they were after, when they were beating you up?"

He shook his head. "No, just say over and over how I not say anything, and I told them how I see nothing and know nothing."

"Yet they didn't believe you."

"No, and they were waiting," he added. "They were waiting for something."

"That phone call probably," Doreen suggested.

Mr. Woo nodded. "Yes, I think so, and then they left."

"And what was the phone call about, I wonder?" she asked, turning to look at Mack.

"Someone saying they found something maybe? Someone asking if they had found the business documents? But who made that phone call?" Mack asked.

"Maybe somebody else was looking for the business

docs," Doreen offered.

"I don't know," Mr. Woo muttered. "I have bad head now." He groaned and shuffled under the bedcovers. "You leave. You go now. You find bad men, so I go home."

"Yeah, that would be a good idea," she agreed, then smiled at him. "You stay here, where it's safe."

"I have business to run."

"It's a good business. Believe me that everybody wants you back where you belong."

He smiled. "Good, good. I make Chinese food, lots for everyone when I'm back."

She chuckled. "Everybody will be happy to have that happen."

As soon as they were outside again, she was relieved to see a policeman on guard. She looked back at Mack. "You have any ideas about what's going on?"

"No, but it seems they were planning to meet Mathew, and he was supposed to give them something, or they thought he had something they wanted." He shrugged. "And either Mathew double-crossed them or planned to cheat them anyway, and maybe they thought they could get whatever it was somewhere else."

"Sure," she agreed, "but an awful lot of *something* and *maybe* are in there."

He glared at her. "I know. What does Mathew deal in?"

"Art, jewelry, business developments, property developments, all kinds of stuff," she replied. "It could be that he owned a property and would give it to them in order to get out of his trouble or something ... maybe?" She shrugged, knowing her speculation had just as many holes as Mack's had. "Maybe a title transfer? Who knows?" she muttered. "Especially with these guys."

"Exactly," Mack stated, "especially with these guys, something is always messed up."

She nodded. "But not my fault."

"Correct." He chuckled. "*This* time it's not your fault."

She rolled her eyes at that. "*This time*? Come on. Most of the time it's not my fault."

"I won't argue the point, but it would sure be nice if we could get a little more information about this."

"If there was a double-cross," she began, "I don't have a problem assuming that Mathew was involved. That's the kind of deal he would do. If he owed somebody and would give him property, maybe in lieu of cash, I can see him signing it over—or saying he would sign it over—but actually sign it over to somebody else instead, … such as a competitor. In fact, I wouldn't put it past Mathew to sell one property to two different and unrelated people, and then wiggle his way out of it."

Mack frowned at her. "Wow. If he's been operating like that for years, no wonder he's dead. So who would know about that?"

"His lawyer, Roger. You should talk to him."

"We did talk to him, but that lawyer only dealt with his personal affairs, like your divorce, and had nothing to do with Mathew's business dealings. Mathew apparently has a separate lawyer for business, but that one's not talking."

"Of course not," she confirmed.

"He won't be talking to us, not until we get some information that we can use to pry open that door a little wider. Knowing Mathew's involved in any dirty business dealings, though, now throws out the confidentiality clause in their contract."

"That's to be expected, I suppose," Doreen muttered.

"Honor among thieves and all that."

"But there isn't any honor among thieves, remember?"

"No, especially if Mathew really was in dire financial trouble. Still, I don't understand why he wanted to talk to me. If he was already selling something or transferring a property or something, it *does* make sense to have all the paperwork ready and waiting. But why see me? It's not as if I have property he can take from me. In fact, with the divorce, as Nick tells me, Mathew should be moving property over to me, not *from* me. Yet, during the marriage, I was always signing stuff Mathew put before me, but I wouldn't now. So, if I wouldn't sign something that day he was here, if I wasn't amiable, then maybe he would have fobbed it off and sold it to somebody else."

"Maybe," Mack conceded, "but we're assuming Mathew had to do *some* kind of a deal, whatever the currency, whether it be drugs, or even just money."

"You're right, but he had no laptop, not at the crime scene. Yet according to Tony, the kid at the car park, Mathew had a briefcase when Tony saw him too."

"When did he actually see him?"

"Tony drove the Jaguar to the airport, handed it over there."

"What?" Mack turned to her.

"Yeah, you didn't know that?" she asked.

"No, I didn't know that," he replied. "I assumed they went to the lot."

"No, Tony took the Jag to the airport and handed over the keys there."

"How did he get back?" Mack asked.

She pondered that. "I don't know. He must have a system. It makes sense that he wouldn't have customers coming and going picking up cars at the car park itself," she noted. "Maybe he called a cab or a friend of his. I don't know." She then frowned at Mack. "What are the chances that Tony's more involved than he's letting on?"

"I don't know, but the stakes are much higher than Tony may realize. So, if he is involved, he probably has no idea how ugly things will get before this is over," Mack muttered. "There's a good chance that kid's life is in danger."

"We need to find out how he got back from the airport," she murmured.

"Yeah, we do." Mack had his phone out and was talking to somebody already. Then he turned to her. "The office said the kid's been let go, and they presume he's gone home." He looked down at his phone, rifled through a couple texts, and said, "I've got an address. I'll go check it out." He looked at her and frowned. "Nope, you don't get to come."

"*Fine*," she said in disgust, frowning back at him. "You don't have to be so very happy about it."

He gave her a big smile. "Hey, I'm just keeping you safe."

"I'm not in danger."

"Really? Do you actually think that, out of all this, you're not the one who everybody wants to get their hands on to get answers?"

"But I don't have any answers," Doreen declared.

"I don't think they really care whether you do or don't. The bad guys are looking for something, and, if they realize that Mathew saw you or tried to see you, they'll look to you next."

She stared at him for a long moment and then nodded. "That makes sense, and we still don't know who the second man is who was beating up Mr. Woo."

"Thank you," he replied, rolling his eyes in frustration.

She gave him a wave of her hand. "It does need to make sense for me eventually. I think the Vancouver PI was the one banging on my front door. Yet I didn't get a good look at him there. Just his profile and his general build. Comparing that guy to the guy in the trunk of the Jag, I can't match his general build unless he's standing up. Plus it was hard to see his face in the trunk—and I didn't touch him of course. So I'm guessing it was Mathew's PI. You can probably match my video with his profile at the morgue." She looked over at Mack to confirm.

Mack nodded. "Yeah, we ran facial recognition, and it was a good-enough match to confirm Mathew's PI was the angry man at your door."

Doreen sighed and continued. "Thank you for that. I get it. You are this person who sees the larger picture and understands an awful lot more than I do, but I'm the one who needs to have things fit into their little boxes in my head."

He sighed and wrapped his arm around her shoulders, as they walked across the parking lot of the hospital. He pulled her up close, then dropped a gentle kiss on her forehead. "I'm really worried because things are at the point where they could potentially blow up. So it's really important that you stay safe."

"I plan on it," she said, but he just stared at her. She shrugged. "Okay, so my plans don't always work out, but I am trying."

"No, they certainly don't, and we don't want whatever is going on to get any worse. We have two dead and one attacked, so we need answers."

"Yeah, I got it," she said. "The answers are the key. As

much as I hate to say it, or to even bring it up, have you guys tried using my phone to set them up or to set me up?"

"It's being discussed, but nobody in the office wants to do that," he admitted.

She smiled. "Well, that's nice to know. Yet it's probably not smart."

He shrugged. "Your phone's in my truck, but I'm not ready to release it just yet." She stared at him, then back at his truck. "Which also means that somebody could be tailing you."

"Maybe. Why?"

"That bug in my phone just puts you into a dangerous position, if they figure out *you* have my phone, instead of me."

He stared at her, his face grim. "In that case I don't want you to be around me to get caught up in that."

"And yet that's when you *could* look after me," she noted, with a chuckle. Although hard to find much room for humor, it was part of the relationship they shared, and she was desperate to keep the status quo, at least for the moment.

He shook his head. "We need to keep you safe. That's paramount."

"*Hmm*, I'm not so sure about that," she countered. "Paramount to me is finding out who's killing people."

"Not at the risk of your getting hurt," he declared, bumping her gently on the nose.

She smiled, but just then came a shout from across the parking lot. She turned to see the kid from the car park.

Chapter 21

DOREEN WALKED OVER. "Hey, Tony," she greeted him, Mack on her heels. "What are you doing here?"

"I was looking for you. The cops told me I could find you here. I, … well, … I thought I'd better tell you something else."

"Yeah, you sure should," Mack declared, his tone hardening again.

The kid looked nervously from him to Doreen. "Will he hurt me?"

"No, of course not," she replied, "but *I* might, if you don't start talking."

Tony stared at her and then back at Mack, who just sighed. "Don't worry, kid. She's joking."

She turned to face Mack and asked, "Am I?"

"Yes," he declared, glaring at her.

She shrugged. "Okay, okay. I'm kidding," she muttered, "but we do need answers, and, so far, everybody is beating around the bush. So, how did you get back into town from dropping off the Jag?"

"They gave me a lift," he said, looking at her.

She stopped and stared. "You delivered the Jag to the

airport, and then they brought you back to the car park?"

"Sure. How else was I supposed to get back? I started to call a cab, but they didn't want that, so they dropped me off."

"Oh." She wondered how any of that fit into this mess. She looked at Mack. "Your turn."

He shook his head, pivoting to the kid. "I would rather hear what you wanted to tell us so badly that you tracked us down."

Tony winced visibly. "I heard something, when I was in the vehicle with them. They were just talking among themselves, and I had my earphones in, listening to music, as I always do. I don't think they really thought about the fact that I was there or that I could still hear them."

"No, but it might have been part of why the driver was killed though."

Tony stared at her in shock. "You think so?"

"I don't know what I think at the moment," she muttered. "Keep talking."

Tony shrugged. "I'm not saying anything for sure, but they were making plans. The guy in the back seat mentioned something about, *After talking to you, if it didn't work out, he could reverse it, but, if things did work out, still would be better in the long term.*"

"Did he say what it was about?"

Tony shrugged, shook his head, and added, "Something about property." He looked at her apologetically. "I thought you knew because he seemed to think it was something to do with you."

"Like what?" she asked.

Tony took a deep breath. "Something might be in your name that somebody wants, and he's trying to either get you to sign or to cancel the divorce or to get a hold of you and force you to sign."

She stepped back and looked at him in shock. "What?"

At that, his tone turned grim, yet with a hint of satisfaction, Mack stated, "*Finally* something is starting to make sense."

She turned to him, frowning. "Glad it makes sense to you, because it sure doesn't make sense to me."

He asked her, "Is there any property in your name?"

She shrugged. "None that I know of."

"Because you didn't know, you probably didn't have Nick do a search for it with the divorce then either."

"No, why would I? If I'd known I owned anything, why would I have come here and scraped by, living off the money Nan kept secretly hiding in my kitchen?"

"Who knows why Mathew put property in your name or even when it happened. But then, when the divorce action started, Mathew must have realized that he was possibly in trouble, once it came to light, and that you probably wouldn't just hand it over to him. Then again, it's quite possible he needed to sell it in order to get clear of some debt. Maybe Mathew had somebody who wanted it and wasn't so willing to sell it or wanted to take it in trade for some money that Mathew owed him, and things got ugly. So, he probably came down here and needed you to sign it over, and, if you didn't, then he was in trouble."

"Except that he always had a way to make it work out in the end, whether I signed or not."

"How? Why?"

"Because he just forged my signature."

He frowned at her. "You're kidding. Is that something he would do, even on a legal document?"

"*Especially* on a legal document. He's done it before," she stated. "I didn't think anything of it at the time, but honestly things were very different then. I was very different then. But now? All this is making me think."

"That's interesting. Maybe not a good-enough signature to get through a court of law, especially considering there's a divorce in progress, but maybe enough to fob off on these people."

"But, if they figured it out later, wouldn't they just come back to find him?"

"Maybe, but maybe by then he would have found enough money to have gotten himself out of whatever financial hole he was in."

She nodded slowly. "I remember a development that he was involved in that wasn't going well, but that was quite a while ago, right before we separated."

"Sure, and he might have held off the investors for quite a while. However, now with the divorce, if one investor got wind of it, … then every investor gets nervous," Mack suggested.

"It's quite possible that is what stirred this up into a huge issue now." She stared at him, nodding now. "In a way that makes sense, yet, in another, it doesn't."

"Tell me what's bothering you about it?" he asked.

She shrugged. "If he already had forged my signature once, … maybe it wouldn't work a second time." She thought about Mathew's hand the last time she'd seen him. "When I saw Mathew last, his hand was wrapped up."

"Damaged from something?"

"Maybe? I don't know, but Reggie mentioned something about Mathew hurting his hand too."

"Right, so in that case, maybe with a bum hand, he

couldn't produce a forgery good enough to get through the legal process—at least not enough to match his previous forgery. Maybe his own lawyer wouldn't even deal with it and wanted a better signature."

"He just needed an even more crooked lawyer."

"Yeah, but Robin's dead."

At that, Doreen winced at the mention of her husband's fling and her own previous divorce lawyer. She sighed, then looked over at the kid. "It sure would have been nice if you'd told us this yesterday."

Tony shrugged. "I wasn't even going to tell you today," he admitted, "but then I got scared, when I thought about the guy in the trunk. I realized I'd been worrying about getting in trouble for the cars, but that won't even matter if whoever killed him thought I might know something more," he shared, with a sad smile.

"Exactly," she said. "Good choice."

Tony looked at Mack, then at her, and asked, "So am I off the hook?"

"Off the hook for what?" Mack asked, staring at him.

"For the rentals."

"No, you're not, and, even if you were, do you really think those car owners won't be all over you?"

Tony winced. "I was hoping maybe you could tell them it's not happening anymore."

"That's fine, but there is still the matter of a beat-up Jaguar that seriously needs its trunk cleaned. I can't imagine the owner's insurance company will let that ride."

Chapter 22

DOREEN WALKED IN the front door of her house to be greeted by the animals, as if she'd been gone for days and days. She bent down, chuckling. "Hey, guys. Sorry. That was an early morning visit to the hospital, wasn't it?"

Mugs woofed and raced around her in circles, putting a huge smile on her face. She headed into the kitchen, realizing she hadn't even had coffee yet. She quickly put on a pot and opened up the back door, inviting everybody outside.

As soon as Mugs was free, he raced to the closest bush and emptied his bladder.

She sighed. "Sorry, buddy. I should have left you out longer before I left." Quickly she checked around the house for accidents and found none, which was a saving grace all on its own. She wouldn't blame them if they'd had a problem, since it was her fault for leaving in such a rush.

With a cup of coffee in hand, she went outside, sat down with her notebook, then proceeded to fill in her notes on what had just happened. She was pretty sure that somehow Robin was involved in all this, but, with the woman no longer around and probably in the same place as her ex, it was hard to imagine getting any answers there.

So Doreen went back to her desk in the kitchen and went through all the previous divorce paperwork that Robin had left for Doreen, hoping she would find something all tied up in a nice little bow that would clear things up, but it was not to be.

Things were never that simple. It seemed Mathew and Robin had left this mess to see if Doreen could figure it out somehow, as if she had all the answers, while they laughed from the grave. Doreen didn't even know what to say about it but returned with her notebook to the backyard, as she updated her information, including comments from the kid, Tony. Doreen still wondered if he was a little more involved than he was saying or if he really was naïve enough to think that coming forward with a little bit of information would let him off the hook.

Even if the Jaguar's insurance company let him off, she couldn't imagine all these rich people not suing him for using their expensive vehicles for personal gain. If nothing else, they would want their cut of the pot. She imagined that some wouldn't care, especially if they were getting paid already because it was just another way to make money.

However, she imagined a good share of them would be horrified at what had happened. It was certainly something to consider, if and when she ever came to the point of needing to store her vehicle. It would definitely not be in a place like that. Not that she was planning on going anywhere anytime soon. Besides, no one would want to rent her old beater.

With her first cup of coffee down and the animals rolling around on the grass, generally just enjoying the lazy day and being outside, she got up and grabbed a second cup. She was hoping that Mack would get back to her, but, knowing

Mack, he would wait until the last minute before he contacted her, particularly if there was anything to update.

What she needed to know was a question that maybe Nick could answer. She frowned, wondering if she should bother him with it. How could she keep asking him to do stuff when she may never have money enough to pay him in the end? She didn't want to take advantage of him. Although she had money coming from Nan's antiques at some point, *the check is in the mail* seemed to be the recurring phrase for her life.

She decided that she would ask Nick, and, if he said no, that was fine. She quickly picked up the phone and called him.

"Hey, what are you up to?" Nick asked. "I've been trying to reach my brother, but I figured something had blown up because he's not answering."

"He probably just doesn't have a moment to get back to you," she guessed, then filled him in on the happenings of the morning.

"Wow. That's some good progress. It seems things are really heating up though."

"Yes, but they're at that point where they can blow and go one way or the other. We just need to keep the information flowing."

"Okay, and was there a specific reason for calling me?" he asked.

"Yes. One of the theories we have is that there could potentially be some property of Mathew's in my name that I didn't know about."

"How would you not know about it, though?"

She hesitated and then in embarrassment whispered, "Because I signed things blindly. He didn't like to be questioned, and eventually I found that life was easier if I just did as he asked. And, worse than that, Mathew was not above forging my signature."

A long moment of silence came from the other end, and then he gave a heavy sigh. "You told me that you have no property in your name."

"Except for this house that I got from Nan, yes."

"All right then. I'll see what I can find." And, with that, he was gone.

He didn't ask for payment, but she was more determined than before to give him something by the time this was all over, providing she had anything to give. She had to remember not to be greedy at that point because that's when people got upset. And, with that, she thought about Reggie. She made a quick phone call and, when he answered, he sounded tired, worn out. "Hey, Reggie. I'm so sorry to bother you. And you sound as if it's been a rough couple days for you."

"Oh my God, it's been exhausting. Between the police—who came and just basically tore apart the house—followed by the slew of lawyers, partners, and developers, then everybody else calling, all of them looking for information and money. It's been pretty rough."

"Ouch. I'm sorry. That must be miserable. Have you spoken to Mathew's estate lawyer, Roger?"

"A little bit, and he did tell me that I'm mentioned in the will, but, until the reading of the will, he won't tell me how much."

"Right, and, of course, we don't trust Mathew at this point."

"No, I sure don't," he agreed cheerfully. "Also there was a time when I used to put property into my name in order to save him on taxes, transferring it back to him later. Then he would sell it, and somehow the money would just disappear. Looking back, I did a lot of those things or put up with that. Now I wish I hadn't."

"I hear you there," she replied.

"Anyway, I'm hoping that Mathew remembered all the things I did for him and that he doesn't screw me over, like he did so many others. Of course you of all people know all about that," he said, with a half laugh, "since you did the same." After a moment of silence, he asked, "Didn't you?"

His tone was odd, and she had goose bumps. "I signed a lot of things because he wanted me to, and I didn't read them because he found that offensive somehow. Frankly, it wasn't worth the potential consequences. But I certainly wasn't aware at the time that I was signing property into and or out of my name," she murmured.

There was another short silence on the other end. "Wow, I wonder if that's what all this fuss is about."

"What are you talking about?"

"Some developers are looking for documents on several properties, but I'm not handling Mathew's business affairs and so keep referring him to the lawyer who is doing that. But even he told me to not forward any more calls, so I don't know what I'm supposed to do now."

"Maybe not answer the phone, cancel the number. I don't know," she suggested. "I'm curious. Did Mathew's business attorney also do your taxes?" she asked.

"Yes." Then he groaned. "Yes, of course he did. Oh my God. Because, of course, he did my taxes and paid the tax on any property transfers but probably used it in other ways to shuffle tax credits and things," he murmured.

"Oh dear, and I'm sure now that the lovely Robin would

have helped Mathew do all kinds of stuff we never suspected."

"Yes, exactly, until she died."

"Right. If there's anything that you can help the police with, the sooner we finally clear up all this, then we can ensure that neither of us had arrears on taxes or are heading to jail for tax evasion that we didn't even know about," she declared, her tone rising. "Jesus, will it ever end?"

"And who needs all that?" His tone was agitated. "All I ever did was my best for him, and I'm far too old to wind up in jail."

"I hear you there, and let's not go down that rabbit hole until we have a better idea. Still, considering that somebody was after him in a pretty serious way, it makes me very suspicious."

Reggie gave a hysterical laugh. "Yeah. I'll feel better if I hear that he left me one million dollars for my pension coming up. If he didn't, maybe I'm better off in jail. At least I wouldn't be out on the street."

"I hope he did. Now try not to worry. We'll get to the bottom of all this. But please help yourself by sharing with the police anything you think of or find out. I know you still feel some loyalty to Mathew, but you need to think of yourself at this point." She couldn't help the heavy sigh that slipped out. "I'm having struggles of my own, since he'd been fighting me on the divorce every step of the way—"

"Partly because he thought it wasn't all over with between you two."

"Yet because of Robin's machinations, I was to get nothing but to walk away."

"Seriously?" he cried out. "You were with him from the beginning."

"I know, and apparently that's why my lawyer is now fighting to get me something, but Mathew hadn't been willing and had fought it tooth and nail all the way."

"Oh, oh, oh," Reggie muttered, his voice trembling. "This doesn't sound very good at all."

"Let's hope he was a better friend to you than he was a husband to me," she stated. "I don't know how we will get any answers, until the reading of the will."

"That's supposed to be in a couple days."

"Is it? I haven't been told."

"Are you in it?"

"I'm not sure." She automatically shrugged even though he couldn't see it. "I believe the police mentioned that I was, but I don't know anything else."

"The attorney should be getting in touch soon, I would think, and I don't know whether you can do it virtually or will have to come down here for the reading."

"I don't know either, though I'm hoping for virtual. Under the circumstances, it would be nice not to have to come down."

"It would sure be nice to see you though," Reggie noted.

She smiled at that. "You're about the only good part of that time of my life," she replied, "and you're right. It would be great to see you. Anyway, I don't want to call the lawyer myself. I don't want to get involved in any of that. However, you need to watch your back because I'm not sure just what all Mathew might have done to get himself out of trouble, and we all are potentially in significant danger."

"I agree," Reggie replied. "Mathew was definitely in trouble. He'd stopped sleeping and was really worried about something. He'd found out something recently that set him off in a big way. I think it may have had something to do with Robin, but I really don't know."

Doreen shook her head. "I hate to say he deserved it, but, with Robin, he did a lot of crooked deals. It seems she may have turned the tables and did a crooked one on him."

"I know," Reggie replied, his tone soft. "Toward the end, Mathew wasn't very clear about where he was headed and what he was after. He did say that he made a big mistake with you."

"That mistake was something he couldn't go back on," she stated. "I'm a very different person now."

"God knows you're better off away from him," Reggie replied, his tone growing stronger. "Anyway I'll have a shot of whiskey and try not to think about any of this for a while. Once it's over, I may have to hire a lawyer or somebody to look into my taxes and all of that to ensure that I'm free and clear. I certainly don't want to go to jail for tax evasion, fraud, or some other ridiculous thing."

"No, me neither," she said, her face wrinkling up. "I'll talk to you later." And, with that, she disconnected and quickly called Nick back.

"I haven't got any answers for you yet," he said calmly.

"I know, and I just talked with Reggie again." She quickly explained what he'd told her.

"Holy cow."

She winced. "That's bad, isn't it?"

"Well, good Lord, I don't even know what to say, but obviously we'll have to do a much deeper investigation into all this."

"I'm really, really not sure what to say either," she whispered. "It'll be bad news if Reggie got caught up in this, not to mention me. But I really don't want to go to jail for tax evasion that Mathew caused."

"You won't," Nick confirmed reassuringly.

"Yeah, you say that, but believe me when I say that Mathew was all about playing games. Plus he had Robin dabbling in the background."

"So I understand, but I'm starting to get a better idea of what the problem was in terms of why he was dragging his feet so much on the divorce and why he kept wanting to talk to you, sidestepping me."

"Yeah, but he didn't say anything to me about this latest turn of events, although he did mention to Reggie several times that I needed to sign something for Mathew."

"Yeah. I'm thinking he may have been done in by his lovely girlfriend, the lawyer," Nick shared. "I really want to laugh, but I won't until I know for sure that there's something here to laugh about. At the same time, he could easily have screwed you over completely. As far as the law goes, you're still married to him. I'll get back to you as soon as I have something." And, with that, he was gone.

She stared at her phone, shock and worry knotting her stomach. She lifted her head, glanced around, and looked down at Mugs. "How do I get into these situations?" she cried out. "Will Mathew ever be done screwing me over?"

At that came a reply from the other side of the fence. "Not until you're divorced and you've got at least a year behind you."

Richard was clearly in a mood, and it showed in his tone. She asked him, "How do you know?"

"Speaking from experience, of course," he snapped. His head appeared over the fence. "And that husband of yours? He was up to no good right from the beginning."

"I didn't know anything about it," she stated.

"That's because he didn't want you to. They're like that.

They're manipulative."

She nodded slowly. "I guess they can be. He definitely didn't turn out to be who I thought he was."

At that, Richard laughed. "He was who he wanted to be, and he allowed you to see what he wanted you to see. Other than that, he was just having a grand old time."

"Do you know anything about tax law? Will I be in trouble if he moved property into my name and then backed out and that sort of thing?"

"Depends how he did it, but, chances are, you will be fine. As long as the taxes were paid in your name and on time, it should be okay."

"I didn't know anything about it, so I don't have a clue if the taxes were paid or if they weren't, but I've got a lawyer looking into it now."

"Good," Richard noted. "I hope for your sake it's all free and clear."

"Yeah, me too," she muttered. "Other than that, I don't know what else to do."

"How is the murder investigation going?"

"We're looking for Mathew's briefcase, but there's been no sign of it."

"The ones who killed him probably took it. Then, if they didn't find what they were after, they'll be looking for the next source of information."

"Which may be Reggie, my ex's *man of affairs*. He oversaw the house and things. He's been in Mathew's employ for a very long time."

He stared at her. "He was that rich that he needed a *man of affairs*? I've never even heard of that."

"Yeah, but I don't even know if that's a good name for him. He wasn't his lawyer or his banker, but he was the one who looked after him."

"Then he would probably know everything."

"He says he doesn't though."

At that, Richard's eyebrows shot up. "Are you sure you trust him?"

"Yes, of course. Why?" She stopped and stared.

"Why would you trust him? Why would you trust anybody who had anything to do with that period of your life?"

"He's quite worried. He apparently was unwittingly involved in some of the real estate transfers and such. Now he's worried he won't even get consideration in the will, as a form of pension, which was always part of their arrangement."

Richard snorted. "Do you think he would be deemed completely innocent and exonerated of all charges, if he allowed all these property transfers in order to save his employer tax? Unfortunately the name for that is tax evasion. So, if he participated, he's guilty of helping your husband at a minimum."

She didn't know what to say to that. "Well, that's very scary," she muttered.

He snorted. "Yeah, hopefully you already filed your income tax this year. Did you?"

She nodded slowly. "I did, but I didn't have any income, so it was pretty easy to do."

"Have you gotten anything back from them?"

She nodded. "Yes, I got a zero assessment on it."

"That's a good sign," Richard declared, "but that still doesn't clear you, not if they find any wrongdoing in the last seven years—or more, if companies are involved." He snorted. "I wouldn't sleep too easy if I were you."

"I'm hardly sleeping at all as it is," she admitted. "I did go see Mr. Woo this morning."

At that, Richard turned and looked back at her. He'd been in the act of getting back down behind his fence again, but his head popped up and over the fence. "How is he doing?"

"He's awake and alert. Apparently two men attacked him."

Richard's eyes grew round. "Wow, he's lucky to be alive."

"They chose his place to wait for me or maybe Mathew," she explained. "However, they didn't realize that Mr. Woo's business was open. So, when they figured it out, they went in to find out what he might have seen."

"That's pretty risky. They should have killed him at the time."

"I guess one of them got a phone call that had them making a hasty exit, after giving Mr. Woo another threat and promising him that they would be back."

"They should have just popped him right then."

"Oh, I agree, but I'm very grateful they didn't. Seems the one guy took off. I wonder if the other one was supposed to have done the job and didn't."

"That makes sense too," Richard replied, nodding. "Just because he was supposed to do the job didn't mean he wanted to or was up for it."

"Oh, I never thought of that," she noted. "Maybe he took off, thinking he could come back later or thinking the other guy could come back and finish it."

Richard nodded. "Depends. It could also mean that Mr. Woo is still in danger."

She winced at that. "He's still in the hospital, but there is a police guard on him."

"Sure, but, if you don't solve this soon, he'll get discharged and will be looking over his shoulder every moment."

"*Great*," she muttered, glaring at him. "Now I have to worry about him too."

"You don't have to worry about everybody, but you sure need to be careful about who your friends are," he pointed out. "And everybody needs to be careful about being friends with you." With that parting shot, he dropped to the other side of the fence again.

She sat here, staring at it, hating the truth behind his words. Yet Richard was right, and this was turning out to be a bad deal for anybody who was connected to her. However, so far, the bad guys hadn't made any attempt to come after her. But then they'd been tracking her, so maybe they were hoping that her ex would take care of her. Or at least get her to fall in line. That would be a completely different story now.

She had to find out what was happening behind her back.

Chapter 23

Wᴴᴇɴ Dᴏʀᴇᴇɴ ɢᴏᴛ a call from Nan a couple of hours later, she was brisk and businesslike right off the bat.

"News?"

"Not a whole lot," Doreen murmured. Then realizing there was something to tell her, she filled her in about Reggie.

"I've spoken to him a time or two over the years," Nan shared, "but Richard's right. You shouldn't trust him."

"I want to trust him," Doreen said.

"Why would you? He was there the whole time throughout your marriage. He knew what Mathew was up to. He knew the man was hitting you."

"He told me how he tried to defend me, and Mathew threatened to fire him if he interfered."

Nan was quiet for a few moments. "And that's quite possible. But then it could also just be a good story."

"He's also an older man," Doreen reminded her. "He'll have a hard time finding employment now."

"No, he won't, and maybe that's why he threw his lot in with Mathew, on a promise of better times."

She didn't like anything about what Nan was saying. Yet everybody was looking for options and theories.

"I do like the idea of Robin screwing over Mathew though," Nan said, with a chuckle.

"Oh, that would be fine with me too," Doreen murmured, "except for the fact that I'm the one who'll pay the price."

"You didn't though. Mathew paid the price."

"Sure, but it's not over yet."

At that, Nan gasped. "Now that's true. Did you ever get a will in place?"

"No, just one more thing on my plate to do."

"Well, you should write down your handmade will and sign it and email a copy to Nick right away."

"We talked about it the other day, and Nick and I were supposed to get together and sign one," she replied.

"You've got to get that finalized. The fact of the matter is, you now have an awful lot of money in limbo, and, regardless of when that money comes through, it's still coming through to your estate. We don't want anybody greedily deciding you might be somebody they can get money from by writing up a fake will and simply killing you off."

"*Great*," she muttered. Her hands shaky, she quickly sat down, while she still talked to Nan, and wrote out a simple will by hand, signed it—even while discussing coming down for a cup of tea with Nan. Then Doreen scanned it in and emailed it off to Nick. "I'll be down there in about twenty minutes."

"Good. Have you had breakfast?"

Doreen frowned. "I don't think I've eaten all day."

"In that case, you get here as soon as you can. I'll get us

some food." And Nan was gone.

It wasn't long after, Doreen hadn't even gotten her shoes back on when Nick called her.

"I got your draft will, but eventually we need to do a proper one," he noted in a flat tone.

"Nan ordered me to," she stated, raising her free hand. "I don't know what I'm supposed to do, but apparently I'm next on the hit list."

His breath caught. "That sucks. I really don't like to think of that."

"And yet according to Nan, I'm worth a pile of money, even though nothing is necessarily settled."

"That's true," Nick agreed. "Everything to Nan, *huh*?"

"Yes, of course. I want to ensure she has everything she needs for the rest of her life."

"Fine. I'll draft up a proper will, but it'll only be temporary."

"Why is that?"

"You'll see soon enough—although that part might take a day, a week, or even a month or two."

Such a note of humor filled his tone that she stared down at her phone. "I'm not really in the mood for games. Did you get the title search back or something?"

"Yeah, I sure did. I've got a call in to Mack about it."

"So, you won't tell me?"

"Do you really want to know?" he asked.

She groaned. "I don't know, do I?"

"Not sure, but you'll have to know eventually. What I found was that several pieces of property were put into your name, and they were done so with your signature and Robin's. The only thing I can surmise is that, somewhere along the line, when you were signing another document,

Robin slipped this in, and you signed it, but she didn't register it right away."

"Why would she not register it?"

"Honestly I'm thinking she probably registered them just before she died, as a way to get back at your ex."

"Oh my God. Was this a one-off to use just in case or what?"

"It's a theory, and really we don't need to know about that, but the fact remains that you signed it. They probably had it all ready in case they needed to do it for tax purposes, in order to transfer everything into your name, to lower the taxes they paid, then sell it and blame you for the taxes. Because that would be something she could do with the same signatures. I don't know whether the forms were even around or not, but she could have transferred the forms right back out again."

"*Great*, like into her name?"

"We need to find out, and we're still doing a lot of that with her estate, sorting out her relationships and the murders, remember?"

"Right, all that property and piles of promises of big scores."

"I suspect it got transferred into your name, and then Robin was using that as blackmail with Mathew. However, realizing what all that was additionally happening in Mathew's life, Robin ended up registering all these so they titled to your name. That would explain why Mathew started to panic all of a sudden because these are worth millions and millions of dollars."

"*Great*, so he really was probably coming up to ask me to sign these things back to him."

"If you had understood what was going on, what would

you have done?"

She shrugged. "I would have given them back to him, of course."

Nick sighed. "And that's why he was trying to talk to you and brought up papers for you to sign."

"So, why would somebody stop it from happening then? Why would somebody kill him in order to make it not happen?"

"Well, who will benefit?"

"Me, it sounds like."

"Exactly, which could make you prime suspect number one in his murder alone," he replied.

"But I didn't even know about this," she argued.

"True. But, on the flip side, if all these properties were in your name, and Mathew was supposed to pay off a divorce settlement or pay off disgruntled investors or whatnot, then Mathew was surely looking to get you to sign them over."

"But that makes no sense. It's already in my name. What threat could he use to make me sign them?"

"But you didn't need a threat, did you?"

"No, but other people apparently think that way," she pointed out. "Just consider how everybody else will assume that I would refuse. He was being a pain about the divorce already, and these properties are already in my name, so why would I transfer them out of my name? That's just what most people would think. However, I don't care how much money they're worth."

"Exactly, so what leverage could they use on you?"

"Only hurting my animals, Nan—and Mack."

"Right, and remember that you *still* have all that property in your name. So, there's a good chance that whoever has the upper hand in this whole nightmare has documents all ready for you to sign them over."

"*Or else?*"

"Exactly. Or else they go after the people you love."

"Meaning Nan and Mack."

"Exactly. Keep the animals close too because the bad guys might try to use one of them as a message." And with that and a warning to stay out of trouble, Nick signed off.

She gathered all the animals close to her and whispered, "Oh my gosh, oh my gosh."

Chapter 24

DOREEN SAT HERE, petting the animals for a long moment, while she tried to figure out what her next move was, but she didn't even get a chance to because Nan phoned right away.

"Are you coming?" Nan asked briskly.

"Things have changed a bit since we spoke, Nan," Doreen muttered.

"Okay, you need to explain that."

Groaning, Doreen repeated her conversation with Nick.

"Oh, my word. Could this get even more confusing? That Robin was quite the little minx. Mathew certainly got what he deserved where she was concerned. Considering what she may have just done, I find myself liking her a little bit more every day. She was clearly a wicked woman, and she certainly screwed you over, but it appears she tried to do right by you in the end."

"Assuming that's really what she did, and, as far as Nick can tell, these properties are in my name right now. That's most likely why Mathew was coming up, to try and convince me to sign them back to his name, so he could sell them and get out of trouble. These properties were probably slated for certain developments, and now those people he's been stringing along have figured out that he's just screwed them over."

"Which essentially he did," Nan stated gleefully.

Doreen groaned. "You know I wouldn't have wanted that."

"No, *you* wouldn't have, but a lot of people would have gladly done it to him. But the bad news is that now there's a ton of money coming your way—the money that a lot of people would do almost anything to get their hands on. You can't trust anybody until this is all settled, and you need to make that will, deciding who and what you'll give money to," Nan reiterated.

"Nick's working on that," Doreen whispered, "and now I've got a pounding headache."

"Of course you do. Don't worry about coffee, as I've already got the kettle on."

"Nick also warned me that the murders were done as a setup, so that I look guilty for them. Also the bad guys will probably try to get me to sign these properties over by threatening those I love."

"Oh, dear. That's inconvenient."

"By the way, I've made sure that, no matter what happens to me, I want you and the animals to be taken care of."

"Of course you do," Nan replied, with a gentle tone.

"But now I'm worried because I don't know who they will target. The last thing you should have to do is suffer between now and the end of your life."

"Don't worry about me, dear. Keep yourself safe. If somebody did take you out, that money would be of absolutely no help for the pain I would be in."

Doreen felt the tears gathering in her eyes. "Ditto," she

murmured. "Okay, … let me get my shoes on, and I'm coming down."

"You be careful on the way and bring the animals."

"Oh, everybody's coming, no doubt. Nick even suggested the bad guys could use one of the animals to send me a message. Can you imagine? I'll be there in a few minutes." She ended the call, grabbed her shoes, and, while she was putting them on, Nick phoned again.

"Okay, I've got a simple will ready. I'll bring it over later. However, when this is over, we'll sit down, and we'll set up a proper will and a proper disbursement for those people you want looked after. There's a ton of money coming at you, and that's just from your divorce."

"Divorce? He's dead. Do I even get divorced?"

"No, because it wasn't legally signed, so it wasn't completed. You'll be considered a widow, not a divorcée."

"*Great*, and does that mean I get anything?'

"We haven't had the reading of course, but, according to what I can see, you're likely to get 99 percent of Mathew's assets, plus all these properties that you apparently already own."

"Do you really think that's fair though?"

"Seeing how Mathew's dead and legally you're still his wife and are getting everything, it's totally fair. He made the choices that put all this in motion."

"Is it fair that he died trying to get these back after Robin screwed him over?"

"Probably not, but considering all the people he has no doubt screwed over throughout all the years, I think it's totally fair."

She groaned. "Is there anything that can come back to bite us in the butt?"

He laughed. "Yeah, probably, to some degree. But you'll have plenty of assets with which to straighten things out, so you have lots of good things coming as well." And, with that, he asked, "So, what are you doing now?"

"We're heading down to Nan's for a cup of tea. As she reminded me, I haven't eaten, and I'm fairly stressed."

"You think? I am too. I'll call my brother again and bring him up to speed. You take care. Ensure you keep things locked up, put on the security, and keep the animals close." Reiterating that same warning for a second time made her doubly nervous, and she almost ran down to Nan's.

As she stepped onto her grandmother's little patio, Nan looked up, smiled, then hopped to her feet and gave her a big hug. "You don't look so good."

"I'm seeing boogeymen everywhere right now," Doreen murmured, as she plunked her butt down on a chair. "It's a scary time."

"It is, but I've got plenty of food, including croissants and bite-size quiches. We'll spend the next hour or so talking about everything *but* all this trouble."

Doreen smiled, and, for the next hour and a half, they laughed at the animals, fed them little bits and pieces, and cherished them for being the characters they were. Richie stopped in, as did several others who lived at the senior facility.

Nan checked her watch and said, "Oh, it's almost four. Time for lawn bowling."

Doreen stared at her, shaking her head. "I think your life is busier now than it ever was."

Nan chuckled. "Agreed. That's okay, and, when I can't do much or don't want to, I'm perfectly capable of just telling them that I'm sitting it out, maybe staying in my room to rest, or, as in this case, having a visit with my granddaughter."

Doreen waved her hand. "You don't need to babysit me, Nan. I'll head on home and see if I can dream up something complicated to cook for a distraction. And by complicated, I mean, maybe a simple pasta with … whatever I have."

"Store-bought pasta, I suppose," Nan guessed.

Doreen rolled her eyes at her grandmother. "Of course. I haven't the guts to make that from scratch yet."

"You'll get there," Nan declared, "but you might want to bake another batch of cookies soon."

"Why is that?"

"Because they were lovely." And then Nan winked at her. "Now go on home, find a good book, and settle in. Do something that's just fun and relaxing."

"I could try," she muttered, getting ready to go. Then she stopped, looked at Nan, and asked, "Has that new detective stopped by to see you?"

Nan nodded. "Yes, she seems to be a lovely lady."

Doreen stared at her. "*Lovely?* Are you kidding? She was mean to me, told me that she thinks I murdered Mathew, and I don't like her one bit."

Nan got a mysterious look in her eyes and nodded. "Ah, that's a whole different story."

Doreen glared at Nan. "What do you mean by that?"

Nan chuckled. "Oh no, you'll have to figure that one out on your own."

Doreen shook her head. "You too? Mack already gave me one suggestion so ludicrous that I got mad at him."

Nan's eyebrows rose. "What was his suggestion?"

"That maybe I didn't like her because she was doing the job I wanted to do."

Nan pursed her lips. "That was very astute of him. I'll have to remember he has that in him."

"He *is* very astute at times," Doreen admitted, "but, wow, that would make me feel very small if that's what it is."

Nan's lips twitched. "I wouldn't worry about that, but you do need to take a few moments and figure out why you feel the way you do."

"It's not that hard to sort out," Doreen declared. "She thinks I'm a murderer. She's not doing her job. She's taking the first suspect and running with it. So I don't like her. She rubs me the wrong way."

"But the question is *why* she rubs you the wrong way?" Nan pointed out and then patted her hand. "Go on home, and we'll sort it all out."

"You're sure you won't tell me what you think it is?"

"Absolutely not," Nan declared. "Trust me. You'll thank me for it later," she added, looking at her with a twinkling gaze. "This is one you need to figure out for yourself."

And sending one last glare in her grandmother's direction, Doreen started walking to the river. She hated it when people seemed to know something she didn't. Not only did it get her curiosity going but it made her feel stupid, as if she didn't know something really important, yet everybody else around her did.

It was that mocking child thing from school all over again. Plus her husband had always treated her that way too. She certainly knew that Nan didn't intend for it to come across that way, but it still stung.

As she slowly walked home, she stopped at the river and played with Mugs in the water. She didn't want to go into the house; she didn't want to go anywhere really. She waded in the water in her shoes, finding the water a little cool, but not too bad considering their unseasonal warm weather. Her shoes would get waterlogged and probably ruined but whatever. It made her feel better at the moment, and right now that was all that mattered.

After playing with Mugs, while Goliath looked on in complete boredom, she smiled. "Okay, Thaddeus. How about you? Do you want to play in the water?"

Thaddeus was sitting on a rock, basking in the sun. He looked up at her and cried out, "Thaddeus is here. Thaddeus is here."

"Glad to hear that, buddy," she said. "I was wondering where you were."

"Thaddeus is thinking," he stated.

She reeled back and looked at him. "What?"

"Thaddeus is thinking," he repeated.

She just stared at him. "Wow," she muttered. "That's a new one. Where did you get that one from?"

"I'm thinking." Then he repeated it. "I'm thinking. I'm thinking. I'm thinking."

She wasn't sure where he'd heard that, although Mack said that quite often, as did she, but it was a whole new phrase that she hadn't expected to come from Thaddeus. She shook her head. "I'm glad you're thinking, buddy. When you get it figured out, let me know, will you?"

"Will do. Will do."

She stopped and stared at him. "Can you really talk and understand what you're saying?"

He glared at her. "I'm thinking."

Closing her eyes, she nodded. "Yes, of course you're thinking."

She was the one going nuts, and these animals were driving her nuts. She loved them to bits, but they could be hard to take sometimes. Thaddeus had been so quiet all day. Ever since they'd found the Jaguar with the second dead body inside, she'd been worried about him. And there was good reason for that. It had been distressing for everybody. But today, since visiting Nan and now getting home, he'd been really quiet and was busy thinking, apparently. She snorted at that, then quickly sent Mack a text, explaining Thaddeus's new words.

He phoned her not long afterward. "You apparently seem to be doing just that."

"I don't know about that," she replied. "I've spoken to Reggie and Nick a couple times, then Nan of course," she murmured, "I'm not really sure what to think at this point."

"At least we've got a better idea of what's probably happening."

"Yeah, but we're still missing one person," she stated, "the one behind all this."

"Correct, and it's hard when we don't know quite what we're looking for. We don't have much of a description either."

"Why is that?"

"We had a description from the kid, but it fit the guy in the trunk, so we figured the driver was the Vancouver PI. Now Tony's waffling on whether the guy that was with Mathew when they got the car was the same guy found in the trunk or possibly somebody else."

She groaned.

He laughed. "The kid mentioned how the one man had a bit of scar, like he recently cut himself shaving, and that's all he could really say. However, if it was from shaving, it's probably healed over by now. The guy in the trunk had no such mark."

"In other words, we really don't know what to believe from Tony's description."

"He was tall and skinny and didn't have much hair."

"Right," she muttered. "So who knows then?" She sighed. "I'll just stay here, while you guys figure it out."

"Oh, wow, that's generous of you," Mack teased.

"Oh no, I'm not listening to that today either," she muttered. "I'm pretty stressed and tired, and I just want to take a time-out."

"That's fine," Mack replied, his tone gentle. "Take a time-out but do so in a smart way, please."

"Yeah, I'll stay home. Will you be here later?"

"I hope so, but it's hard to say at the moment. Things are really starting to break, and that's what we need."

"Good," she murmured. "What about Mathew's will?"

"Yeah, there's a reading apparently. Oh, I was supposed to tell you."

"Tell me what?"

"That you're supposed to be there."

"Can we do it virtually? I did hear from Reggie that he and I are in it, but I was told to wait for the lawyer to contact me."

"Yeah, I told him that I would tell you."

"That seems unprofessional of him. Shall I contact him?"

"Yeah, why don't you, and find out if you can do it virtually. Tell him you're too tired and worn out from all this to travel."

She liked his excuse, even though it wasn't quite true. Doreen quickly picked up the phone and called Roger. When she explained who she was, he perked up.

"Oh, good, thanks for calling. I should have called you

directly. I'm sorry, but I wasn't sure. When the detective said he would let you know, I wasn't sure whether that was appropriate or not."

"No, that's fine. He did tell me, but I wanted to hear it from you."

"Good, good," he replied in relief. "That's smart. Yes, you are named in the will, and we need you as part of the reading."

"That's part of the reason I'm calling. Can I attend the reading virtually?"

"Yes, absolutely. And the others are—"

"No thanks," she interrupted him. "I don't need to know who else is in the will."

"Wills are public documents anyway, so, after this initial reading is completed, you can see everything about it, and you'll get a copy."

"Okay, that's fine," she said. "I don't need to know anything else for now."

"All right then. Hold on, and I'll get you the details for calling in."

They set up a time for tomorrow morning, and she ended the call. It helped to know it was in the works, but not enough. She would have to wait for the reading to see just how much she may have gotten and whether Mathew had provided for Reggie or not. She was really worried about that aspect. But what was she supposed to do about it? Just another one of Mathew's little games. She wasn't fond of that sort of thing and wanted to stay as far away from it as possible.

Finally, with the day turning slightly chilly, as the clouds moved overhead, she came inside and made up a simple pasta dish. As she sat down to eat, she smiled. "Not very highbrow or classy, but I did it by myself," she muttered.

As she sat here, she noted a message on her phone. She'd shut it off when she was down at the river, not wanting to be disturbed. As she checked the ID, it read Private Number. She frowned and tried to call it back, but it wouldn't go through.

It rang again, just when she was checking her voice mail, as a Private Number again. She answered, but nobody replied on the other end. She frowned. "This is the second call," she muttered. "Stop calling me." But there was nothing in response. Just a *click* as they disconnected.

It was pretty disconcerting, and she quickly sent Mack a text message, saying she'd had two hang-ups from a Private Number. She wasn't sure if that was something to bother him with, knowing it was one of those days, but at least he had the opportunity to know, and he could decide if it warranted a follow-up.

Happy at taking decisive action that put the ball in somebody else's court, she finished up her pasta and decided on an early night. She grabbed the book she hadn't been able to get into all day, then went up and had a shower, got into cozy pajamas, and curled up in bed. It was only seven, but, with the book, she could read for a few hours, and it felt like a gift to be here in bed and to relax.

The animals didn't appear to argue and seemed totally okay with it. When Mugs wanted outside to go to the bathroom at nine-thirty, she realized that was the downside to going to bed early. She had to get up out of a warm and cozy bed and let them out.

With a groan she got up, and, with Goliath now protesting, she led the way downstairs and shut off the alarm and opened the door for Mugs to go outside. As she stepped out on the deck, a hand wrapped around behind her, and Mugs took a blow to the side of the head, knocking him down. She fought as she realized the animals were being attacked right in front of her, only to have another blow come down out of nowhere and hit her on the side of the head too.

The last thing she remembered was seeing stars.

Chapter 25

DOREEN OPENED HER eyes and groaned. Her head was killing her. Her hands and feet were tied together.

"There you are," said a man, with a slightly familiar voice, but one she was still struggling to place.

With her eyes closed, she whispered, "What do you want?"

"I want an awful lot of properties, properties that we were supposed to make a lot of money on," the man said.

"What did you do to my animals?"

"They're all right here," he replied. "I figured they would at least keep you calm. Apparently you're some crazy animal lady now."

That statement had her opening her eyes again, but darkness was all around her. "So," Doreen began, "let me get this straight. I'm supposed to sign paperwork to give you all the properties, so you can turn around and make lots of money, and then you won't hurt me, right?"

"Gee, look at that. You figured it all out."

"Except, if you let me go, then, chances are, I'll tell the cops, and you'll get in trouble. So, no way you'll let me go, so why would I help you?"

After a moment of ugly silence, a shadow stepped into the light. "Can you see me?" he asked.

"No, I can't. It's dark here."

"Plus you've got on a blindfold," he muttered.

"Well then, how could I see you?" she snapped. "Good God, are you really the brains behind this?"

Another ugly silence followed, and then the man came closer and said, "That's enough out of you. I took enough of you with that kind of attitude before."

She opened her eyes and tried to wiggle away the blindfold, but suddenly it was ripped off, and she found herself staring at the man who had hit her. "Reggie?" she asked in disbelief.

"Yeah, it's me."

"Did you kill Mathew?"

"Sure I did, once I realized what was going on and that Robin had cheated him out of everything. He was so furious, and, if it hadn't been my money involved too, I would have been absolutely over the moon at what she'd done. However, then I heard how she'd gotten you to sign all these transfer forms and then filed them, which is a whole different story than just having the paperwork on hand. Mathew didn't find out until he went to deal with the property title issues and realized that Robin had legally changed the titles on all these properties."

Doreen groaned.

Reggie continued. "Everything is yours. *Everything*. Every single one of those properties that had nothing to do with you, that you would never have gotten, *ever*, are now in your name," he snapped. "All my money, all my pension, everything I've worked for all this time," he said, sounding almost hysterical, "went up in smoke because of that lawyer, that stupid female."

"Right, that stupid female lawyer who Mathew also screwed over," she added.

"Which has nothing to do with me."

"Or me," she declared, staring at him. "There's a reading of the will tomorrow. Why aren't you waiting for that?"

"Waiting for what?" he snapped. "Waiting to find out that Mathew didn't give me anything but a little bit of money? You think I haven't looked at that will time and time again, wondering what I would do about it?"

She stared at Reggie. "What's in the will?"

"Everything goes to you," he snapped. "*Everything.* I get like twenty thousand dollars. Do you know how far twenty thousand dollars will go?" He shook his head. "Nowhere, it will go nowhere."

Considering she was doing quite well with five thousand dollars, she wanted to pipe up and say something but figured he wouldn't take it well.

"I've learned to live on almost nothing," she muttered.

"Yeah, good for you," Reggie snapped. "I'm not interested in learning to live on almost nothing. He owes me."

With that, she had to agree. "I totally agree with you. That was a bad thing for him to do, but it's also Mathew we're talking about here. So you should know that anybody who screws others will probably screw you too."

He stared at her for a moment. "How is it you can still be so nice?"

"What do you mean?"

"You would have signed those papers if he'd asked, wouldn't you?"

"Of course," she said, with a shrug. "It wasn't my property."

"In that case, you can just sign them over to me." Then he slammed a stack of papers down in front of her.

Looking at the formidable pile, she frowned. "How many properties did he want me to sign over?"

"A lot, and not only were they not yours, but a lot of them weren't his either. They were all part of a custodian group, and he was the leader of it. We all trusted him because we'd done deals with him before. However, this time, his lawyer screwed him over. Once everybody got wind of that, his life got difficult in a hurry."

"Oh my God," she muttered. "Everybody got screwed in the deal?"

"Everybody."

"And how many times have you guys done things like this, where you screwed other people?"

Reggie shrugged. "That was the name of the game."

"So, it's the name of the game, as long as you're not the one getting screwed out of your life savings, is that it?"

He nodded. "Absolutely."

"Didn't you just say you made a lot of money on all these deals?"

"Sure, but we had more money coming."

"And that's why you're upset. Not because Mathew screwed you over but because he was fool enough to get screwed over himself."

"Yes, we trusted him. We thought he had it together and that she didn't have him by the balls, but, boy, were we wrong."

She just stared at him. There was something surreal, farcical, and satisfyingly comical about the whole situation. "How many people got screwed over?"

"Six investors. A couple of them are furious and are

claiming losses because they were in a position where they have enough money that they can do so. Others don't have a clue what to do and aren't sure if they have any recourse. But me? I won't sit around and wait. I want those properties."

"But you don't want just what you are owed," she noted calmly. "You want all of them."

He gave her a nasty smile. "You see? Mathew thought you were too stupid to understand business, but he didn't get you at all, did he?"

"No, he sure didn't," she stated, eyeing Reggie carefully. "He assumed because I was quiet that I was stupid, but that's not true."

Reggie nodded. "I get that, and I told him that he was making a mistake getting rid of you because you would come back to haunt him."

"I'm not coming back to haunt him, but apparently Robin did."

At that, his face twisted in disgust. "Oh, that witch," he snapped. "She treated me like dirt. You might not have seen me half the time, but that one made sure not only to see me but to grind her heels into me. Mathew laughed and told me that I was way too sensitive and needed to get over myself."

Doreen didn't know exactly what to say to that, but she gave it a shot. "I'm sorry. Robin was apparently accustomed to a certain lifestyle. Yet she didn't come by it naturally, so she felt everybody owed her."

"Yeah, ya think?" Reggie said, with a headshake. "Why exactly is that?"

"Just the stuff that makes life very difficult for everybody," she said. "Let's find out what the will says."

"Did you not hear me? I know exactly what the will says, and it says it's all yours, except twenty thousand to me."

"The trouble is, these properties weren't even in the will, were they?"

He shook his head. "No, because they were all under corporations, trusts, and dummy accounts, and now that they've all been transferred, you basically money-laundered them."

"I didn't do anything," she snapped.

He laughed. "No, and, if anybody got a hold of them from here, it's free money."

She stared at him. "How could Mathew possibly get me mixed up in this?"

"It wasn't him. It was Robin, that lawyer. That constant scam of his, moving ownership around in a tax dodge, required him to have signed documents on hand all the time, but it bit him in the butt this time. He didn't even realize that Robin had done this. He thought he had all those papers from her, but one of the last things she did was file them. You should have heard him when he found out." Reggie chuckled. "I was inside the house at the time, and he just about destroyed the entire place."

Doreen nodded. "I can imagine," she said faintly.

"Yeah, it was pretty ugly," he said, "and you can bet I was deliberately absent when he started to call for me."

"I'm sure you were," she whispered.

He stared at her, rubbing a hand on his head, and asked, "Like my bald head?"

"Last time I knew, you had a full head of hair."

"Yeah, I did, but that's what living with Mathew these last few months has been like. The stress has been so terrible that I ended up bald really fast, but whatever. I don't really care about that, but I do care about the fact that I'm about to lose everything."

She looked at him shrewdly. "No, you're not about to lose everything. What you're not happy with is losing whatever you put into this, and what you want is to screw over everybody else and take it all for yourself."

He gave her a fat smile and nodded. "Exactly, and you're the one who will make it happen. *You* will."

"What if I don't?"

He smiled at her, then at her animals. "I killed Mathew and his PI. I should have finished off the Chinese guy, but I'll do that later. So I don't have a problem killing people. Do you think killing an animal will be a problem?"

She glared at him. "So, these innocent animals that have done absolutely nothing to you, … that's who you'll hurt?"

"Sure, why not?" At that, Mugs walked over, and, since he'd known Reggie for years, he rubbed up against him and snuffled. Reggie smiled, bent down, and scratched him. "Although I might keep this guy. He and I had a bond back then."

She stared down at Mugs, feeling a sense of despair. "It would be nice if you would keep him," she said softly. "I would hate to think you would kill him just because he's mine."

"I will if it makes you sign the paperwork. That can certainly be arranged."

"But, even if I sign it, who will you get to file all this stuff?"

"That's my problem, but don't you worry. I can get a lawyer to take care of this in a heartbeat."

She thought about it and then nodded. "You probably have a lawyer in the consortium, so you can share the profits with him."

"I'm not sharing the profits with anybody," he snapped.

"My days of sharing and getting screwed are over."

"So, how do you stop the new lawyer from cheating you out of this?"

He hesitated and then shrugged. "I pay a flat fee, that's what. I'll get somebody who doesn't know me, who doesn't know anything about this mess. We file it, and it's all mine, and then I disappear to a nice Pacific island."

"I don't know if the Pacific islands are quite what they're cracked up to be," she shared cautiously. "Think about it. They have hurricanes and ugly weather, and, with the pandemic, there are all kinds of supply issues and related headaches."

"Stop all that talk and start signing." Then he tossed a pen at her.

She looked down at her hands, secured with zip ties. "I can't sign anything tied up like this and have it look like my signature," she stated. "I'm surprised Mathew didn't try to forge my signature and handle it that way."

"He did try, but, because everything had to be checked and double-checked, it didn't work, since he'd injured his hand."

"Yeah, but he could have hired someone. Surely he had access to someone skilled in forgery."

"He figured he would ask you first," Reggie said, with a shrug. "I told him that it wouldn't work, but he seemed to think it would."

"I would have signed them," she declared. "I've never been interested in taking what wasn't mine. All I've ever wanted was enough to live on."

"That's good for me, I guess," he said, rubbing his hands together. "Then you won't have any trouble giving it to me."

"Oh, but things have changed. The property is mine

now. And since Mathew is dead and gone, and it won't save his butt, why would I help you, when you're the one who killed him?"

He stared at her. "How do you know I killed him?"

"Who else would?" she snapped. "Besides you just admitted it."

He stopped and glared at her, his hands on his hips. "So what if I did?" he finally said.

"Ah, now we're getting somewhere. And what about the private detective? Did you have to kill him too?"

He shrugged. "Yeah, he knew too much, and he would have put it all together."

"Do you really think that the others in the consortium won't figure it out when they do a title search down the road? Surely someone in that group has the brains to figure out that you've taken all these properties for yourself and ran?"

He stared at her. "Just the one guy is on my case. He's getting impatient, calling me all the time. However, I'll be long gone before he finds me and the others figure it out. They're so flummoxed that they won't do anything but wring their hands for a while. Meanwhile I'll be out of the country."

She stared at him. "Reggie, you know that's not true. You know that's not the way this will work."

"Sure it will," he stated almost desperately. "Otherwise I don't have enough money to retire. Don't you get that?"

"Yeah, I get that," she replied. "What I don't get is how you think this will ever work out in your favor. These men will come after you, and you won't even see it coming. Who knows? Maybe they'll do the same thing to you that you're trying to do to me and make you sign everything away."

He shook his head. "No, I won't do it."

"But don't you see? They'll find something you care about, and they'll force you."

"I don't have anybody," he snapped. "Working for Mathew made sure I didn't have anybody."

She stared at him. "No family?"

"No, and thank you for asking fifteen years after we met."

She winced. "You're quite right. Particularly by the end stage of our marriage, I didn't even know how to do anything but walk the hallways like a ghost."

"He used to call you that, you know? He told me how it was creepy the way you just whispered through life," he admitted.

"Sure, and, anytime I spoke up, I got beat down."

"I really did argue with him over that. He told me that it was good for you, but, when he kept making all those comments about you being a ghost, I realized how much of an effect it had on you."

"If I could have kicked him myself, I would have. I even wanted to when I found him dead because a part of me wanted to have killed him myself. I just can't believe you killed him down at the Chinese food place."

"He was the idiot who thought he could sit there and wait for you. Mathew thought he was so clever to find out about your movements, to know where you were and what you were up to," he said. "Why not just go to your house?"

"Because the neighbors were always watching for Mathew because he made such a stink the last time. Because the cops have alerts out to watch for him when he returns to town. Because the cops also have told him not to bother me at home."

At that, his eyebrows raised. "I didn't hear anything about that."

"Oh, he didn't tell you that? My friend was all over Mathew for creating such a disturbance and trying to assault me."

"I didn't know that, but it certainly explains a lot."

"It might explain a lot to you," she said, "but it doesn't explain a thing to me."

"Sure it does," he said, with a smile.

And then it dawned on her why he was being so smug. "Where is Goliath?"

"The cat? He's here somewhere. He didn't take kindly to being picked up." He glared at her. "Bloody cat, he scratched my hand." He pulled back his sleeve to show her his scratched-up arm.

She nodded. "Cats are like that."

"Which is why he'll be getting a bullet," he stated, glaring at her.

"Thaddeus?" she asked warily. He pointed, and there, sitting off to the side, was Thaddeus, just watching the proceedings.

"Thaddeus," she said in a soft tone. "Doreen loves Thaddeus."

He tilted his head and whispered back, "Thaddeus loves Doreen."

Reggie looked from one to other and nodded. "Oh, isn't that sweet," he muttered. "At least I know who I'll kill first."

She looked back at him. "So you think killing the bird will stop this?" And such a cynical tone filled her words that she was proud of herself.

He glared at her. "If you want the bird to live. They have a long lifespan, you know."

"I do know that," she stated, "if they get a chance, of course."

"*Right*," he agreed.

She looked around the room, her eyes slowly adjusting to the light. "Where are we?"

He shrugged. "Doesn't matter where we are."

"It does matter. It really matters."

"No, it doesn't," he countered. "You're someplace where nobody will find you."

"So, a warehouse? That's almost too cliché." He glared at her, then she looked at the side wall where there was a bit of paneling and frowned.

It looked familiar, but the light was bad enough that she couldn't quite see her surroundings. Then she cried out, "This is my basement."

"Yeah, it's a good basement too," he noted. "I almost missed this floor. Who would have thought there would be doors from the garage connected to this basement?"

"I know. It's a very strange layout for a house, but it's my house," she said in delight. "I'm really glad to be here."

"Well, it was convenient."

"Of course it is," she said, with a smile.

"Nobody is likely to come down here, at least not for a few days."

She nodded. "Of course not. Mugs will have to go to the bathroom." She looked around, and Mugs was already whining at the door, running back to her and to the door and back again.

Reggie glared.

She suggested, "If you open up the side door to the garage, he can run out to the backyard."

He contemplated it for the moment and nodded.

"You're not going anywhere, so I'll leave you to think about the fate of the other two animals." Then he followed Doreen's instructions, and Mugs ran up the stairs to the double doors at the top. He opened them and let Mugs out the side door of the garage, then Reggie came back down.

"Presumably he'll come back when he's done."

Chapter 26

"OF COURSE HE will," Doreen replied, but mentally she was urging Mugs to go find Mack. At that, with the door still wide open, Thaddeus flew out above Reggie's head, crying and cawing. She cried out, "Find Mack, Thaddeus! Find Mack!"

Although Reggie tried to jump up and grab him, Thaddeus darted around him, and then she noted Goliath slipping through and racing upstairs as well. Reggie ran up behind them, trying to slam the door shut, but they were already out.

And, with that, she smiled, as a great sense of relief washed over her.

Reggie came back down, glaring, and swearing a blue streak.

"That's terrible language, you know."

He turned and stepped toward her, his wrath raising his hand in fury.

She nodded. "That just makes you like Mathew."

Immediately he froze and slowly dropped his hand. "He really did like to punch you, didn't he?"

"Until I stopped reacting. He didn't like that, and he

found another outlet."

"That was the boxing hobby he picked up," Reggie muttered absentmindedly. "That was my suggestion actually. I told him that one of these days he wouldn't be able to hide the bruises, and then he stopped beating you. So, just for that, you should sign the paperwork anyway."

"Maybe, but I still can't sign anything with my hands like this."

He stared at her and said, "I don't trust you."

"I can't help that. You expect me to sign when I can't hold a pen properly. The signatures won't pass inspection, especially when compared to my earlier signatures. You don't think they'll have to be verified as legal documents?"

He nodded. "I wondered how that process worked."

"I had also already assigned Robin to be my lawyer to make all these decisions and to act on my behalf," she explained, "but I don't know what happens in your case. I presume Mathew had something figured out, but he was my husband, so that's a different story. In your case, I don't know."

Reggie's face twisted in fury, as he realized it might not be as easy as he had hoped.

"I'm sure, if you get a crooked lawyer, they'll find some way to forge my signature onto a document, making them my legal representative, but you should know it'll cost you a pretty penny."

"Everything costs in this world," he snapped.

She nodded. "That's very true. Everything costs." At that, she heard Mugs barking outside.

"What's his problem?"

"Mugs wants back in."

Reggie hesitated, then looked up at the door, as the

barking got louder and louder, sounding more frantic.

Finally he turned to Doreen and asked, "What's wrong with him?"

"Maybe he wants me," she said. "Did you ever think about that?"

He snapped, "Doesn't matter if he does or not. I'll have to kill him if he doesn't shut up. He'll bring somebody over to check on you."

"Yeah, he sure will," she agreed. Soon she heard a cat howling, and she smiled. "That's Goliath."

Then they suddenly heard a raucous high-pitched voice calling out, "Police, police! We need police, police!"

Reggie stared at her in horror.

She shrugged. "Thaddeus is pretty smart and can speak. All my animals are pretty smart. And that would be them outside, causing a ruckus."

He paled as he stared at her. "Good God, what are you running here, a zoo?"

"Kind of," she said, with a nod. "They love me, and they know when I'm in trouble."

"They do not," he snapped. "That's total nonsense. I'm not that gullible."

"No, but Mathew also mentioned how you weren't the smartest cookie in the jar."

His expression turned ugly, as he stepped toward her.

She nodded. "He really wasn't very fond of you, and I'm sorry for that. You deserved better."

"I sure as hell did. And I did a lot of deals with him."

"Yeah, I know, but that doesn't mean he treated you right in those deals."

He pondered that and then shrugged. "I can't kill him a second time," he muttered, "so it doesn't really matter."

"I understand," she said, "and this way, you're still not getting full justice, which is also hard. I'm sure Mathew took you to the cleaners on a few other things in life, and you probably didn't even see it coming."

"He told me that it was an accident on one."

"Yeah, well, it wasn't. Nothing Mathew did was an accident."

Reggie stiffened, as he thought about it. "Maybe not, and all the more reason for me to get this payoff now and get out of here."

But outside the crazy din continued, and now people were starting to yell, "What's going on? What's going on?"

"Reggie, you have one chance to get out of here before the cops come running," she warned him.

"The cops won't listen to this. They'll bring in animal control."

She smiled at him with pity. "You don't understand who these animals are though."

"Are you some celebrity or something?"

"Or something," she replied, with a nod. Outside, Thaddeus was kicking up a scream, like she'd never heard out of him. Even Goliath was howling at the top of his lungs. She didn't know who could possibly not hear it. If Richard was home, he would be calling the police, as would the neighbors on the other side, although she hadn't had a whole lot to do with them. Hopefully anybody would be calling for the cops right now. At least she hoped so, and that hope was enough to keep her going.

"I can't leave without these papers. Hurry up and sign them." He tossed them closer to her.

She held up her bound hands. "No, not until you undo my hands," she repeated in exasperation. "It's simple. You want me to sign? Undo the zip ties."

And, with that, he glared at her and then brought out a pocketknife and quickly cut the ties between her hands.

She slowly rubbed at her wrists. "Look at that. They made me bleed."

"So what," he snapped in an ugly tone of voice. "That's nothing compared to what I'll do to you if you don't sign those darn forms."

She glared at him. "You don't have to be so mean."

"You don't have to be so stupid," he yelled. Pointing to the pen, he bellowed, "Start signing now!" And he held the pocketknife in such a way that she knew he was nearly out of control, and the din outside was terrifying him too.

"You should run," she repeated calmly, as she picked up the papers. "Absolutely no way you'll get away with this." She looked at the paperwork and, even in the darkened basement, she could read enough, then started to smile. "Wow, sure I'll sign these." And she picked them up and started to sign each one of the documents.

"Thank God for that," he said fervently, and he snatched them from her hands.

"You didn't read them, did you, Reggie?"

"Why do you say that?" he asked, turning to look at the papers, frowning to get a good read of them.

"All this does is sign them back over to Mathew, but who do you think is inheriting everything anyway?"

He stared at her in shock and started flipping through the papers. "No, no, no, I copied off the right ones."

"No, you didn't. You copied the ones Mathew had saved, which already had his information filled out," she explained. "These can never be filed because he's deceased."

At that, Reggie started to scream in outrage. She

couldn't do a whole lot because her feet were still bound, but still, she struggled to lift the chair legs, realizing he'd strapped each of her legs to one chair leg. She had to get one leg kicked out past the chair leg and free, and then the other.

Meanwhile he was still staring at the papers in horror.

"Better luck next time," she called out, as she made a break for the door. He came running after her, and halfway up the stairs he caught her by the waist, pulling her back. She tumbled down the stairs, crying out in pain as she landed at the bottom.

"No way, no way."

"You can't fix it now," Doreen said, "so you better run, before the cops get here."

He stared at her in a full panic, looking around, before deciding that a hasty retreat was the best bet, at least for the moment. He scrambled up the stairs, threw open the double doors, and bolted into the garage, only to come up against a very solid wall.

A wall named Mack.

Chapter 27

DOREEN HUDDLED IN the kitchen, a blanket wrapped around her shoulders, as she waited for the coffee to drip.

Mack sat beside her, one arm holding her close. "Are you sure you don't need to get checked out?"

"I'm fine. I just fell down the stairs."

He gave her a wry look. "*Just fell down the stairs*? People die that way all the time."

She nodded. "I know, but I didn't." Thaddeus was curled up on her shoulder and, every so often, kept nudging her, whispering, "Thaddeus loves Doreen."

"I love you too, big guy," she whispered back.

"Big Guy, Big Guy," he cried out.

She winced. "Yes, I know. You're due for another visit with Big Guy, aren't you?"

He cried out, "Thaddeus loves Doreen. Thaddeus loves Doreen." With almost a hiccup and then a sob, he tucked up against her neck and hummed gently.

She sighed. "They are very special."

"They are, indeed," Mack agreed, watching Thaddeus, "and obviously just as affected by emotions as you are right now."

"I can't believe you were on the way over anyway."

"I was, but then I got Richard's phone call right away, telling me that something was very wrong, how all the animals were outside, raising a ruckus. I raced through the house, then realized the only other place you could be was in the garage or in the basement."

"Yeah, perfect timing," she muttered. "And now Reggie knows what it's like to hit an immovable object." Laughter rumbled from his chest, and she curled up closer. "Is it over now?"

"Yeah, I think it is," he said.

"Good, we need to tell Mr. Woo." At that, she yawned, closed her eyelids, and tucked up closer.

Mack just sat here and held her close, his chin resting on top of her head.

The police were here, including the new detective Doreen really didn't want to deal with. Finally, hearing a bit of throat clearing, Doreen opened her eyes to find the detective in front of her. She frowned. "Now? Really?"

"Yes, now," Insley stated firmly.

She sighed, looked at Mack, and said, "Fine. What do you want to know?"

"Everything," she muttered.

"Everything? Well, good luck with that," she muttered, and then yawned again. In a monotone voice, she proceeded to explain everything that had happened.

"You signed the papers?" Mack asked.

"Sure. I was stalling for time, hoping help was on the way, but they're not legal anyway. They're all filled out for Mathew. Reggie had copied them off Mathew's laptop, getting himself a copy that he thought I could sign. But he didn't read them carefully. They were already set up to transfer to Mathew. He thought he would fill that in afterward."

"Of course he did," Mack replied, with a sigh.

"Mathew always said Reggie wasn't the sharpest."

"No, but that doesn't mean he's actually stupid."

"No, but it was all to the good. Just so there's no confusion, do you think we should put a big line through those papers, to ensure there's no chance for confusion or for somebody else to pull a fast one?"

"Good idea," he replied.

"We do have them, don't we?" She looked over at the detective who passed them toward her. Taking them, Doreen asked Mack, "Do you mind if I just rip these in two?"

"Go for it," Mack said.

"Wait. Let me take photos of them first," Insley stated.

"I can do better than that. I'll scan them in for you." Doreen slowly got up, then keeping the blanket wrapped around her, walked over to her printer, quickly struck through her signatures, then scanned each page in and emailed them to herself. From her phone, she forwarded a copy to Mack.

"Now you have copies," she declared. "These weren't even Mathew's though, at least not completely."

"How so?" Mack asked.

"He ran some shadow company with property developers. Apparently he was the boss of the outfit, and they had bought properties at a steal and planned to turn around and sell them for big money, then build up developments. All the typical hype that goes along with these guys. Anyway Robin filed the documents, putting all those properties into my name to get back at Mathew. She was feeling remorseful just before she died, using the very same documents they'd made me sign earlier—in case he needed to do it temporarily for tax purposes. *Tax evasion purposes.* Reggie told me that Mathew would slip extra forms into something legitimate, tricking me into signing forms, just to have on hand when he needed them. You might think that was stupid of me, but honestly refusing to sign was asking for a beating, and, by the end, I mostly just did as he asked."

Doreen collected herself in order to continue. "Apparently Mathew didn't know Robin had filed her changes, until he did a title search recently because of the divorce in the works, trying to ensure he knew exactly what properties were where and whether he could shuffle anything around, so it wouldn't be included in the division of assets. That's when he realized all these properties were in my name."

At that, Mack stared at her.

She shrugged. "What can I say? It's a typical Mathew-type deal."

"Yet you came out smelling like a rose," Insley declared, with a sigh of disgust.

"Sometimes people come out smelling like roses," Doreen stated, "and other times people just get what they deserve."

"So, you're saying you deserve all these properties?" Insley asked in a mocking tone.

"No, but, if you'd been married to him, you might understand why I feel the way I do right now."

At that, Insley frowned.

Doreen walked over, sat down beside Mack, and whispered, "I really don't want to talk anymore right now."

Mack wrapped his arm gently around her shoulders and scooted his chair closer to hers. "I'll tell her."

She nodded at that and yawned again. "Will you update Mr. Woo?"

"I will. Now you need to get to bed and rest."

"Yeah, that sounds good, … though I'm not sure I'll sleep."

"With the protectors you have here, you should be just fine."

She looked down at her animals. Mugs was curled up on her feet now, and Goliath was under her chair, watching everybody with that haunting look of a cat who doesn't like what's going on. "You're right," she agreed, managing half a smile. "We'll be fine."

"Tomorrow's the reading of the will, correct?" Insley asked.

"Yes, I'll be calling in to the meeting," Doreen replied.

The detective hesitated and frowned.

Doreen looked at her. "What? Do you need to be there for that too?"

"No, not necessarily, but we do need a copy of the will."

"You can get one afterward. Apparently it's public record, once the reading is over."

"Okay, that's fine." Insley then looked over at Mack. "We need to go."

"Yeah." Mack got up, leaned over, and gently kissed Doreen. "Will you be okay for the night?"

"Yeah, I'll be fine. Go do your police work."

He chuckled. "Probably more like paperwork now. All that boring stuff that comes after the excitement is over."

"Right, the stuff you never liked to do. Okay then, I'm going to bed." She got up and, as soon as they stepped outside, she set the security, stumbled upstairs, and crashed into bed.

Chapter 28

THE PHONE WOKE Doreen the next morning. She groaned a weary greeting. It was Nan.

"The news is full of it. Why didn't you tell me?" she cried out.

"Tell you what?"

"Tell me that you solved the case," Nan said, almost in happy tears.

"Will you make any money on it?" Doreen asked, as she stared at the ceiling, listening to the long silence. "You hadn't mentioned gambling for so long that I figured maybe you decided to not do it anymore."

"What? Of course not." Then she got cagey and added, "I finally just decided it was a conversation that upset you, so I didn't mention it this time."

"So, who made money on me last night?"

"Richie," she declared in disgust. "Richie cleaned up on this one."

"How much did he get?" she asked, with a sigh.

"Seven hundred and twenty pennies," Nan announced.

Doreen chuckled. "That's quite the haul. Good luck to

him taking that to the bank."

At that, Nan added, "Sorry I woke you up, sweetie. When you're feeling better, give me a call." And, with that, she disconnected.

As Doreen lay here, thinking about 720 pennies and how irritated Nan was about Richie winning, Doreen burst out laughing.

Those were the kind of betting matches Doreen could handle. Just fun and games. She was sorry she hadn't called her grandmother last night, but Doreen really had been done in, and letting Nan know had escaped Doreen's attention. Doreen was moving gingerly at first, unsure how getting hit in the head and falling down the stairs might feel this morning, But, a little while later, all showered, dressed, and downstairs with coffee, she realized that, for the most part, save a few scrapes and bruises, she really was okay. More important, she knew it was over. Really over.

She stepped outside and called out to Mugs, "Come on, buddy. Let's go down to the river."

Richard called out to her from over the fence, his face popping up over it. "Good morning. Are you okay?"

"Hello, Richard. I'll be fine, and I want to thank you for whatever part you had in calling the police."

"Did you hear the animals?" His eyes went wide. "What a racket. One way or another, the police were bound to come, even if I hadn't called."

She giggled at that. "So, did you hear that I was being held prisoner in the basement?"

He shook his head, his jaw hanging open. "Oh, good Lord. Could you just stop this for a while? I want to sleep, and all this trouble is making it impossible, never knowing what'll happen next."

"If it makes you feel any better, I'm not exactly sleeping very well myself," she muttered. "So, yeah, I vote for no more trouble too."

"Sounds good, but you really are okay, right?"

"I'm okay. Thank you for asking." *Especially considering I got knocked on the head, tied to a chair in the basement, then tackled before falling down the stairs trying to escape,* she thought to herself, with a smile.

Richard beamed and retreated behind the fence on his side.

Slowly, cup of coffee in hand and the animals at her side, Doreen carefully wandered toward the river, where she sat down and just relaxed. It was another day and a whole new world, as far as she was concerned. Still, it would take some time to process Mathew's death and what that would mean. She didn't have to get a divorce now. And all that time and effort Nick had put into trying to get a divorce for her was obviously for naught, but maybe it was a good thing they had gotten this far and no further. And today was the reading of the will.

As a matter of fact it was at nine this morning. She checked her watch and noted she had only fifteen minutes left, before she had to set up for the meeting.

By the time she finished her coffee, it was time, and she walked back up to the house with the animals. Propping the kitchen door open, so they could come and go, while she was online for the reading of the will, she opened her laptop and set it up.

Just before it was due to start, she heard a truck pull in her driveway. She got up and walked to the front door and saw Mack hopping out. Looking at him, she asked, "Decided you guys needed to attend after all?"

He shook his head. "No. I decided I needed to be here … to support you."

She looked at him, then a slow smile dawned. "Thank you, Mack. That's nice, lovely even." She reached up and gave him a gentle kiss. He really was here to support her, despite several times during this investigation where he seemed to be more about supporting *Insley*. Her smile grew bigger, and her heart filled.

"Come on. It's almost time," he said.

She walked back to the kitchen table to see the lawyer on the laptop screen. He looked at her, and she nodded. "Good morning, Roger. Mack's here with me too."

He nodded. "I understand from my conversations with the police this morning that there was quite a show over at your place last night."

"Yeah, that's a perfect description. Reggie attacked me and tied me up in my basement. He was trying to get me to sign all these property documents, transferring them into his name."

Roger just shook his head. "Good Lord, I'm glad to hear that's all over with."

"Yeah, me too. So, what is in this will that's causing all the drama?"

He looked at her and smiled. "Because of Reggie's recent activities, his bequeath will be tied up for a time, while he enjoys his right to due process. However, should he be found guilty, he'll be excluded. So, in the end, basically everything is yours."

"But what does that mean? I don't even know what Mathew had." He stared at her, and she shrugged. "For all I know, he sold the house after I left. I have no idea what he's got."

"Your attorney handling the divorce proceedings has the list of all that. I don't understand. Did Nick not give it to you?"

At that, Mack leaned forward and explained, "I can vouch for the fact that she made it clear to her divorce attorney that she didn't want to count on anything, so she didn't want anything to do with the numbers during the process. Her instructions to him were to negotiate something fair that would give her enough for a modest living."

Roger's jaw dropped.

Mack nodded. "I know, but that's what she's like," he said, with a note of pride.

"To sum it up, if you were in a poker game," Roger told Doreen, "you just won the whole pot."

"So, how about telling me what is in this pot?"

"That includes the properties transferred to you because they were transferred legally. None of the people who were involved have any claims. It's not even a legal corporation. It's a shell corporation, where they were money-laundering. So, when I say you won the pot, you won the whole pot." After summaries of those properties, he began to list the properties in Mathew's name alone.

By the time he was done, Doreen stared at him in shock. "Why would Mathew have so many houses? You can only live in one at a time."

Roger's lips twitched. "He had four houses here and one in France."

"France?" she asked in shock. "We never even went to France."

"It was a recent purchase, something I believe Robin was interested in. All the furnishings and contents and the artwork are included."

Doreen rolled her eyes at that. "Fine, so that's the property listing. Is there anything else I should know about?"

"Yes, there are the contents of the safes in the house here. I have a listing, which includes jewelry, some of which may have been yours and would have been part of the divorce settlement."

"Yes," she agreed.

"There is more jewelry than that—some pieces that he bought as investments, for example. Then there are stocks, bonds, and multiple bank accounts. In summary, the total value is well over twenty million and could run as high as thirty and even more. I don't have true values on many of his paintings and jewels."

She sat back, stunned, then turned to Mack but couldn't get any words out.

He burst out laughing, then leaned over and gave her a big fat kiss. "Thank you. She seems to be at a loss for words. Is there anything that she needs to do right now?"

"As estates go, this one is simple in some ways and quite complicated in others. As such, we'll want to be very diligent as we go through probate to ensure we get everything done correctly and position ourselves to address any claims against the estate that may arise. Anything we expect to be challenged, we'll hold back until that is resolved. What was intended for Reggie will be held until such time as he is convicted or exonerated, which doesn't seem likely. So, Doreen can definitely have access to some assets. Other things will take longer. Virtually everything was left to her."

"Next step?" Mack asked.

"I'll sort it out and send the paperwork. There will be plenty enough to keep her busy, figuring out how best to deal with it all." The lawyer nodded to Mack.

Then he focused on Doreen. "Doreen, I'll detail this in a letter coming with the paperwork, but this is a big deal and no doubt overwhelming. You should get yourself some trusted advisors and take some time to think about what you want to do with this. Unless you have any questions now, we're through here, and you can expect an email soon with some documents attached, including a copy of the will itself. So, if you don't have any questions for me now, we'll talk soon." He looked at her and Mack, and they both nodded. "Thank you. I'll sign off then."

As soon as the screen went blank and the call was terminated, Mack looked at her and started to laugh. "If you could only see your face right now," he said. "He's right, you know? As far as a poker game goes, you just won big."

She shook her head, but still no words would come out.

Seeing the need to get some blood circulating through her body, he reached for her hands, pulled her up, then twirled her around in his arms. "Guess what? You can have steak now, if you want."

She beamed at that thought, seeming to come alive. "Does that mean I can have, I don't know, soup?"

"That's the richest thing you can come up with in your brain?" he asked, chuckling.

"Brain? Are you kidding? My brain stopped working about halfway through that call," she said pitifully, "so take it easy on me."

He smiled, cuddled her close, and declared, "You can have soup. You can have lobster. You can have anything you want because you are a very wealthy woman."

"Not yet. I don't have it yet. It has to be real." She sighed. "You know I didn't even care about that, right?"

"I do know that. You only wanted to ensure you had

food for the animals and that you had enough to get by. But you always took better care of them than yourself," he stated, glaring at her. "We weren't made to live on plain pasta and coffee."

"Now there's enough food for all of us," she declared, still beaming. "And plenty for you too."

It was slow coming, but his smile slowly transformed his face, and it was beautiful to see.

She reached up and kissed him gently on the chin. "Wow. I get that there's still a ton of paperwork to do, and I can't even begin to imagine the massive amount of stuff to deal with, but wow."

"Wow is right," he muttered, shaking his head. "Now add in all the antiques you've yet to get paid for, and you are beyond a very wealthy woman. Like Roger said, you should find some good financial advisors to guide you, to give you suggestions," Mack pointed out. "You'll be up in Bernard's level."

She shook her head. "Nope, there are no levels in my world," she announced. "I'm just me, and I plan to stay that way."

Mack picked her up, hugged her close, and whispered, "I'm so glad because I think *just you* is pretty perfect."

Epilogue

Over the Next Week ...

SEVERAL DAYS LATER, after Doreen had had a chance to really relax, the police had gotten statements from Reggie, and, of course, he would spend the rest of his life behind bars for the murders. She'd gotten copies of the will from the lawyer and a ton of paperwork to deal with, and it would just be the tip of the iceberg.

Thankfully Nick was handling a lot of it for her, and she promised that, this time, she would pay him. He just laughed and noted that, in light of her change in circumstances, he would happily accept payment. Then he looked at her and stated, "Now, just tell me that you'll put poor Mack out of his misery."

She looked at him. "You may find this surprising, but people say that to me all the time. Call me slow, but I've never really understood it."

He chuckled. "Something else you need to figure out."

"What now?" she asked, frustrated.

"Did you ever figure out why you don't like the new detective?"

She glared at him. "Not you too?" she snapped.

But Nick just laughed, and, since he was walking out the door anyway, he just kept on walking.

Mack drove over a little bit later and came inside, greeting all the animals and hugging Doreen. He asked, "How's it going?"

"Crazy," she muttered.

His eyebrows shot up. "Crazy in what way?"

"Just all the paperwork the lawyer sent. Thankfully your brother will handle it for me, and this time I'll pay him," she declared, with a grin.

"I'm sure he would like that," Mack said gently.

"I would have figured out how to pay him anyway. I just didn't quite know how to make that happen since I didn't really have any money," she explained.

"Cookies?"

She burst out laughing. "That would require a lot of cookies."

He chuckled at that. "Yeah, but who doesn't like cookies?" Then he looked at her and asked, "Did you ever figure out why you don't like the detective?"

She glared at him. "Not you too. That seems to be a popular topic of conversation today and even earlier."

"Yeah, it is in some ways."

"I mentioned it to Nan, and she just gave me this mysterious look and said that I would figure it out eventually. I probably will," she admitted. "How about you? Any new cases to tell me about?"

"I don't need any new cases," he declared, glaring at her. "I'm done with cases. So should you be."

"What? Are you retiring and didn't tell me? Shame on you. Besides, one doesn't have to be working to get involved in cases. Plus, just because I have money coming in now, there is still work to be done on the cold case files. Ooh, and Solomon's files when I don't have anything else to work on."

He chuckled, shaking his head. He looked at her and opened his mouth to speak, then frowned and shut up.

"What? Come on. Tell me."

"It's just that you're a very wealthy woman now, and you could do a whole lot better than some country bumpkin cop like me."

She frowned at him, walked over, and pushed him back, so he was sitting on a chair, then plunked herself down in his lap. "Yeah, and who was there for me when I didn't know how to cook or even how to buy the most basic foods and was living off of peanut butter and jelly sandwiches?" Poking him in the chest, she continued. "Who was there when I didn't know how to work an ATM or turn on the oven?" She sighed happily, as she looked up at the strong features of his face and the lovely expression there.

"It doesn't have anything to do with money. True wealth is all about what's inside," she stated, tapping his heart. "So don't you worry about that. I'm perfectly happy with a *country bumpkin* cop, exactly like you." She leaned over, kissed him gently, and said, "But that still doesn't mean we're not getting cases."

"I, for one, would very much like for this town to calm down and to not have anything else happen for quite a while."

"*Quite a while* is fine with me," she replied "We can go like this for days and days. Hey, even weeks or a few months would be great."

First Part of November

DAYS LATER DOREEN and Mack were sitting outside, having a barbecue, when his phone rang. He checked the Caller ID, then looked down at her.

"A case?" she asked, looking at him.

He got up, glaring at her, and stepped a few feet away, so he could take the call in private. Finally the call ended, and he turned around and shared, "Apparently we've had enough of a break."

"What's up?" she asked, looking at him excitedly.

"A body was just found in a flower garden."

"Where?" she asked.

"Behind the juice processing plant."

She frowned, as she thought about that. "A garden's back there?"

"Yeah, a community garden," he added.

"They're quite popular in town, aren't they?"

"They are, although maybe not so much after this."

"Why? Is it not a natural death?"

He shook his head. "No, he was tased." When she gave him a blank look, he explained, "You know, *zapped with a police zapper thingy.*" He laughed when understanding dawned on her face. "Oh my God, you're making me crazy. Now I'm even coming up with your ridiculous descriptions."

"It worked though, and now I understand completely. So, was it the fault of a cop?"

"No, I don't think so," he replied, looking at her. "At least I hope not. Sounds like the guy was found in a special place that contains the flower garden, among those spikey things."

"Spikey things?" she asked, frowning at him. "You mean, *cactus?*"

"No, the flowers, the long spikey ..."

"Multipetal zinnias?" she asked.

He raised both hands, stupefied. "Yeah, those. How did you figure that out from what I said?"

She shrugged. "I didn't. I just considered what flowers would still be blooming in Canada at this time of year. But a greenhouse in the community garden would be good cover for these flowers come wintertime."

Mack shrugged. "Don't know for sure until I see the crime scene myself. And don't forget we've been enjoying an unseasonably warm fall and so far we haven't had a killing frost. They could be still flowering quite nicely."

Then Doreen's smile on her face grew and grew.

"What?" He looked at her in confusion.

"It's the *Zapped in the Zinnias* case," she declared, with a chuckle.

"Oh no, no," he argued, "we're not going with that name."

"Yes, we are, and you know it. You can't stop me."

He glared at her. "If you go with that name, I want something from you first."

"What's that?" she asked.

"I want to know why you don't like the new detective."

She flushed, looked at him, and asked, "Are you leaving right now for the crime scene?"

"Yeah, I am."

"Okay, in that case, I'll tell you."

He slowly raised his eyebrows, clearly surprised. "Okay, so tell me then." He slipped his phone in his pocket, grabbed his jacket, and reached for his keys.

"I don't like her because she's too close to you."

He stared at her for a long moment. "Seriously?"

"Yes, seriously," she declared. "I don't want anything to come between us. Particularly a determined, good-looking, sexy cop you're around all day," she snapped, glaring at him. When his lips twitched, her glare deepened. But when he burst into laughter, she stomped her foot and crossed her arms, still glaring at him, "It's not funny, Mack."

He stopped laughing and smiled. "No, it's not funny," he agreed. "It's absolutely delightful." He picked her up, gave her a huge hug, then a big kiss on the lips, and stated, "You just made my day." After giving her a second big smacking kiss on the lips, he headed for the front door, whistling. Then he called out, "*Zapped in the Zinnias* it is."

"That was easier than I expected," she muttered, following him to the door.

"Hey, I'm always happy to compromise, particularly with somebody like you."

"What do you mean, somebody like me?" she asked.

He flashed her a grin and, stepping out the door, said, "Somebody I love."

And, with that, he was gone, leaving her standing in the doorway, staring after him, her mouth gaping.

This concludes Book 25 of Lovely Lethal Gardens:
Yowls in the Yarrow.

Read about Zapped in the Zinnias: Lovely Lethal Gardens,
Book 26

Lovely Lethal Gardens:
Zapped in the Zinnias
(Book #26)

Riches to rags ... When endings happen ... new beginnings start ... Chaos fills the middle!

With Mathew's murder done and dusted, and her future now wide open, Doreen turns to sorting out her financial world, particularly as her antiques are sold. And helping others is moving up her list of things she wants to do. Especially after finding a young woman who wants to get out of the streetwalker world and to move back home.

Of course a decision like that doesn't come without strings, and Doreen and her animals are soon embroiled in pimps and madams. A world she knows nothing about but is quickly learning. Mix that up with Nan getting kidnapped, only to bail her kidnapper out of jail, and Doreen's world is chaos as usual.

Corporal Mack Moreau has a plan, but implementing

that plan requires a special moment—the right moment.
And trying to figure out when and what that moment looks
like is a challenge. Especially as it involves Doreen …

Find Book 26 here!
To find out more visit Dale Mayer's website.
https://geni.us/DMSZapped

Author's Note

Thank you for reading Yowls in the Yarrow: Lovely Lethal Gardens, Book 25! If you enjoyed the book, please take a moment and leave a short review.

Dear reader,

I love to hear from readers, and you can contact me at my website: www.dalemayer.com or at my Facebook author page. To be informed of new releases and special offers, sign up for my newsletter or follow me on BookBub. And if you are interested in joining Dale Mayer's Reader Group, here is the Facebook sign up page.
http://geni.us/DaleMayerFBGroup

Cheers,
Dale Mayer

About the Author

Dale Mayer is a *USA Today* best-selling author, best known for her SEALs military romances, her Psychic Visions series, and her Lovely Lethal Garden cozy series. Her contemporary romances are raw and full of passion and emotion (Broken But ... Mending, Hathaway House series). Her thrillers will keep you guessing (Kate Morgan, By Death series), and her romantic comedies will keep you giggling (*It's a Dog's Life*, a stand-alone novella; and the Broken Protocols series, starring Charming Marvin, the cat).

Dale honors the stories that come to her—and some of them are crazy, break all the rules and cross multiple genres!

To go with her fiction, she also writes nonfiction in many different fields, with books available on résumé writing, companion gardening, and the US mortgage system. All her books are available in print and ebook format.

Connect with Dale Mayer Online

Dale's Website – www.dalemayer.com
Twitter – @DaleMayer
Facebook Page – geni.us/DaleMayerFBFanPage
Facebook Group – geni.us/DaleMayerFBGroup
BookBub – geni.us/DaleMayerBookbub
Instagram – geni.us/DaleMayerInstagram
Goodreads – geni.us/DaleMayerGoodreads
Newsletter – geni.us/DaleNews